The
Rocky Raccoon Revival

MICHAEL C. DUELL

Vigorous English 2014

THE ROCKY RACCOON REVIVAL
Published by Vigorous English
Noblesville, IN 46062 U.S.A.

This is a work of fiction. Names, characters, places, and
incidents either are the product of the author's imagination or
are used fictitiously, and any resemblance to actual persons,
living or dead, business establishments, events, or locales is
entirely coincidental.

ISBN-10: 0996006508
ISBN-13: 978-0-9960065-0-7
eBook ISBN: 978-0-9960065-1-4

Cover Art by Matthew Merchant

www.michaelcduell.com

To Lisa
Thank You

The Wanderer

Michael Sinclair was finally near the end of his eastward journey, which had started long before that day's twelve-hour drive. He observed a seemingly endless parade of road signs proudly proclaiming the area's rich history. Although he deftly adapted to the universally accepted Bostonian disregard for the rules of the road, it did not prevent him from getting lost along the North Shore's twisting roads. He experienced an unexpected and unwelcomed chill on an otherwise hot August evening, which was soon replaced by a dark sense of foreboding. Upon seeing the street sign, "Witch Way," he surmised that he was in Salem, and navigated his way through its serpentine roads to 1A North. The ominous feeling quickly passed and was forgotten as he drove across the Veterans Memorial Bridge leading into Beverly, Massachusetts, home of the world renowned Easton Theological Seminary.

He soon arrived at Easton's entrance amid a clearing of trees, which was effectively hidden to anyone unaware of its existence. Its long and winding driveway was lined on both sides with a continuous menagerie of ancient trees that arched over the road. He emerged from the darkened tunnel of foliage and saw a

1

grand Victorian home garnished with ivy that overlooked a stagnant, algae covered pond. A modest blue sign with gold lettering indicated that it was the residence of Easton's famed president, Dr. Peter Casper. An accompanying sign directed him to continue driving up the massive hill that dominated the campus's topography.

Michael carefully guided his now steaming car into the first available parking space at the Lewis Center. He popped the hood and slowly stepped out with a one-gallon carton of distilled water. He carefully lifted and secured the open hood, and poured the water into the old car. He stood up straight and stretched his back as he casually placed his gold cross necklace under his sweaty t-shirt. He took a drink from the carton while he surveyed the islands of posh residences and white steeples interspersed amidst the surrounding ocean of trees in the New England landscape.

He wiped the water and sweat from his face, which was sporting a few days' growth, and matter-of-factly rubbed his dirty hands on his ripped jean shorts. He gently closed the old white car's hood and then patted it, as one would affectionately thank a faithful horse after a long ride. He found that he had to consciously command his legs to move following his long drive, but he quickly regained his natural gait and entered through the main doors of the Lewis Center with a spring in his step.

"May I please see Peter Casper?"

"I'm so sorry," said the receptionist. "*Dr.* Casper can only be seen by appointment."

"But of course," he said and smiled. "I actually do have an appointment. My name is Michael Sinclair."

The receptionist looked at Dr. Casper's calendar and then glanced back up at him. "You're Mr. Sinclair?"

"For better or worse, that's me," he said with a laugh.

"Ah, yes, right. I will let Dr. Casper know that you are here to meet with him. Please have a seat and he will call on you shortly."

"Well thank you very much. Do you mind if I just look around a little bit? I've been cramped inside my car for half the day and would love to stretch my legs a little. I promise not to drift too far away."

"Sure."

"Great! Incidentally, what's your name?"

"Uh, my name? My name is Meredith. Meredith Steele."

He extended his hand. "Nice to meet you, Meredith. I'll soon be working here with you."

"Wo-working with me?"

"Well, here at the seminary anyway. I'll be working in the cafeteria."

"Oh, I see. Well then, welcome aboard."

"Thanks, Meredith. I'm just going to walk into the hallway here."

"Okay. I'll get up and find you when he's ready."

* * *

Michael walked through the hallway, reading bulletin boards and perusing through literature on educational and ministerial opportunities. His nose led him to the cafeteria. Dinner was being served, and it looked as though most of the seminary was present. He started to walk into the cafeteria when he heard the steady echo of pounding footsteps heading his way.

"There you are, Mr. Sinclair. Dr. Casper will meet with you now."

"Thanks, Meredith," he said, but she had already turned around and started back to her desk.

3

Michael went directly to Dr. Casper's office, but then paused for a moment and took a deep breath before knocking on the president's door. Dr. Casper opened the door and smiled. "You must be Michael Sinclair. You look just as Bob described. Please come on in and have a seat."

"Thank you, sir," Michael said as he sat down on the first available chair. "It's an honor to meet you."

"You took the words right out of my mouth, young man."

"You know, I had actually asked Bob not to tell you about my past."

"I know," said Dr. Casper. "I forced the issue."

"You don't like my being here?"

"Are you kidding? Do you know how much restraint it's taking for me to not run out of this office and tell the whole world all about you? The only thing that's holding me back is my promise to you and Bob."

"Why then did you force the issue? Is there something about this arrangement that doesn't sit well with you?"

"Not exactly. It was just a highly irregular request, even from an old friend like Bob. It was only after I had turned him down that he revealed your past to me. Please know that he only told me as an absolute last resort to change my mind."

Michael nodded.

"For what it's worth, even before disclosing the remarkable events of your life, Bob spoke very highly of you," Dr. Casper said as he sat down behind his hundred-year-old antique oak desk. "He described you the same way Jesus described the Spirit. He said that you are like the blowing wind, going wherever it pleases. Nobody knows where you are coming from, or even where you are going. You're unpredictable and free."

"I'm not sure if he necessarily meant that as a compliment."

Dr. Casper laughed. "Well, be that as it may, he did mention that you have quite the servant's heart, and are quite willing to get your hands dirty in service to others."

Michael offered an appreciative smile.

"With that being said, let's discuss your arrangements. You will be working in the cafeteria as promised. It pays better than a lot of similar local jobs, and it will also provide you with three free meals a day. You'll start tomorrow morning at eleven since we don't offer breakfast until the semester begins Wednesday. You'll shadow the staff, learn their system, and then you'll be good to go on Wednesday.

"Additionally, we have made arrangements for you to live and work in Tuttle Hall. You will be given a room, albeit a pretty Spartan one, and you'll keep the dorm's kitchen and lavatories clean, as well as taking care of the refuse.

"Also, though you are not an Easton student, please feel free to sit in on any class, activity, and, of course, chapel whenever you are able."

"This is great, Dr. Casper. I really appreciate all that you have done to make this possible."

"All I can say, Michael is that the Lord truly does work in mysterious ways. Welcome, at last, to Easton Theological Seminary."

A Sort of Homecoming

Michael decided to forgo dinner following his quick stop at the housing office. He still had some snack food from his long trip, and opted to drive down the hill to Tuttle Hall to unpack his car.

A tall slender man met Michael as he approached the dorm's side door near the parking lot. "I see you've got your hands full," he said.

"I'm one of those guys who like to get everything in one trip."

"Seeing as how we're not expecting anyone else this evening, I'm going to wager that you're Mike."

"Got it in one, my friend."

"Excellent! I'm Jim, and I'm the R.A. of Tuttle Hall. If you need anything, just stop by my room, number twenty."

"Thanks, Jim."

"What do you have planned for tonight?"

"Frankly, I just need to get some sleep. I've spent the entire day traveling and I'm exhausted."

"Sounds like a good plan, man. I'll catch you tomorrow and introduce you to the guys."

"I'd like that. Thanks."

6

"Have a good night and welcome to Easton!"

Jim walked to his car and Michael walked into the dorm, looking for room number twenty-four.

* * *

Michael's room was just as Dr. Casper had described. His guitar case fit neatly under the bed, the closet, a single steel rod located in the hallway outside of the room, easily accommodated his one suitcase of clothes, and his books were placed on the windowsill. In a matter of minutes, he was home. He spent fifteen minutes praying and then fell quickly asleep.

Walking Distance

Michael woke up early and started the day with some quiet time in his room reading from his Bible and praying. He then proceeded to clean the kitchen.

Jim staggered in for his morning coffee. "Good morning, Mike."

"Good morning, Jim!"

"Have you met any of the guys yet?"

"Not yet. I guess they're enjoying the last day they can sleep in," Michael said with a grin.

"They'd better be getting up soon. Some of them have orientation and need to register for classes. What's on your agenda today?"

"I'm going to check out the library this morning, and then I'll head over to the cafeteria. I'm supposed to be shadowing the staff today during lunch and dinner to learn the routine. After that, I really want to meet some of the people here."

"You have a busy day ahead of you."

"Well, to be honest, that's how I like it."

"Steven, one of the guys here, is throwing a party tonight and you're welcome to come. We're just going to hang out in his room and watch a movie."

"That's great," Michael said. "I'll be sure to stop by later then."

"Excellent," Jim said as he grabbed his coffee. "I'll let them know to expect you."

*   *   *

Michael walked outside into the cool of the morning and took in a deep breath of fresh air. He was simply in awe of the beautiful campus. Its well-kept grounds were reminiscent of a professional golf course. He noticed a family of deer congregating in peace and gave them a neighborly nod as he respectfully strolled by them.

He opted to take the sidewalk that led up the steep hill to the Lewis Center and go "people speed" rather than drive up as he saw others doing.

"Good morning," he said to a student walking in the opposite direction.

The young man looked past him as if he weren't there and kept on walking.

"He must not have gotten the classes he wanted," Michael said quietly to himself.

He finally reached the top of the hill and stopped to catch his breath. "Tomorrow I start working out."

"Wow. Most people wait till New Year's Eve," he heard a pleasant voice reply.

He turned around and found an attractive Filipino woman behind him, whose short stature and petite build did not match her surprisingly loud voice.

"Who said I didn't say it on New Year's, too?"

"Hi there! My name is Becky. What's yours? Or should I wait

until you get some more oxygen?"

He laughed.

"My name's Michael. It's a pleasure to meet you."

"Oh, don't say that. You haven't gotten to know me yet."

"Fair enough! Are you a new student here?"

"Me? No. This is my last year here. You're a new face though. I take it this is your first year?"

"Well, yes, so to speak. I'm not a student though. I'm working in the cafeteria and Tuttle Hall."

"Tuttle Hall is the fun dorm. You'll like it there. I'd say it's the closest thing we have to a frat house." She laughed.

"Great, I think I'll fit in just fine then."

"Are you on your way to the cafeteria now?" Becky asked.

"No. They don't start breakfast till tomorrow. I'm just on my way up to the library."

"Really? What for?"

Michael's eyebrows rose at the question. "I'm an avid reader. I try to read about three books a week."

"Whew! Three books? I'll go to you if I need any help in my classes!"

"I'm in room twenty-four. Knock anytime."

"Great! Maybe I will. Look, I need to go register for classes. I'll see you later at lunch, okay?"

"See you then, Becky." He smiled and then continued on his way to Easton's famous library.

* * *

Michael happened to glance at the clock on the wall and realized that he was late for work. He dropped his book on the nearest table and ran to the Lewis Center with his pounding shoes echoing throughout the former monastery's hallway until

10

he burst into the kitchen.

"Hi! Sorry I'm late!" he said as he ran into the kitchen and nearly slid by the entire staff on the slick floor.

"You must be, Michael," said a large black man wearing an apron that read "Pray for your food."

"Sorry I'm late. I was reading Kierkegaard and lost track of time."

"Oh, sure. I hear that one *all* the time," he said with a serious look before busting out laughing. "Don't sweat it, kid. We were all late today. No one had the key to the refrigerators. Anyway, it's really nice to meet you. Just call me Sam."

"Nice to meet you, Sam. What can I do to start?"

"Mostly, you just need to watch me. I'll also have you working out on the floor keeping the place tidy. These students may one day lead sheep, but some of them can still be like pigs." Sam laughed out loud.

"Great, let's get started!"

Moments of Transition

Michael ventured out to wipe off some tables and take out the trash after the lunch rush slowed down. He exchanged greetings and handshakes with a group of Korean students sitting together conversing in their native tongue. He shared a laugh with a table of African-American students who were exchanging anecdotes from their respective summer breaks. He took some trays for the female students sitting at another table, and tidied up after some of the professors were finished at their table.

"Hey, Sinclair! Come here for a sec!"

He turned his head and saw Jim at a table full of students.

"Come here and meet some of the gang."

He wiped his hands with a clean rag and straightened his soiled apron as he approached the jovial bunch.

"Everyone, this is Michael Sinclair. He just arrived from Ohio last night and will be living with us in Tuttle this year."

Jim's introduction was greeted by a general welcome from the entire table.

Jim started to introduce those sitting at the table. "This is Steven. He's the one throwing the video party tonight. He's working on his Master of Divinity."

Michael and Steven nodded.

Steven was a Maryland native in his mid-20s with dark red hair that matched his well-trimmed beard. With his tilted khaki ball cap, he resembled a young Ernest Hemingway.

"Fan of the Beatles, I see," Steven said as he observed Michael's t-shirt. "Good taste in music, my friend."

"They're the best," Michael said with a smile.

"This here is Chip Park, our resident genius—and graduate of Yale I might add."

Chip was a New Jersey native in his early 30s and a Korean-American. He was noticeably short and a little overweight, but looked comfortable in his athletic attire.

"Nice to meet you, Michael," Chip said. "Your name sounds really familiar to me. Have we ever met?"

"I don't believe so. I never forget a name or face."

"You'll have to excuse Park," said Jim. "Ever since he won a series of trivia contests, including college week on *Jeopardy*, the guy thinks he knows *everything*."

Chip laughed and offered playful punches to Jim sitting next to him.

"This is Rick, our resident circus star," said Jim. "He can perform magic, ride unicycles, throw knives, walk on tightropes, and do all kinds of mischief with computers. In other words, he's the ultimate youth pastor!"

Rick, a native of Michigan, had a tall, athletic build and blond hair with a matching goatee.

"I'm beginning to see why Becky referred to Tuttle Hall as the frat house of Easton," said Michael.

"Ah, you met Becky," Steven said. "She and a few other girls will be at the party tonight."

As Jim was making other introductions, he was interrupted by a voice from across the aisle yelling, "Hey, Jimbo, leave the hired help alone and let the man do his job!"

"Knock it off, Tom," Jim said without any hint of the same good-natured ribbing seen moments earlier.

"Don't be so touchy," Tom replied. "I simply noticed that the garbage was running over onto the floor, and the guy whose job it is to take care of it is busy jawing with you."

Jim looked up at Michael. "I'm sorry about Tom. He may be the top student here, but he seriously lacks people skills."

"He didn't used to," Steven said in a somber whisper as he picked at his food.

"Don't sweat it. I didn't take it personally. He's right. I have a job to do, and I'm falling behind."

Michael walked over across the aisle to greet Tom, who casually looked around the cafeteria noting his peers' shared gazes.

"Hi, I'm Michael."

"It's really nice to meet you, Mike. I hope that you quickly make yourself at home here at Easton. It's a great school. Are you a new student?"

"No. I'm actually here to work and hopefully get a chance to get to grow as a Christian in this incredible place."

"Well that's great. We all have our reasons for being here. Speaking of which, let me give you a hand. You've already got your hands full, my friend. I can take our table's trays over with you."

Tom wore the smile of a man campaigning for mayor as he slowly walked down the aisle side-by-side with Michael and helped him with their collective pile of trash. He shook hands with Michael and then returned to his table.

"That's the guy I told you about earlier," Meredith whispered to Tom.

"Really? I wonder why he met with Dr. Casper."

"He probably didn't know that human resources handle the workers," she replied.

"Well, he's certainly not here to get a degree, that's for sure," said Tom.

* * *

"I heard you met Tom," said Sam.

"I did," said Michael. "I hear he's the top student here."

"He's probably going to be valedictorian this year and win the Aberdeen Scholarship."

"What's the Aberdeen Scholarship?"

"It's a $50,000 award to study at the University of Aberdeen in Scotland for a year. They say that it's a great experience, but the award looks even better on your resume," said Sam.

"It's typical that someone like Tom would win," Jeff, a fellow cafeteria worker muttered.

"Why's that?" Michael asked.

"The guy comes from a pretty rich family. I bet they're worth a few million dollars," said Sam.

"How do you know?"

"Well, for starters, the guy doesn't keep it a secret. Whereas most people here have a car that runs well enough to serve their purposes, Tom has an SUV, a sports car, and a motorcycle," said Jeff.

"Well then, I feel sorry for the guy," Michael said.

"What? Why? Are you crazy, man?" Sam asked.

"Yeah, no doubt. Do you know what you could do with that kind of dough?" said Jeff.

"I can imagine," Michael said as he walked out of the kitchen to wipe off the now vacant tables.

THE ROCKY RACCOON REVIVAL

* * *

After an uneventful dinner and some time spent at the library, Michael walked back down to Tuttle Hall to join Steven's party in progress.

He didn't know which room was Steven's, but given the small size of the dorm and the loud noise of laughter, he had a pretty good guess. He walked down the hallway and went to the source of the commotion, finding the Tuttle gang, Becky, and her friends enjoying a comedy.

"Hey! We thought you got lost," Rick yelled from across the room, which was met by a collected "shhhhh" from those waiting for the next punch line.

He walked over the bodies lying on the floor to sit next to Rick. Other people started to look over and acknowledge him. As the movie played, he fidgeted, squirmed, and looked around the room as the others stared at the television. Rick noticed Michael's growing discomfort but said nothing about it.

After the movie, the co-ed group of seminarians laughed, joked, talked among themselves, and if the topic was hot enough, everyone got involved. Chip, however, looked dejected, so Michael went over to see what was wrong.

"He'll live!" said Jim.

"What's wrong?" Michael asked.

"He lost a battle of wits against Simon the Great…*again*," one of the girls said.

"Who's Simon?"

"Simon is a guy down at Harvard who eats Christians for lunch," said Jim. "He frequents Café Veritas down in Cambridge, which is the fashionable establishment to go for all the intellectuals and Bohemian wannabes of Harvard and MIT."

"I like Café Veritas," Becky said. "They have lots of

16

discussions, poetry readings, and live music."

"Chip and I went down there this evening, and Simon was there giving philosophical lectures on why he's not a Christian, and why no one else should be either," Rick said.

"The scary thing is, this guy really does influence a lot of people, which is the main reason we keep going back," Chip explained.

"The problem," Jim added, "is that Simon is one brilliant guy. We can't out-debate him."

"Why not?" Michael asked.

"I've debated a lot of people in my life," Chip said, "but this guy has a way of countering every argument that you make. He really humbles me."

"Is humility such a bad thing?"

"It is when it makes Jesus look bad," said Chip.

"I see," Michael said as he looked down at his feet while scratching behind his ear.

"You know what I mean," Chip said.

"I do…but God will never place more on your shoulders than you can bear. Don't seek to add any more to it. I don't think that the point of seminary is to create a bunch of Christian Atlases, hunched over carrying a world that is already in the palm of His hand."

Chip nodded.

"Promise me that you'll take me to meet Simon next time you go," said Michael.

"Why not? I'm sure he'll like some fresh meat for a change!" Chip laughed.

"Hey, everyone. Tomorrow is the first day of class, and I have Greek at 8:30 in the morning," Steven informed his guests. "It's been real. Now get out!"

17

Rocky Raccoon

Michael woke up early, read a chapter from Proverbs, prayed, and then went jogging in the cool of the peaceful New England morning. He concluded his first fun with a victorious limp and a hand firmly pressed against the unrelenting cramp in his side.

Michael quickly learned that breakfast time offered little to no work or interaction as most students didn't eat breakfast, or they simply got coffee and a bagel to go. He seemingly enjoyed the light mornings as much as he did the busier lunch shift, when he served food to the students in line. It was a great opportunity to meet everyone, and he was already addressing most everyone by name on his second day.

Tom stood in line along with the other members of his clique listening to their fellow students praising Michael for his incredible gift for remembering names.

"Michael," a student named Hannah commented, "I've only known you for a couple of days here and there on campus, but I must say that you've really impressed me."

Tom rolled his eyes and looked back at his friends.

"Really," said Hannah. "You have made such an effort to get to know people, and I saw what you did for that man in

18

downtown Beverly yesterday when you didn't think anyone was looking. I bet you didn't tell a soul, did you?"

Michael smiled and subtly shook his head no.

"There you go then." She smiled. "It's refreshing to meet a man who understands the true meaning of compassion. Unfortunately, there are not many Christian men like you. I'm sure your example will influence many here. Have a nice day, Michael."

Tom now stood before the esteemed new cafeteria worker.

"Well, hello there. Remember me?" Tom asked.

"But of course," he replied. "What can I get for you, Tom?"

"How about another shirt for starters."

Michael looked down to see that he was wearing another Beatles shirt, which was just like the one he wore when he first met Tom. Tom looked up and was momentarily startled when he saw Hannah's disapproving stare. He then slowly reached into his back pocket and pulled out his wallet.

"Here, buddy. Take this $50 and go get a new shirt. Okay? My treat."

"Thanks, but no thanks."

"Why not?"

"It's just not necessary, that's all. I really appreciate the offer though," Michael replied as he looked down and stirred the baked beans.

"Come on, take it. It would make me happy. Anyhow, I'm sure the health department wouldn't want you wearing the same shirt each day like some kind of ragamuffin," he said with a chuckle.

"Actually…" Michael started to reply until Sam interceded.

"You're causing a logjam in my line, Tom. What do you want to eat today?"

"Sorry, Sam. I was just trying to do a good deed, like in Luke

19

10:33. You know, the Good Samarian. Hmmm, let's see. Let's see." Tom looked over the food selection again. "Hey…Rocky Raccoon," he said, looking Michael directly in the eye, "I'll take a hamburger and fries."

Michael simply raised an eyebrow.

Martin laughed and asked his best friend, "What are you talking about?"

"*Rocky Raccoon* is a Beatles song, right?" asked Tom.

Michael nodded as he handed Tom his food.

Meredith, who followed behind Tom then said, "Hi, Rocky Raccoon," and looked over at Tom for approval. "I'll have the spaghetti."

Michael smiled and fixed her plate.

"Thanks, Rocky!"

"That's why I'm here," he replied while acting busy with the empty ladle.

"Hey, there…Rocky Raccoon," said Martin.

The rest of the clique followed along with the same joke. Word quickly spread around the cafeteria. Most people were appalled by the joke, but no one said a word.

Jim, Steven, Rick, and Chip entered the cafeteria, unaware of Michael's newly acquired nickname.

"How's it going, Mike?" Jim asked.

"As Paul said, 'Rejoice in the Lord always.'"

"Great!"

As Jim walked over to the table where the Tuttle guys usually sat, Hannah leaned over and told him what had happened. He didn't say or do anything at first. He simply stared darts over at Tom, who looked back at him and smiled.

Michael later walked down the aisle that divided the cafeteria toward the garbage. As he was pulling out the trash bags, Tom stood up and yelled, "Hey, Rocky Raccoon wait a second!"

Jim and Rick both stood up to intercept Tom, but he had already run by them and handed Michael his garbage. "Just trying to ensure your next load to the dumpster's a little lighter."

"Thanks, Tom."

"No problem, Rocky! That's why I'm here."

Michael offered a smile as he brushed back the hair away from his eyes that had fallen out of its tie.

"Just watch out for the other raccoons by the dumpster. I hear that they're pretty territorial," Tom said as he patted Michael on his back. "Hey there, you know I'm just playing, right?"

Michael placed the trash bag down on the floor and extended his soiled, sticky right hand to Tom, who took a step back.

"I can see that you're busy," said Tom. "So I'll let you go, okay? Take care and God bless you."

Jim and Rick, both athletic guys over six feet tall, made a beeline for the door to talk to Tom before he left, but Michael stopped them.

"You can't let him talk to you that way," Jim protested.

"Beating him over the head isn't the answer."

"Maybe, maybe not. An eye for an eye, and a tooth for a tooth," Rick said.

"There's a reason Jesus came to change that, you know. If He didn't, we'd all be toothless and blind. Please don't do anything. I'll be fine. I greatly appreciate your friendship and support."

"Okay," said Jim. "We'll make sure that we nip this whole Rocky Raccoon thing in the bud."

"Thanks, but no thanks."

"I beg your pardon," Jim replied

"Tom's done me a great favor. Look around this place, guys. Everybody saw what just happened. Given how public he has made this silly nickname, everyone will know my name. Anyhow,

I'm impressed that he knew a fairly obscure Beatles' song, if there is such a thing!"

"I don't think Tom was using it as a term of endearment," Rick replied.

"Possibly…even so, I've studied history, and sometimes we Christians get labeled with many different names, such as 'Jesus Freaks,' which we usually find ourselves ultimately embracing rather than shunning. If it's all the same to you, I'd like to keep the nickname."

"I can't say I understand, or even agree, but if that's what you want, then I guess we'll call you Rocky Raccoon," Jim said as Rick walked away in disgust.

"Actually, Rocky will do just fine."

The Ivory Tower

Word quickly spread about Rocky Raccoon at Easton. Even Dr. Casper heard about the incident. He promptly arranged for a meeting with Tom to discuss the matter.

"What on earth were you thinking, Thomas?" Dr. Casper asked.

"I'm afraid that this is all a misunderstanding. He's a new guy, and I was just ribbing him, just as I do with Martin and the other guys. I was hoping that would make him feel more welcome."

Dr. Casper sat silently, looking at his finest student. "Do you really think that naming him Rocky Raccoon would be perceived as a call to fellowship?"

"He's apparently a big Beatles fan. I picked one Beatles song out of a hundred. If I had called him 'Ringo' we wouldn't be having this conversation."

Dr. Casper paused and sat quietly looking at Tom, who now squinted as the morning light shining through the window had crept its way up to his face where he sat.

"I wasn't there…so I cannot say for certain what was said…or how it was said."

"Yes, sir."

"Just know this, Thomas. The strongest argument against Christianity is Christians. Hypocrites. Those who say one thing and act another way."

"Yes, sir."

"Conversely, though, the single greatest argument for Christianity is Christians. People who live what they teach, like Billy Graham and Mother Teresa."

"Yes, sir," Tom said as he continued to nod his head.

"It's up to you to decide which side of the argument you want to be on."

"Thank you, sir. I'm terribly sorry for the misunderstanding. It won't happen again."

"Tom, you're the top student here. You will certainly be valedictorian and more than likely will win the Aberdeen Scholarship. Still, let me offer you some advice."

"Yes, sir."

"You watch Michael, or Rocky Raccoon, if that's what he wishes to be called. You watch, and you learn."

"Sir?"

"You're dismissed. I'll see you later in class."

Tom walked out of the office and was greeted by Martin and Meredith, who were waiting out in the hallway.

"What happened?" Martin asked.

"I have no idea," Tom replied.

*   *   *

Rick went into the cafeteria for breakfast and found Rocky sitting alone at a table eating cereal.

"How goes it?" Rick greeted Rocky.

"It's a wonderful morning, my friend. I'm thankful to be alive and I genuinely love God's creation out there," he said, pointing

24

out the windows to an ocean of color provided by the trees along the New England countryside.

"I wanted to ask you a question, Michael."

"That's fine, but please call me Rocky."

"Okay then, fine. I noticed that you were extremely uncomfortable at the video party the other night. Am I wrong?"

"No, you're not. I'm sorry, I didn't mean to be that obvious."

"Well, you weren't really. Everyone was busy watching the movie. If I hadn't been next to you, I wouldn't have noticed either."

"Well, I guess it comes down to this. How much sin do you want to willingly let into your life?"

"I don't understand. Did the movie offend you?"

"It may have been a silly comedy, but I didn't personally care for the cavalier attitude toward sin. At some point you have to ask yourself if it is really edifying to hear the Lord's name taken in vain a hundred times in one movie, or see sexual acts or extreme violence. Once you have lived a life as sinful as mine once was and you have become free of it through the grace of Jesus, I guess you just don't want to expose yourself to it and welcome the sin back in."

Rick sat very still and then replied, "Okay, I see what you mean. I suppose that I don't monitor what I watch or listen to as closely as I should."

Rick then stood up, paused, looking as if he were going to start a new conversation, and then pushed his chair in to excuse himself.

"Is there anything else you'd like to talk about?"

Rick did not answer right away. "No, I'm fine. I really need to get to class now."

"Which class are you off to?"

"Dr. Casper's theology class."

"Oh, my gosh! I had planned on going to that myself today. If you give me one second, I'll let Sam know that I'm leaving," said Rocky as he back peddled toward the kitchen.

"That's fine, Rocky. I'll wait right here for you."

* * *

Rocky walked into the class and stopped in the doorway. He looked around the classroom wide-eyed, like child in a toy store. Rocky sat down next to Rick and Jim. He noticed Becky sitting in the middle section with some of her girlfriends, and also saw Tom and his clique sitting on the left hand side of the small auditorium. Rocky offered a nod toward Tom who just glared back at him.

Dr. Casper walked in and made his way down the right aisle stepping past Rocky's seat. Dr. Casper was not only a world-class scholar but also a well-dressed man who wore the latest fashionable suits and ties and had a nice, slender build to wear it well.

Dr. Casper took a moment to wipe off his glasses and looked up to see Rocky in attendance. "Good morning, class. I hope that you all enjoyed a nice summer break."

The students collectively replied to his energetic greeting with an almost inaudible mumble acknowledging their presence in his class. The veteran professor knew what to expect the first day of autumn class, and was not caught off guard by the lethargic response. He simply took attendance, already familiar with these second and third year students, and was soon prepared to start class.

"I would like to take a moment to introduce a new person in our community. Michael, would you please stand up and introduce yourself?"

"Oh, hi, good morning. I'm Michael, but please call me Rocky."

Tom rolled his eyes and let out a sigh in disbelief.

"I'm from Ohio and I love Jesus with all my heart. I'm here to learn more about Him and how to teach others the Gospel."

Rocky sat down and the class offered a polite round of applause, with the notable exception of the left side of the classroom.

"Thank you, Rocky, and welcome. You have come to the right place to learn about Jesus. Today, class, we will be talking about the Jesus Rocky knows, and debating the major millennial views pertaining to His second coming."

Upon hearing this, Tom sat up in his seat and whispered something in Martin's ear. Martin sat back with a smile and gave his grinning friend a playful high-five.

Dr. Casper began the class with a short lecture, outlining the main tenets of the major millennial views of Jesus' second coming. Rocky sat up and listened carefully.

After the introductory lecture, Dr. Casper turned the class over to the students for discussion. The format quickly went from an academic setting to that of an afternoon TV talk show format, where everyone was quick to offer their opinions, but no one seemed prepared to listen or change their minds.

Julie was the first to speak. She was the daughter of two prominent missionaries in Ukraine and was pursuing her Master of Arts in World Missions and Evangelism at Easton. "Postmillennialism is the most logical of the three main views. I think it is entirely reasonable to believe that the preaching of the Gospel, that is, following the Great Commission, will see the world converted to Christianity."

Dr. Casper saw the hands going up all around the room, presumably to disagree, but he wanted Julie to state her case before her colleagues challenged her. "Please continue, Miss Poblenz."

"The millennium you speak of does not occur in the future, but is *already* here. Even Augustine cited Mark 3:27: 'In fact, no one can enter a strong man's house and carry off his possessions unless he first ties up the strong man. Then he can rob his house.' Augustine's understanding of this verse was that Satan is the strong man, and the plundered goods are the Christians that were formally under his control. At Christ's first coming, Satan was bound and is no longer able to deceive the nations. That's why missionary work can succeed now, because Satan is not able to deceive the nations. And before anyone starts doing the math, the millennium shouldn't be viewed as a literal thousand years but simply as the time period of the Christian church."

Dr. Casper nodded and smiled. He now looked around the room and called on Martin over Tom.

"You're kidding, right?" Martin asked. "That or you are definitely a 'cup is half full' kind of gal. You're not a postmillennialist. You're an optimillennialists."

"I'd rather be an optimillennialists than a pessimillennialist," she replied.

"Let's be realistic," Martin said. "The twentieth century, the bloodiest and most ungodly century of them all, should alone poke a few holes in your argument. Your view seems to indicate that things should be getting better in time, not *worse*."

Dr. Casper acknowledged the good points and deferred back to Julie. "Well, the twentieth century was just a setback, that's all."

"Oh, come on, Julie!" Tom interrupted. "No offense to your parents, but missionary success and evangelism has declined, not increased. There are parts in this world completely closed off to Christians, such as in many Muslim nations…."

"That's what they used to say about communist countries like the Soviet Union," Julie replied.

"Look, I know your parents are doing great work in the Ukraine, but let's look at the overall facts and not just some isolated cases. Islam is growing much faster than Christianity. History and demographics aside, even Jesus said in Matthew 24 that there would be great wickedness and a cooling off of the faith before His return. There's simply no Scripture to support this optimistic viewpoint."

"Thank you, Thomas," Dr. Casper said. "Your references to Scripture, as always, are very thoughtful."

Rocky cocked his head to the side upon hearing Dr. Casper's praise.

Dr. Casper then offered Tom an opportunity to share his point of view.

"I'll defer to Jim and let him get a word in. I don't wish to *hog* the discussion," Tom said with a smirk.

Jim did not appear to appreciate being put on the spot but sat up without hesitation to address the class. "Okay, I'll be happy to go. Thanks, Tom. Although I respectfully disagree with Julie, she's right that Augustine's view was probably postmillennial, but just look at the context of his life. He was living in a time following the conversion of Constantine, where Christianity was enjoying tremendous success in the empire that was once its worst enemy. If I lived back then, I would consider this optimistic viewpoint as well. However, as Tom mentioned, things have unfortunately gotten worse, not better. I also agree with Julie, that the millennium referred to in Revelation 20 should not be taken literally, and in fact, being an amillennialist, I don't believe that there will be a millennium. Nor do I see there being an earthly reign of Christ, as the Church represents Christ's spiritual kingdom. Christ is presently reigning from

29

Heaven, and Satan, who is not bound, will continue to be active till the second coming of Christ. The final judgment will immediately follow the second coming."

Not as many hands rose in the air this time. Rocky did note one lone hand waving, trying to catch Dr. Casper's attention.

"Thomas. What a surprise. What say you?" Dr. Casper asked and then stepped back for the show.

"Jimbo, if the thousand years is symbolic rather than literal, what then does it symbolize?"

"Numbers have special meaning throughout Scripture. Look at numbers such as three, seven, twelve and forty...."

"What about a thousand, *Jimmy*?"

"I'm getting to it, *Tommy*. Many believe that it represents the idea of perfection and completeness. In Revelation 20:2, it represents Christ's complete victory over Satan, and in Revelation 20:4, it symbolizes the perfect joy and glory of the redeemed in heaven."

Dr. Casper appeared pleased with Jim's explanation, and the class was visibly happy to see Jim stand up to Tom.

"That was an excellent recitation of about four different scholars. Don't worry about it though, Jimbo. As Picasso said, 'Good artists copy, great artists steal.'"

Tom's clique laughed, and other raised hands quickly fell.

"Since Jimbo brought up Revelation 20, I would like to ask my good and dear friend to explain the difficulties in his argument."

"Could you be more specific, Tom?" asked Jim.

"But of course. I won't belabor the issue of the one thousand years. However, I would like to know how you explain the two resurrections mentioned in Revelation 20, given that your amillennial view states that the first resurrection is spiritual and the second physical. John was speaking of two physical resurrections involving two separate groups."

"After a thoughtful reading of Revelation 20:6, 'Blessed and holy is he who shares in the first resurrection! Over such the second death has no power,' one must conclude that the first resurrection is a victory over the second death," said Jim. "The first death is not mentioned, but I think it can be implied to be spiritual."

"Oh, give me a break, Jim! You might as well go back to Dr. Jennings's hermeneutics class 'cause you're way off base. Saying that the first resurrection is spiritual and the second physical is inconsistent. The exact same Greek term used twice in the same context. So how could it have two separate meanings? I'll spare Jim having to quote the amillennial party line, but the amillennial explanations that there two different types of resurrections, or two spiritual resurrections, is out there with other scholarly work like the origin of the pyramids involving little green men from outer space."

Rocky lowered his head starring blankly at his old canvas shoes.

"I believe that my good buddy Martin adequately disarmed the postmillennial view, and I clearly demonstrated that amillennialism does not have a leg to stand on, given that one passage in the Bible can diffuse it. That leaves us with premillennialism, the view that upon His return, Jesus will reign on earth for a thousand years, if you desire to take the time period literally. Contrary to Julie's point of view, Scripture teaches that there will be no gradual growth of the kingdom, but that it will be ushered in by a cataclysmic event."

As Tom spoke, most of the class had already stopped listening. Rocky listened, but wouldn't look in Tom's direction. Tom continued to talk at length and then came to his conclusion.

"Unlike the other millennial views, there are no biblical passages that premillennialism cannot address. The amillennialists do not have this luxury," he said looking over at Jim. "Lastly, premillennialism is not based on only one passage of the Bible."

Looking around the room, Tom realized that the attention was not on him, but on the clock. He sat down and looked over at Rocky and smiled.

Dr. Casper surprised the class by not offering a concluding remark or a challenge to Tom. Rather, he posed a question to one lone individual.

"Rocky, I'm curious as to what you think about it all."

Tom and his clique subtly grinned at each other, eagerly awaiting Rocky's observations.

"The reason I'm asking you, Rocky, is because you are in a sense the audience that all these folks will be addressing once they stand before their own congregations or go out onto the streets or into the jungles of a distant land. You heard the three main views. What do you think?"

Rocky did not offer an immediate answer. He looked around the room at Julie, Jim, Martin, and Tom, and then slowly stood up to face the class.

"A family had just gotten word that Johnny was coming home from the war. His momma said, 'Johnny will be coming home by train.' His papa disagreed and said, 'No, Johnny will be coming home by bus.' His brother spoke up in protest and said, 'No, Johnny will be coming home by car.' They continued to argue and debate the matter until they heard the doorbell ring. They opened the door and saw Johnny. They were all so happy to see him home safe and sound that they all forgot about the debate they had on how he would get home and were happy just to have him home."

Rocky slowly sat back down in his seat. The room was silent at first, and then a few students started to clap, followed by a few more students, until the majority of the room was clapping. Tom and his friends were not clapping but were astonished to see that Dr. Casper was equally impressed with Rocky's simple parable.

*   *   *

Following class, Rocky hurried to get to the cafeteria on time. "Hi, Sam!"

"Hello there, Mr. Raccoon." He laughed.

"I'm still getting used to that myself." Rocky chuckled.

"Well, I hate to ruin the experience for you, Rock, but what you did yesterday for training is basically what I need from you everyday. Can you handle the monotony?"

"Life's complex enough. It's nice to have something simple and easy to look forward to."

"Well then, I'm going to be the bringer of much joy." Sam cracked himself up. It wasn't hard to do.

*   *   *

The line was growing outside of the cafeteria, so Sam agreed to start moving them in early. Rocky reported to his position at the entrée station on the food line and initiated what had already become known at Easton Seminary as the "Meat & Greet."

"Hey, Bobby, pick your poison," Rocky asked the first student in line.

"I heard that, Rocky!" Sam yelled from the kitchen.

"Hi, Rocky," said Bobby. "I really appreciate that you call us all by name. I used to always feel like cattle coming in here to eat."

"Thanks, Bobby. Speaking of cattle, would you prefer the hamburgers or whatever animal this stuff here came from?"

"I heard that!" Sam's voice again echoed from the kitchen.

"Sorry, Sam. I try to entertain the troops while I feed 'em!"

Many of them already knew of Rocky by his public incident with Tom. Those who did not know of him for that were now getting an earful in the line and at the tables regarding his parable in Dr. Casper's theology class.

Each person in line made a point to greet Rocky as he addressed them. Those who were in attendance in class earlier congratulated him for a very fine response to Dr. Casper's question.

"That was a fantastic answer you had today, Rocky," one girl named Lynne said.

Rocky smiled and simply said, "Thank you."

Tom and Martin were in line observing the endless greetings and compliments directed toward Rocky. Martin shook his head and looked at Tom.

As they got closer to Rocky, Tom just turned around and left. Martin decided to stay and eat.

"Hi, Martin, where'd Tom go?"

"How should I know? I'm not my brother's keeper."

"I respectfully disagree with you," Rocky replied.

"Yeah, well, whatever."

* * *

Near the end of lunch, Rocky was able to grab a bite to eat and sat down with his friends from Tuttle Hall.

"Hey there, Rocky!" Steven yelled.

"There's the man!" Rick said, as though introducing the

34

world heavyweight champion.

"Hi, guys. Mind if I join you?"

"Not at all, buddy. Sit down," said Jim.

"We were just talking about you and what you said in class," Rick said.

"Oh?"

"You really hit the nail on the head. Everyone else is debating this timeless theological issue, and here you come in from out of nowhere and basically settle it by reminding us of what really matters," said Jim.

"Well, I guess I'm not one to argue about how many angels can stand on the head of a pin," Rocky replied. "Anyhow, in my opinion, prayer is the most accurate theology, for God is the I AM and not the IT IS that some make Him out to be."

"Exactly!" Steven said. "You're real. That's what people respond to. No one outside of seminary cares about these issues we debate in theology."

"I still think they're important," Rocky said. "I just think that we should not lose focus on what's really important, that's all."

Salem

Chip and Rick invited Rocky to go to church with them. Rick drove them in his little white hatchback. Rocky had his face pressed up against the glass watching the sites of Salem. He marveled at the sheer number of witchcraft shops and satanic themed stores there were.

"Do they realize that those who died during the Salem Witch Trials were not really witches?" Rocky asked.

"It doesn't matter to them," Chip answered.

"What do you mean?"

"The town has become synonymous with witchcraft because of the trials. They're not going to let a little thing like the truth get in the way," Chip said.

Rocky continued to look out the window until they had arrived at the church. Once inside, he recognized a few professors and a dozen students from Easton. Once they had found their seats, Rocky got up and made a point to not only greet those whom he already knew, but he also introduced himself to several of the members already in attendance for the morning service.

"Look at that," Rick said to Chip, who was sitting beside him

36

reading through the bulletin. "Rocky has only been here for ten minutes, and he probably knows more people than we do."

"It's a little embarrassing actually, considering that we've been coming here every Sunday for two years," Chip replied.

Once the service began, Rocky returned to his seat. He turned around and noticed a man enter the sanctuary and sit down in the back pew. The man was dressed in all black, with the exception of his silver rings, necklace, and earrings, which all featured a snake. Later, during the offering, Rocky made a point to ask Chip and Rick about the man.

"He's a Satanist," Chip whispered.

"Wow. That's quite progressive of the Church of Satan to attend Christian services."

"No," Rick corrected him, "he's not here to worship or participate. He's here praying to Satan against this church."

"Impressive," said Rocky.

Rick and Chip stared back at him.

"What I mean to say is, here's a guy of a false religion coming to pray against us. His beliefs are obviously not 'theologically sound,'" he motioned his fingers with air quotes, "but his faith is admirable. How many times do we go to their church to pray for *them*?"

Rick and Chip continued to stare at him.

"So why is he praying against this church?" Rocky asked.

"This church is pretty active, especially on Halloween," said Chip. "During Halloween, Salem gets several thousand visitors. About half are here to celebrate witchcraft and Satan."

"Who's the other half?"

"Underage smokers and drinkers," Rick replied

"This church prays all night long against the satanic forces active in this community and engages in true spiritual warfare," said Chip.

"And the Satanists believe that they can weaken the church by praying here to Satan?" Rocky asked.

"That's about right," Rick whispered.

The pastor then began his sermon, and the conversation ended.

* * *

After the service was over, Rick asked Rocky, "So, how'd you like Pastor Chuck?"

"He's great. I especially liked the Beatles reference," he said as he started to walk away.

"I thought you would like that." Rick laughed.

Rocky didn't stay long enough to talk. Instead, he ran to catch up to the faithful Satanist.

"Hey, wait up!" Rocky yelled.

The man in black kept on walking, and those who didn't hear Rocky chasing after him before did not miss him yelling even louder, "Hey, mister, wait up!"

The man kept walking like a commuter about to miss his train. Rocky ran up to him and started to walk alongside him.

"Good morning. My name is Rocky Raccoon."

The man suddenly stopped, turned around to face Rocky. "What's your name?"

"Rocky Raccoon."

"That's what I thought you said. What do you want?"

"I just want to talk. Is this a bad time?"

"Talk about what?"

"About you. I imagine you're an expert on the subject, so I thought I'd ask you."

"I really don't want to talk," the man insisted as he began to walk away from Rocky.

38

"I just wanted to commend you on your faith."

The man stopped and again turned to face Rocky. "What?"

"I wanted to say that, though I don't share your beliefs, I admire your faith."

The man looked long and deep into Rocky's hazel eyes. "I'm going to get some coffee. If you want to talk, you'll have to buy your own," he mumbled.

"Fair enough," Rocky said, while subtly taking inventory of the change in his pocket.

"By the way, what the hell kind of a name is Rocky Raccoon?"

"It's better than having no name at all, I suppose."

"Oh, yeah. My name is Snake."

"Your parents must have hated you."

"No more than yours did, apparently," he said and shrugged.

Rick and Chip stared out at Rocky and Snake as they walked farther away into downtown Salem.

"What should we do?" Rick asked.

"I guess he'll call us when he's ready to come home," Chip replied.

* * *

Rocky and Snake walked into Brubaker's Café, a popular coffeehouse a few blocks away from the church. Rocky held the door open for Snake, and they both walked in and sat down in a booth. Snake was personally greeted from across the room by one of the staff.

Rocky looked over at the counter and then looked back at Snake.

"She already knows what I want," said Snake. "You'll have to go up and order your own."

"Fair enough. I can't read the menu from here anyway."

When Rocky returned, Snake was already enjoying his coffee.

"So what do you want, Rocky Raccoon?"

"I wanted to get to know you better, that's all."

"You know, you're the first person in that church who's ever taken an interest in really getting to know me. I mean, I have had some of the elders give me a couple booklets about becoming saved and all, but that's as far as they went. They didn't want to know me, just dump their literature on me."

"I'm sorry to hear that, Snake. I can tell you that I've had a few bad experiences at some churches too, usually because I wasn't dressed the way they wanted me to dress."

"That's what I'm talking about. They're hypocrites!"

"Of course there are hypocrites in church. Church is a place for sinners to go, including hypocrites. Especially hypocrites! If you're perfect and have it all together, you don't need to go to church, now do you? You can simply stay at home watching football pre-game shows on TV with all the other perfect people Sunday morning."

Snake sat back and said nothing.

"So, what did you think of their literature?" Rocky asked.

"It looks great on paper. I've never seen it lived out though. It's like seeing a romantic movie and then going home to a broken marriage. To me, it's all theory."

"And you chose the Church of Satan as an alternative?"

"I never said I was with the Church of Satan. They're contemporary Satanists," he replied and then took a sip of his coffee.

"I'm sorry, I thought that you were a Satanist."

"I am. I'm a *traditional* Satanist."

"What's the difference?"

"The Church of Satan is altogether different. They don't even really believe in Satan. It's more of a philosophy about the individual. Haven't you ever heard of Anton LaVey?"

"I've heard of him, but that's where it begins and ends for me."

"Well, he's the founder of the so-called Church of Satan. It's just a fashionable philosophy for people who think too highly of themselves. Traditional Satanism, on the other hand, is the oldest religion in the world."

"So you do worship Satan then."

"Not worship, per se. Emulate. I admire how he rebelled against God."

"Most people like you usually pick James Dean as their role model."

"James Dean didn't give us free will," Snake replied. "Just read Genesis 3."

"Neither did Satan. God gave him the freedom to rebel, just as he gave to Adam and Eve."

"According to your Bible maybe."

"You're the one who cited Scripture, Snake. You can't quote as fact one moment, and then discredit it the next."

"It's not infallible, if that's what you're getting at."

"Do you agree with 2 Corinthians 4:4 that Satan is the god of this world?"

"Yes, I do. He opened the door to this world, rather than allowing us to be trapped in the world of blissful ignorance in Eden."

"If Satan rebelled against God, that would make God the authority he was rebelling against, right?"

"Yeah, that's right."

"Likewise, if Satan acquired his position of god of the world from Adam who gave it up, that would infer that God, who gave Adam the world, is the Creator of the world as the Bible teaches."

"Sure, why not? What's your point?"

"That Satan is not equal to God, my friend, and he's not infinitely powerful like God."

"Okay, so you're saying that God really will win out in the end, just as the Bible claims, so therefore, I should reconsider my whole belief system?"

"Well, if you're with Satan, you will share his fate, just as the Bible states."

"Oh, really? And what if Satan wins? Have you ever considered that the Bible got it wrong?"

"Satan will not conquer God but will suffer in hell."

"Says you."

"That's right. Think about it for a minute. This isn't the same as Dr. Frankenstein being ultimately destroyed by the monster he made. God is infinite. Satan is finite. How could a finite creature conquer its infinitely powerful Creator? I think you should really reconsider, Snake," Rocky said as he sipped his now lukewarm cup of coffee.

Snake was still and quiet. He looked at his watch then looked up at Rocky.

"Thanks for the good conversation, Rocky Raccoon, but I have to be on my way to work now."

"Think about what I said, okay. Also, look over what they gave you at the church. It might be helpful."

"I'll see you at church next week, Rocky."

"I'll see you then, Snake."

* * *

Rocky called Tuttle Hall, and Jim answered the phone. Within twenty minutes, Jim arrived at Brubaker's Café to pick up Rocky.

"I heard you left with Snake after church," said Jim.

"I did. Pray for him. I really believe that he's a seeker. He hasn't found God yet, but he will."

"What makes you think he'll find God? He seems pretty committed to his beliefs."

"I think he's seeking the truth, and God promises that all who seek shall find."

Jim smiled.

As he turned his car back into Easton's long and winding driveway, Jim asked, "Hey, the guys and I wanted to know if you would like to join us tomorrow morning for the Nile Books warehouse sale?"

"What's Nile Books?"

"Nile Books is the largest Christian book distributor in the nation, and their warehouse happens to be about ten miles from here. They have an open warehouse sale at the start of every quarter. You can get a lot of Christian books dirt cheap."

"Sure, why not?"

"Great!" We'll get you up around 4:00 a.m.," said Jim.

"What?"

"Trust me, you'll see what I mean tomorrow."

Deadly Sins

In parts of Russia, 4:00 a.m. is referred to as "The Hour of the Wolf." It's that time in the morning when a person is unable to sleep because of feelings of regret about past decisions that have led to the present state of discontent. Rocky had not had to deal with the wolf much since becoming a Christian, but he was now facing a far worse foe, Steven knocking on his door at 4:00 a.m.

Rocky slowly got up and was amazed to find the whole dorm wide-awake, drinking coffee and watching TV.

"Have you all gone mad?" Rocky asked.

His question was met with collective laughter.

"Rocky, this is tradition," said Rick. "You're either in, or you're, well, you have to be in. We won't let you stay out!"

"Swell."

"All right! Now get ready before we're late," said Chip.

"Late? How early do they open their doors?" Rocky asked.

"7:00," Jim replied.

"Then why are we getting there so early in the morning? I thought you said it was just a few miles away."

"You'll see," he heard one of the dorm's residents reply.

"Okay, let me grab a jacket. It's going to be chilly out there,"

Rocky said.

"That's the spirit!" Chip said.

* * *

The gang from Tuttle Hall arrived in their caravan at Nile Books at 4:40 a.m. As they got out of their cars, Rocky looked at the line that was already forming.

"Oh, my gosh! Are we also meeting the President of the United States?" Rocky asked.

"Like I said, they sell books pretty cheap here," Steven replied.

"I'm not here to shop," Rocky said. "I'm just here to behold your quarterly tradition."

"Come on now. Let's get in line," Jim said.

Rocky was amazed to see many familiar faces in line from Easton Seminary. Not just students but professors as well. There were students from other local seminaries and colleges, as well as several local pastors and laypeople. There was a genuine sense of community among those in line.

"What should I expect when they open the doors?" Rocky asked.

"Okay, here's the drill. When the doors open, the line will move very quickly. You gotta be ready," Chip said.

"Ready for what?" Rocky asked.

"When you get in there, you will see a huge pile of empty cardboard boxes to your left," said Chip. "If you're planning on buying any books, be sure to grab one. In fact, grab one anyway, as you may change your mind."

"Okay, I grab a box. Then what?" Rocky asked.

"Be sure to tell him to go to the center tables first," he heard Steven add.

"Center tables?" Rocky asked.

"Yeah," said Chip. "The books that are the cheapest will be on the center tables. If you go for a book that is on the shelves or have to request a book from the stacks, then it will be cheap, but it won't be nearly as cheap as those on the bargain tables."

"Okay. That sounds easy enough," said Rocky.

"You'd think so, wouldn't you?" Chip replied.

* * *

The main doors opened at 7:00 a.m. sharp. Everything went just as Chip had described. Rocky had to jog at a slow pace just to keep up. He walked through the main doors, grabbed a box, and then stopped. He couldn't move his legs to go and seek out the great deals. He just marveled at the crowd of future and present pastors and laymen fumbling over and running into each other for a good deal on a Christian book. It looked like the day after Thanksgiving, when the natural born shoppers tear each other's hair out to buy that year's popular toy, which typically would be sold in short supply.

Rocky watched as the whole line entered. He stood there for several minutes observing the phenomenon. A gray haired man wearing blue overalls with a green patch on the left knee and a red handkerchief hanging out of his back pocket walked up to Rocky. The man stood next to Rocky and started to chuckle.

"You just gotta laugh at these folks," said the old man.

"Laugh or cry. Hi, my name is Rocky."

"Howdy, Rocky. It's nice to make your acquaintance. I'm Gus. I'm the custodian here."

"It's nice to meet a colleague. I'm one of the custodians at Easton."

"Ah, yes, the Protestant seminary. I'm Catholic myself."

"Really? So which of the Seven Deadly Sins are we witnessing here, Gus?"

He shook his head as he and Rocky saw two people wrestling each other over one book, as they both already held boxes filled with dozens of other books.

"Well, sir, I'd say that you're definitely witnessing firsthand greed, gluttony, pride, and envy."

"Four out of seven? Why pride and envy?"

"Young man, I've been around here for a long time and have come to know a lot of these seminary types pretty well. Most of all of them are really good people, but some of them suffer from pride when it comes to these books. I see it all the time. Did you see those two guys practically fighting over that one book a moment ago? Did they really need that book? Did they really need it now? Why do they need it? I'd betcha a day's pay that after they buy these books that they go and display them proudly in their rooms with no intention of actually reading them."

"You think so?"

"Call it a hunch. I could be wrong, young man, but I doubt it."

Tom walked out of the crowd pulling a wagon full of books.

"Hey there, Gus. I see you've met Rocky Raccoon."

"Why, yes, I have, Tom Cat."

"I'm glad that I found you, Rocky," Tom said as he turned to grab something from his book filled wagon. "Here you go. I saw this and thought of you."

Rocky accepted the book, *The Complete Guide to Christianity for Morons.*

"Uh, thanks, Tom."

"No problem, Rocky. I'll see you around, Gus," Tom said as he left pulling his wagon.

"What a nice guy," Gus remarked.

"Tom?"

"Yeah, he gave me the same book too because I was confused about a few things that he and I had discussed, and it really did help clear some stuff up for me. The title seems rude, but that's just how it's marketed to us layman." Gus laughed. "Tom even confessed a couple years ago that he owns that book too, but joked about how he kept it under his mattress so that none of those arrogant, know-it-all students would tease him about it."

"*Really?* You *know* Tom?"

"Not as well as I used to really. When he first moved out here to attend Easton a few years ago, he was quite the whippersnapper, if you know what I mean. The kid came straight out of college on fire for Jesus, and he told everyone that he saw about Him. Never saw a young person with such a heart for Jesus. I've stood here every year for fifteen years, and he's the only person to actually stop and get to really know me. That's special."

"That is, Gus."

"Why sure it is. You can't be a preacher if you're afraid to talk to people. I've seen him come here just like today, and buy a bunch of books, only to stand outside and give them away as people left. I know the kid comes from money, but he doesn't have to do that kind of stuff."

"Does he still do that?"

"I don't know really, but he did give you one though."

Rocky nodded in agreement.

"However, now that I think about it," Gus thought aloud, "I do remember near the end of his first year that he seemed sad. Not quite himself, you know?"

"Do you have any idea why?"

"It's not like I saw him all the time, just at these quarterly

48

sales, which made the change more obvious to me maybe, than to those who saw him every day. He did say to me that he felt pretty overwhelmed in school at times. Even though he scored perfect grades, he said that he felt pressure from upper classmen to be 'more intellectual.' Like that's what the world needs, more eggheads." Gus laughed.

"Tom's the top student now. I would have never guessed that he felt this way."

"Well, here's something that I have learned in my own humble life. I'm not a rich man, nor am I a famous man. I probably never will be, unless I hit the lottery. When I die, there won't be many people who will remember me, let alone visit my grave. However, I've found contentment in wanting to please Jesus and not others. Young Tom Cat struggled with that, and maybe he still does. I really don't know. He's a good kid, but sometimes there's a temptation to want to esteem yourself, especially in a place like Easton, which isn't what the Good Book teaches. For that matter, the book Tom gave you doesn't teach it either. I guess that's what I mean by pride and envy I suppose."

"I see what you mean. Well, I hate to cut this short, but I had better meet up with my friends. It was nice talking with you, Gus. I'll see you around"

"My pleasure, young man."

Rocky gazed out into the crowds noting that his friends weren't going as crazy as the others. He placed his cardboard box back where he found it. When he'd picked it up, there was a mountain of boxes. Now, his lone box made a molehill.

The Devil's Brew

Rocky sat contently in the cramped backseat of Rick's old foreign compact on their way Salem Presbyterian Church. He leaned forward and said to Chip and Rick, "I want to thank you both for praying for Snake this week. I really sensed that God was softening his heart to receive the Gospel message last Sunday."

"It's entirely possible that, though he was going to church to pray against it, that, on a subconscious level, he heard and understood God's Word," Rick observed.

"Maybe he is a true seeker, and God revealed Himself to him through church and your talk," said Chip.

"I've met Satanists before," said Rocky, "and Snake doesn't fit the usual profile."

"Yeah, I've noticed a lot of Christians wearing all black, tattoos, and snake jewelry!" Chip laughed.

"I know he looks the part," said Rocky, "but his motives are questionable."

"What do you mean?" Chip asked.

"I've talked to some Satanists before, and frankly, I've never spoken to one who was so willing to hear me out, or even agree with the logic and theology of my arguments. There's more to this guy than the Satanism. I think he feels hurt or betrayed by God."

"How do you figure? Did he say so?" Chip questioned.

"No, but I've been there before. I grew up in a Christian family but drifted away from the faith. I grew to be angry with God, blaming Him for my troubles, especially when my parents died. No matter how mad I got though, I still longed for Him and never forgot that He really was in charge."

"I think this is the first time you've ever really told us much about your past," said Chip.

"Yeah, maybe so," Rocky replied as they pulled into the parking lot, "but when I became a Christian man, I buried my past along with my sins."

*   *   *

Once inside, Rocky looked around for Snake.

"He normally comes in right as the service starts, probably to avoid any contact with the members or clergy," Chip said.

They sat in the back row and waited for Snake. When they saw him, Rocky stood up and motioned to invite Snake to sit with them. Snake appeared almost outwardly happy to see Rocky.

"Good morning, Snake," said Rocky.

"Hi there. I wasn't sure if you'd be here," said Snake.

"I promised you I'd be here. Please have a seat."

Chip and Rick both looked around nervously as many of the members in attendance turned around to observe Snake taking a seat next to them.

"Snake, I'd like you to meet my friends, Chip and Rick."

"Hi, guys. I'm glad to meet someone here not named after an

51

animal," Snake said with a grin.

The joke really seemed to break the ice, and Chip and Rick both cheerfully greeted him.

The service started, and the four of them stood up for the first hymn, *Amazing Grace*. The pastor looked at them in both amazement and joy. Even though Snake wasn't singing, this was the first time the pastor had ever seen him stand up during a hymn or participate in any fashion.

* * *

Salem Presbyterian Church was offering communion this Sunday. As the bread, symbolizing the broken body of Jesus, was passed down the pew, people took a piece and ate it. Rocky noticed that Snake didn't take communion, but Pastor Chuck did explain that only Christians could participate in the sacrament.

The ushers then passed the communion tray that contained little cups filled with red wine, symbolizing the shed blood of Jesus. Snake noticed that Rocky was trembling as he passed him the tray, causing the little cups to spill out some of its contents.

"What's wrong? Are you okay, Rock?" Snake asked.

"I can't drink this," said Rocky as his shaky hands passed the rattling tray to Rick.

Rick leaned over to Rocky. "Is it against the rules of your denomination to drink alcohol?"

"No. That's not it…I'm a recovering alcoholic. If I drink this, it would be *bad*."

Snake, looked up at Rocky, whose eyes were welling up with tears, patted him on the shoulder.

Rocky got up and walked out of the sanctuary. Snake motioned to Rick and Chip that he'd go check on him.

"Shouldn't one of us go too?" Chip asked.

"I don't think we should make a scene," Rick replied.

Chip then turned to Rick and said, "It's weird, but after Rocky's confession, he seemed holier than ever before."

"I don't think he looks at it that way," Rick answered. "I think he's just really honest with others and with himself. I don't know where he's been or what he's done, but he has clearly confessed to God and seems freer than anyone I've ever known."

* * *

Snake caught up to Rocky and walked alongside him to Brubaker's Café without saying a word. Rocky and Snake arrived at Brubaker's and sat in the same booth they had occupied the last Sunday. Rocky once again ordered his own coffee at the counter and then joined Snake.

"So, Rock, how long have you been sober?"

"One year, ten months, and 15 days."

"I admire the strength of your character. I believe that most Christians would have risked drinking the wine in order to save their pride or maintain the *perfect* image."

"Perfect image?" Rocky said with a chuckle. "Now that's an accusation no one's ever thrown at me."

"I can see it in your friends' eyes. They look up to you. I imagine that others do too, whether you notice it or not."

"The only thing holy about me is that I'm human. God created us to be human, and that includes all the screwing up, failing, confessions, and healing. In Vegas, I struggled with many sins and fell badly with alcohol. It's still a temptation," Rocky said, still visibly shaking.

"How did you overcome it?"

"I haven't. No alcoholic is ever cured. I look at it no

differently than I do sin. Although I can sin, I do not plan on it. If I don't sin, I find that I don't miss it at all. During my time in Vegas, Satan was trying everything he could to separate me from God. He robbed me of my understanding that I am a child of God, and, once I lost that, I really had no boundaries. I committed sins that still haunt me, and the sins that scare me the most are the ones I don't know because I was either too high or drunk to remember."

Snake sat wide-eyed listening to Rocky. "How did you overcome those sins?"

Rocky finished taking a sip of his coffee, looked Snake in the eye and said, "My appetite for sin is stronger than anyone I've ever known or read about. Only now, my love for God is much stronger."

Snake nodded his head and said nothing.

"When I was feeling low, I figured I lost God's favor, and that He no longer loved me. I really didn't believe that my life had any kind of spiritual or eternal value."

"What happened to change your mind?"

"One morning I woke up on the doorstep of some building in downtown Las Vegas. I didn't know how I got there, but judging by the empty bottles and the dried up vomit all over my clothes and in the beard I had back then, I knew that I had spent the night drinking and doing drugs. Or as I called it back then, 'having a good time.' I remember lying there, unable to even get up. As I was sitting there on the doorstep, trying to regain my balance, the wandering child of a tourist came by and stood right in front of me and stared. She offered me a piece of gum and smiled. Next thing I know, I hear a woman screaming, 'Don't look at that filth!' She ran over and dragged the kid away from me by her arm."

"I'm sorry, Rocky."

"Don't be. The next voice would be the one that changed my life. As I sat there, hurting from the woman's biting judgment, another voice offered a kinder message. I looked up and saw a Franciscan priest standing over me. He sat down with me and told me how God loved me. I started to cry and confessed every sin that I could possibly remember and rationalized how God could never possibly love me. He responded, 'There is nothing you can do, son, to make God love you more and nothing you can do to make Him love you less.' That got my attention, and I listened to him on that step till I was physically able to get up with his assistance. He then took me to get cleaned up, and later we went to have a nice breakfast and lots of coffee. Grace always precedes redemption."

"He sounds like a good man."

"He is. He commented that it's people like me, who are broken underneath the wheels of life who are more likely to accept the Gospel of Grace than those who are living in some pietistic illusion. He also told me that Scripture teaches us not to get too hung up in our failures, weaknesses, and addictions, because God still loves us. He said that it was impossible to overestimate the value of anyone. Even me," Rocky said with a smile.

"I'm glad that he found you."

"How could he not? I was sitting at God's address."

"Where's God's address?"

"It's at the end of your rope."

Snake sat quietly and was so deep in thought that he sipped his ice-cold coffee as though it were a fresh steaming serving.

"It's amazing that you're alive to tell me this story," Snake finally said. "I've never met anyone like you, especially a Christian."

"Thanks, I think."

"I'm amazed that they let you in at the seminary. Don't they have some sort of agreement or statement of character, promising that you didn't do certain things in recent years in order to be accepted?"

"Yes, but I'm not a student."

"Really? What are you then?"

"I'm a janitor, and I also work in the cafeteria."

"You've got to be kidding! You're the most convincing person I've ever met from that place, and you're the *janitor*?"

Rocky nodded.

"I can't believe what a wild turn your life took."

"Make no mistake about it though, I went through absolute hell getting cleaned up. God loved me as I was, but He wanted much more for me than the life I was living."

"I've tried to give up cigarettes many times and still drink more than I should, but I can't imagine what you went through. I wish I knew you back then, but something tells me that you've done more for me now as Rocky Raccoon in Salem than you could have ever given me in Las Vegas."

"Thank you."

After a deep breath, like someone about to dive into a swimming pool, Snake said, "Believe it or not, I grew up in a very devout Catholic home."

"Really?"

"Yeah. Really. I had a great childhood, mind you. I'm not one of those people, like those celebrities on TV talk shows, who cry about having a horrible childhood. I had a great time growing up. I loved to wake up every summer morning with no plans, finding a new adventure with my brother and the neighborhood kids. I used to love going on a Sunday drive after mass with my parents and brother. My dad would simply ask us which direction we'd want to go, and we'd go, even at the risk of getting lost, which we often did."

"Those are great memories."

"Well, that's about all I have left to me now. God seemed to delight in taking it all away from me. My Dad died too young. He worked at his job for 29 years and 11 months. The company after his death said that they would not be giving the family any pension benefits, as Dad technically didn't work there 30 years."

Rocky nodded.

"Yeah, I know. My mother blamed the company for that and continued to raise her sons, and then my little brother Craig died in a car wreck, and my mom's faith in God died the same day. I hated what had become of my mother, and I had no idea why God would permit it to happen."

"Is it fair to say that your decision to follow Satan wasn't about worshipping him, but rather following his rebellion against God?"

"That's a funny question really. It stands to reason that an act of rebellion is about our only recourse against God. Right? How else do you hurt an all-powerful God? You go for His heart. That's what He did to me."

Rocky sat quietly.

"I think we've a lot in common."

"Like what?" Rocky asked.

"We've both spent a lot of time at God's address."

"It's just like the hymn we sang today. We were lost but found, blind and can now see. I did not save myself, nor could I. Satan separated me from God with lies and temptations, just as he has done to you."

Snake said nothing but seemed noticeably surprised to find himself nodding along.

"Look, Rocky, I appreciate you and your friends sitting with me today. I also want to thank you for always being so honest with me. I do need to get going now. I have to go to work. Will I see you next Sunday?"

"You don't have to wait till Sunday. You've got my number. Call me anytime. And, yes, I will definitely see you next Sunday."

Snake smiled, put on his jacket, and walked outside.

After Snake left, a young woman in the booth behind Rocky turned around and said, "I know this is going to sound really rude, but I was listening to everything you just said to that young man."

Rocky turned around to find a middle-aged woman with tears in her eyes. He slowly got up and sat across from her. "Do you wanna talk?"

"Can we?"

Rocky spent the next hour and a half talking to a woman he did not know who was struggling with a destructive addition of her own. No one would ever know about this conversation, and he would receive no recognition for his time and compassion. However, it served as a reminder to him that God might have brought him to Brubaker's for reasons other than Snake that day. God does work in mysterious ways.

Confessions and Lamentations

Michael called Tuttle Hall to see if anyone could pick him up following his unexpected encounter at Brubaker's Café. Rick answered the phone and said that he would be there in twenty minutes.

Rick came in and sat down across from Rocky who was reading the café's courtesy newspaper. Rocky looked up, happy to see his friend and his ride.

"Let's get going!" Rocky said as he scooted out of the booth.

"Would it be okay if we stayed and talked for a while?"

Rocky eased himself back into the booth and said, "Sure Ricky. My time is your time."

"A while back, I wanted to talk to you during breakfast," Rick said.

"Yes, I remember that you had something on your mind that morning. What is it?"

"I don't know who to talk to, and after finding out that you're dealing with an addiction, I thought that maybe you might understand."

"I'm conscious of my sins, but I still struggle with them daily. What's on your heart?"

59

"I have a problem. A big problem that started off as a very little one," Rick said in a hushed voice, looking around to see if anyone was listening before he continued. "I have a sexual addiction."

"Do you mean that you are sexually active with others?" Rocky asked.

"No, not that. I'm not *that* bold. I mean…I have an addiction to pornography."

Rocky looked into Rick's eyes, which were red with the strain of holding back the shame he felt. "I do understand, Rick."

"I knew you would, Rocky," Rick said, relieved of some tension. "As soon as I heard that you're battling an alcohol addiction, I knew you'd understand."

"Well, yeah, but I am also battling the same addiction you are. I took it a lot further than porn though. That's where it starts, until the 'high,' if you will, is no longer satisfied, and then you go look for a new way of satisfying your addiction, like strip clubs, and then prostitutes."

Rick said nothing, but his eyes spoke volumes.

"Ricky, only by the grace of God do I not have any diseases, let alone AIDS. My drug and alcohol habits really damaged my thinking, and I really got into some deviant activities because I let Satan in."

"That's my concern. I don't want Satan to have a hold on me, but I cannot quit, no matter how hard I try. I'm seriously considering withdrawing from Easton and pursuing a different career with my degree in history."

"I think that would be a tragic mistake. You should flee temptation, not God. I found out firsthand that I am at my weakest when God isn't my top priority. When I am fervently praying, reading the Bible, and attending church, sexual temptation never crosses my mind. When I'm not praying or

60

reading the Bible, then my thoughts do wander."

"I know what you're saying, Rock. I know James wrote that we are purified when we draw near to God."

"Doesn't it make sense? If we draw near to God, and He draws near to us, then temptation is weakened. Before we can approach victory, we must draw near to God."

"Why doesn't God simply intervene and cure me? He created the universe and everything in it, yet seems unwilling to help me overcome this addiction."

Rocky gave a crooked grin and massaged the five o'clock shadow on his chin. "I used to ask myself that all the time, and even asked the Franciscan priest who literally picked me up out of the gutter the same question."

"What did he say?"

"Remember that passage in Luke, where Jesus went to that man's house whose daughter just died?"

"Yes, that man was Jairus."

"Yes. Anyhow, he told me that Jesus took her by the hand and told her to rise. After she did, he instructed the others to get her something to eat."

"I don't get it."

Rocky smiled. "I didn't get it at first either. Why did Jesus bring her back to life but not fill her stomach with something filling and nutritious? Why did He tell the others to get her some food to eat?"

Rick was non-responsive, leaning forward to get the answer quicker.

"Could it be, Ricky, that God does the impossible, but He requires us to do the possible?"

"I understand what you're saying, but I'm not sure if I can do it. I feel as though I really need help, but I have always been afraid to ask for obvious reasons."

Rocky's head lowered for a brief moment. "That's why sexual addictions are more complex than any other addiction, especially for Christian men. Trust me, I've battled them all!"

"Different in what way?"

"If I walked into a church and asked people to pray for me because I was battling pride, alcohol, gossip, greed, or any other sin, they would. One failing of the church is that Christian men feel ashamed, or are made to feel ashamed, to confess their struggles with sexual temptation, which allows Satan to continue to put a stranglehold on their walk with Christ. How many times has a man come to you and asked you to pray for his sin of sexual lust? How many times has a man requested his Bible study or Sunday school class to pray for him as he lusts for his neighbor? Men can admit a lot of sins but not sexual temptations. Unfortunately, the church is often times not as receptive to helping a man through this addiction as it is other sins."

"And that's what I fear. I feel such shame. I know what I'm doing is wrong, and I've tried to stop on my own, but I always fail. I have prayed to God literally thousands of times for Him to give me strength, and after I fall, I must have prayed a thousand more times for His forgiveness," Rick confessed while looking down at the now moist sugar packets he played with in his hands.

"I'd say that this is a big step, and I'm honored that you trusted me enough to share this with me. We'll get through this together."

"Thanks for listening. I feel as though the world has been lifted off my shoulders."

"So, you have a degree in history? That's great. Before I left for Las Vegas, I was a history major at Ohio State University," said Rocky.

"I didn't know you went to college."

"Went? Yes. Graduated? No."

"What made you want to leave school for Las Vegas?"

"The same thing that is making you consider leaving here. My addictions got the best of me. They don't have to get the best of you. I'm not going to lie to you and tell you that it's easy to quit a sexual addiction. From my experience, I struggled every bit as much with overcoming my sexual addictions as I did with heroin, alcohol, and smoking."

Rick looked over his shoulder and scanned the café to see who may have overheard Rocky's confession as Rocky sat back and took a sip of his coffee.

"What do I do now?" Rick asked.

"First, be thankful that you even know that you have a problem. That first step is the hardest. Second, you shared your desire with God and me to clean up. If you don't see it, these are basically the first few steps of Alcoholics Anonymous Twelve-Step Program."

"I greatly appreciate your help, Rocky. Just confessing this to you has strengthened me."

"I'm here for you, buddy, but I'm not an expert. I didn't overcome all the stuff that controlled me by myself. I had professional help, many good friends, and God. I will help you find some professional help and will stand by your side with honor as your friend."

"I don't know how you do it. We both suffer the same sin, yet I was about to quit seminary, and here you sit, the most Spirit-filled Christian I've ever met."

"It's not me," Rocky said as he shook his head. "My identity and security is not in living a lie that I'm some pious man with impeccable morals. I'm not, and I'm okay with that. I'd rather live on the verge of falling and trust in God's grace rather than seeking security in my own morals, which can change or disappear at any time."

"I still feel like God wouldn't want me preaching to His people," Rick said as he sank back into his seat.

"Rick, King David also battled and fell to the sin of sexual temptation. He committed adultery with Bathsheba. Though he was punished through the death of the child of that affair, God still used the union of David and Bathsheba to give birth to one of Israel's greatest kings, Solomon, and, ultimately down the line, Jesus. God's love will even take the lowest points in our lives and use them for His glory."

"I know."

"Rick," Rocky paused, choosing his next words carefully, "do you believe everything Jesus said?"

"Yes, of course I do."

"You have a servant's heart, which is one of the reasons I imagine you're looking to become a missionary. Am I correct to assume that you believe that whatever you do for the least of us, you do for Jesus?"

"Yes, that's in Matthew 25, and I certainly try to live my life much like you do, serving those who are poor, hungry, and neglected," Rick said, as though he was answering a question at Easton.

"As a Christian, you are willing to help out anyone, especially the poor, thirsty, hungry, and naked. Are you willing to get your hands dirty with a person that society has tossed aside like litter on a highway?"

"Yes, Rocky, I am."

"One day, not too long after I rededicated my life to Christ, I had a revelation."

"What was it?"

"At that time in my life, I discovered that the one who

needed my love the most, the one I could love the most, the one that I could help with my love the most, and the one whom my love would have the most meaning was *me*. I found that, at that time in my life, I was the least of the brothers of Jesus. I needed to love me, which helped me find my way to sobriety, as well as following Christ."

Rick lowered his head and let out a slow, deep breath.

"Rick, I know that, theologically speaking, you believe that God loves and forgives you and accepts you just as the father welcomed back his prodigal son, and He does! Be aware, though, that to battle Satan in this territory, you have to also love and forgive yourself too, and know for a fact that your life has value and that God has a plan for you."

Rick sat up with a glimmer in his steely blue eyes, which was absent during the entire conversation. "Thanks, Rocky. I think you're right."

"Well, don't sound so surprised!"

"Perhaps *we* can talk to Dr. Samuels tomorrow," said Rick. "I know he's a professor of evangelism, but he's also a licensed psychologist."

"That sounds like a great idea. Just let me know when, and I'll be there."

"So how did you get to be so wise, Rocky?"

"By learning that I wasn't."

The Legend of Rocky Raccoon

The beautiful bouquet of autumn's glory that decorated the North Shore had slowly crumbled away, exposing the stark stony landscape that inspired generations past to move west for more fertile ground. Rocky, like the determined New England farmers of old, planted seeds wherever he went, and his reputation grew as he served the Lord. His ministry was as overt as volunteering at a homeless shelter in downtown Boston and as covert as simply acknowledging everyone that he encountered with a friendly greeting. He oftentimes discovered that those whose existence he affirmed were desperately in need of acceptance by another or had already been praying to God for some sort of sign that He still cared.

In just two months, Rocky was arguably the most popular person in Beverly, Massachusetts. He could walk into any store, bank, or restaurant, and most everyone knew him by name. Incredibly, he remembered their names too. Steven once commented that Rocky was a gifted listener in an academic setting where everyone else wanted to be heard.

Rocky made an effort to limit his time at Easton to when he worked and slept, though he still attended Wednesday chapel

66

and sat in on a class every now and then. He started to spend an extraordinary amount of time off campus. His heart was in spending time with those whom society often neglected, such as the elderly, teenagers, the homeless, mentally challenged, disabled, and the sick, especially those stricken by HIV. Though complimented for his time and effort, Rocky stated that he was only following the Lord's "Great Compassion," which he cited from Matthew 25: "Whatever you do for the least of these brothers of mine, you do unto me."

* * *

Snake fidgeted and looked around the café anxiously. He looked to Rocky like a shaken can of pop about to explode if someone dared to open it.

"What must I do now to get myself back on the right track?" Snake blurted out. "I mean, I really do understand the theology and the steps to getting saved. After all, I think I have the best attendance of anyone in that church!" He laughed as he kept trying to sip coffee from his empty cup.

"You know, that's probably true." He laughed along with Snake. "Let me first say that I didn't become a Christian because of some philosophy on life. I became a Christian because of what Jesus did. When I was at my lowest point, I knew the basics of the faith as well. Still, I needed help to take the steps in the right direction. In my case, I had to give up all the things that were separating me from God, which is the very nature of sin. I gave up the drugs, alcohol, sex, gambling, and all my other vices. In your case, you need to sever all ties with the people involved in your present faith. Get rid of all the literature and paraphernalia that might lead you astray. Also, focus on the truth. You seem like a guy who is seeking the truth, and Satan gave you just enough to confuse you. You need to turn to God's Word and know Him through Scripture and through prayer. Also, keep going to church. I'll be there, and I will help you as best as I can."

"Truthfully, I have already thrown away all the satanic stuff in my apartment. My friends have noticed a change in me. Word got out that I was spending a lot of time with you. In a sense, they've already cut ties with me."

Rocky nodded.

"I know that I need to accept Jesus as my Savior, but I'm not sure how."

"Snake, just know first off that you can never earn your way into Heaven. That fact seems to escape many Christians, even those studying and teaching at Easton. Satan will try to trick you at times and make you feel unworthy. God loves you as you are and not as you should be. To accept Jesus, you need to admit that you're a sinner, and you must be willing to turn away from that sin. Also, you must believe that Jesus died on the cross for your sins, and receive Jesus into your heart and life through prayer."

"I guess if you can be saved, then I know God will take me in!" Snake laughed out loud. "I appreciate everything that you've done for me, Rocky. I know that you have not only spent a large amount of time on me but have done so at the expense of your own reputation."

"I'm not too concerned about my reputation. In my mind, I could repeat the Apostles' Creed over and over again till I'm blue in the face, but if I don't love others, I cannot call myself a Christian."

"You've shown me so much love, and I know that it comes from God."

"Thanks. That's honestly the nicest thing anyone has ever

said to me."

"Well, I hate to cut this short, but as usual, I need to get to work now. Thanks again for everything. I'll call you later this week."

"It's been my pleasure, and please call me *anytime.*"

"I'll see you next Sunday at church," Snake said as he put on his jacket.

"I'll see you there," Rocky said as he got up and gave Snake a hug.

At the door, Snake turned around and said, "The name's Adam."

"God bless you, Adam." Rocky smiled from ear to ear.

"He has. He really has."

*   *   *

"I don't get it!" Tom said to Martin in their campus apartment. "I have worked my butt off for *three* years here at Easton, and no one seems to care, because they're all falling over themselves to praise some janitor!"

"Well, to be honest, the guy has done some pretty incredible things," said Martin.

"Like what? Cleaning Jim's toilet? Oh my gosh! I'm up to my neck in more nuts than a fruitcake!"

"Look, man, I know he's getting a lot of attention lately, but some of it's deserved. I would have never guessed that Snake would become a Christian."

"Who cares?"

Martin stood silently and stared at Tom.

"You know what I mean, Martin. I'm happy that the Snakeman is saved."

"What is it then? What's your problem?"

69

"I honestly feel, with every ounce of my being, that I'm going to be the next important theologian whose books and teachings are going to impact the world. I have never mentioned it to anyone, but I had a dream one night tell me this."

"So, in other words, you think God promised you a certain position, and you've worked your butt off to make it happen."

"That pretty much sums it up, I guess," Tom acknowledged.

"Perhaps you should reread the accounts of Abram and Sara and see what happened when they tried to fulfill prophesy."

Tom put on his Stanford letterman jacket and walked out the door.

Rocky Raccoon Is Missing

Reading week had finally arrived, and not a moment too soon for the students of Easton Seminary. Reading week was a designated week during the semester when the students did not have any classes to attend so that they could catch up on all their reading. Typically, Easton professors assigned their students anywhere from 1,500 to 3,000 pages of reading each semester. Although reading week was designed to generously provide students with an opportunity to catch up on their schoolwork, most students took the week off to relax, work more hours, or even go on vacation.

"Hey, Jim, where's Rocky?" Rick asked. "I haven't seen him for a couple of days now."

"You know, I was wondering the same thing. I told him to take some time off here in the dorm since the cafeteria is closed for reading week. I figured he could take a break from work."

"Well, his car is still in the parking lot. It's been four days now since anyone's seen him," said Rick.

"Maybe he told Steven or Chip where he was going," Jim said.

Rick and Jim quickly made their way to Steven's room where

71

they found him playing a computer game.

"Steven, have you seen Rocky around?" Jim asked.

"Last time I saw him, I dropped him off at the train station. He was heading to Boston."

"Did he say when he needed to be picked up or when he was returning?"

"No. He said he'd come back when he was ready and would find his own way home," said Steven.

"Do you have any idea where he was going?" Jim asked.

"I don't know, but given how he was dressed, he definitely wasn't heading to the ballet. He dressed more like someone going to a factory. He did have his Bible with him."

"Well, no one has heard from him since, and we're getting worried that something may have happened to him," Rick said.

"Maybe we should contact Dr. Casper," Jim said. "From what I've heard, he's the reason Rocky is even here. He may know something we don't."

* * *

Dr. Casper, unlike his students, was working rather hard to catch up on his work for the semester. The work of a seminary president is never finished. He heard a knock on his door as he graded several midterm research papers.

Jim, Steven, and Rick all walked in upon hearing Dr. Casper's invitation.

"What can I do for you, gentlemen?"

"We're concerned about Rocky," said Jim.

Dr. Casper stopped what he was doing and was now giving Jim his undivided attention. "Yes, go on."

"Well, sir, he seems to be missing. Steven dropped him off at the train station four days ago and we haven't seen or heard from him since. He didn't have any bags or suitcase," said Rick.

"I see," said Dr. Casper. "Well…four days without any suitcase does seem rather odd, even for Rocky. He's been unaccounted for now long enough to at least call the police. I'll take care of it and call you if I hear anything."

* * *

Jim, Rick, and Steven did not go back to the dorm, but chose instead to wait outside of Dr. Casper's office. Forty minutes later, Dr. Casper called them inside of his office.

"Gentlemen, I appreciate your concern for Rocky. It turns out that Rocky is fine."

"Great! We were really worried," Rick replied. "Where has he been?"

Dr. Casper had a crooked grin on his face and took a few breaths before answering Rick's question. "He's been in a Boston jail the last four days."

"Rocky's in jail?" Steven said. "What did he do? Kill someone with kindness?"

"No, Rocky's fine," he said with a laugh. "I spoke with the lieutenant of that division for about twenty minutes. Rocky volunteered to go to jail for the week so that he could preach to the inmates more effectively. Apparently, Rocky asked around and happened upon one that was run by a strong Irish Catholic who thought it was a great idea."

"So let me get this straight," said Chip. "While most of the seminary is blowing off reading week, no offense, Rocky is busy preaching the Gospel inside of a downtown Boston jail."

"Was he going to tell us?" Jim asked.

"I don't know. My guess is that he had no intention of telling anyone."

"Dr. Casper," Rick said, "why did you find this so funny?"

"Well, from what I hear, it's just typical of this guy."

"What *have* you heard?" Rick asked.

"Well, you know…I hear the same things you guys hear."

"Yes, sir."

Rick, Jim, and Chip excused themselves so as to let Dr. Casper return to his work. On the way back to the dorm, they passed about a dozen students telling each of them what Rocky was doing. Again, word was spreading about the deeds of Rocky Raccoon.

* * *

The next day, Tom turned on the local news, and following the requisite stories on fires and crime was a feature story about a "remarkable Christian." Tom sat up in his chair and watched in disbelief as the screen focused on Rocky Raccoon standing outside of a Boston police station.

"I was amazed at what grace had already accomplished here," Rocky said. "God was here before I ever set foot in this cell. I even came across an inmate who so desperately wanted the Word of God that he borrowed another inmate's New Testament and copied the Book of John word for word onto notebook paper. God is doing incredible things here in Boston."

The feature then offered a sound byte by Dr. Wiggins, a professor at Easton Seminary who commented, "Studies have shown that we live in the most well read region of the nation, yet we also live in the region that reads the Bible the least. Perhaps people like Rocky Raccoon will help bring the much anticipated and prayed-for New England revival."

The news reporter concluded, "Rocky Raccoon wouldn't comment on himself, but I found out that the most amazing part

74

of this story is that this young man is not one of Easton's shining stars of academia as was originally reported, but rather he is an hourly employee who serves cafeteria food to Easton's best and brightest. I guess it just goes to show that appearances can be deceiving. In this case, I would have to agree with the passerby who commented a moment ago that Rocky looked more like John the Baptist than he did Billy Graham."

Tom turned the TV off and crawled into bed.

Citizen Armstrong

Rocky, Rick, Chip, and Adam were walking to Brubaker's Café for some coffee after church. Along the way they talked about the sermon, college football, and of course, girls. As they approached the coffeehouse, Rocky stopped and stared at a newspaper machine.

"What's that still doing there?" he asked.

"What's what doing there?" Adam asked.

Looking at the Salem newspaper, Rocky pointed to the top left hand corner, which had the silhouette of a witch on a broom with the Moon as a backdrop. "Why is that still on their paper? Halloween's over."

"That's there year round," said Rick. "It's the town's main claim to fame."

"Wait a second," Rocky paused, much to the dismay of the three cold men standing before him. "A town noted for killing twenty people wrongly accused of being witches embraces this as a *good* thing? I guess there are some newspapers in Warsaw that have starving Jewish Holocaust prisoners on their papers then too."

"I don't think people look at it that way, Rock," Adam said.

76

"I think they're trying to distance themselves from it by presenting the cartoon image of a witch, instead of those who actually died."

"Seeing it everyday on the front cover is not the best way to forget," Rocky said.

"Well, perhaps it's best that no one forgets, so that history doesn't repeat itself," said Rick.

"This is such a screwed up town. You have a huge witch population here, even though those whose deaths made this place famous were not really witches. If anything, they've become martyrs to a cause they never belonged to or believed in. Secondly, this town takes some sort of sick pride in it!"

"Well," said Adam, "it's also a black eye on the church, so who are we to throw stones?"

"How do you figure that?" Rocky asked.

"Well, it's the Christians who burned the witches at the stakes after all," said Adam.

"Actually," said Chip, "no one was ever burned at the stake in Salem, they were hanged."

"Oh, I guess that makes it all better then!" Adam laughed.

Chip grinned and then continued, "I think what Rocky's getting at is that it was the Christians who helped to stop the hysteria and the subsequent killings. Prior to the Salem witchcraft trials of 1692, New England Puritans only accepted the evidence of two unimpeachable witnesses, in accordance with Deuteronomy 19:15. The problem was that some judges decided to allow 'spectral evidence,' which basically said that the witness did not even have to see the accused commit a crime, but rather, if they saw a ghost or a specter which showed them the accused committing a crime, then it was acceptable."

"I think I remember the whole spectral evidence issue from Arthur Miller's *The Crucible*," said Adam. "I guess I always interpreted it as meaning the Christians were behind it."

"No," said Chip. "It was both Increase Mather and his son Cotton, two Puritan pastors from Salem, who openly spoke out against the trials. Increase Mather even wrote *Cases of Conscience*, which demanded the return of the two-witness system of the Bible, and the killings stopped. Without any doubt, Increase Mather stopped the trials," Chip concluded.

"Does this guy know *everything*?" Adam asked Rocky and Rick.

"Yeah," Rick said, "he's a *College Jeopardy* winner!"

"I really regret ever telling you guys that!"

"This has been really interesting and very educational, but I really want to get inside and have a cup of hot coffee," said Rick.

"Yeah, I'm sorry," Rocky said. "Let's get in before we catch a cold. I think a storm is coming our way."

* * *

Later that evening, Rocky sat in the Easton library with the C.S. Lewis classic *The Screwtape Letters* in hand, but his attention kept returning to the newspaper shelves where he fixated on the Salem paper. Rocky tried to continue reading his book, but after spending twenty minutes on the same paragraph, he closed his book and approached the seminary's computer lab. He proceeded to research the details of the newspaper's ownership. He quickly found a name, Vincent Armstrong. Some additional research yielded Vincent Armstrong's home address courtesy of a police report involving an attempted burglary at his estate.

He left the library and drove down to Tuttle Hall. He stopped his car, looked up at the lit up dorm rooms as he listened to his wipers mopping his rain-drenched windshield. He put his car back in drive and carefully drove down Easton's winding road out to the main road.

He discovered that he was the only driver on the road. The wind had grown much stronger, but the rain had finally stopped. Still, these were not ideal driving conditions, especially when trying to find a house in the dark.

He finally came upon the country road he was seeking. He could immediately tell that each house was worth millions. Each home was separated not only by several acres, but also a complex maze of security fencing.

He stopped in front of a gate and double-checked the address to verify it was Vincent Armstrong's residence. He got out of his car and approached the gate. The wind had caused a lot more damage here than it had at Easton. One of the trees at the gate was broken in half, and blocked a portion of the entrance. He couldn't reach the intercom box to buzz Mr. Armstrong but noticed that the gate was partially open and walked inside.

He admired the grand Victorian design of the mansion and, in spite of the wind damage, marveled at the landscaping. He finally reached the front door and rang the doorbell.

Rocky heard a rushed set of footsteps running toward the door and instinctively took a step back. An older man whipped open the door and yelled, "My God, man, get in here quick!"

Once inside, Rocky noticed that the man was no longer moving frantically but instead just stood there looking at him.

"Hi, sir, I'm really sorry to disturb you this evening, but I wanted to talk to you tonight about your newspaper."

"Didn't you see the sign out there?"

"No, sir, one of your trees fell down on top of the main entrance, so I wasn't even able to buzz you at the gate. That's why I walked up to the front door."

"Young man, I'm not mad. I'm just thankful that you're alive."

"Sir?"

"The tree that fell over must be covering our warning sign. We have attack dogs on our property. I have no idea how you made it to the front door alive, son."

"Well, it may be because God placed a message on my heart that I wanted to share with you."

"What? Say that again."

"I don't mean to be intrusive. However, I felt strangely moved today by God to come and talk to you about your paper."

"Wait a second! Okay?" The man said as he walked away backwards, and started to yell out, "Blanche! Blanche!"

Rocky could hear a conversation in the other room. "What is it, Vince?" he heard a woman reply.

The conversation lowered to a barely audile hum, and he couldn't make out what they were saying.

Vincent, accompanied by a petite lady in a snow-white silk nightgown and purple robe, walked hand-in-hand into the entrance where Rocky remained standing.

"This is the young man who came to our door tonight because *God* asked him to," said Vincent.

Blanche extended her hand, which had enough jewelry on it to pay off a third world nation's debt. "It's nice to meet you, young man. I'm Blanche, Vince's wife."

"Nice to meet you, ma'am. My name is Rocky Raccoon."

"That's an odd name. Were your parents hippies?" Blanche asked.

"No, ma'am," Rocky replied with a smile, "It's a nickname I've recently acquired."

"I'm sorry, son. You started to say something earlier about the paper and I interrupted you," said Mr. Armstrong.

"That's quite all right, sir. The reason I'm here is I wanted to talk to you about your use of a witch on the front page of your newspaper."

"You don't like it?"

"No, sir, I don't."

"Okay, it's gone," said Vincent. "Come into the Great Room, and let's talk."

Rocky looked like a confused hospital patient who had wandered out of his room without permission as he trailed behind the Armstrongs who strolled into the Great Room still holding hands.

*   *   *

"Thank you for stopping by," said Blanche. "It was a miracle that you weren't killed by the attack dogs, but it's not a coincidence that you are here tonight."

"It isn't?"

"No, dear, you see, we were talking quite candidly tonight about backsliding in our faith and about other personal matters that were leading us astray. Money can do that to a person, honey."

Rocky nodded.

"Yeah, Blanche and I did something that we never do tonight. We prayed to God for a sign, and here you come walking right up to our door, avoiding the dogs like Moses parting the Red Sea. This must be an act of God. You can't deny that this is an answered prayer."

"I wouldn't dream of it, sir."

"Do you mind if we talk for a while, and maybe answer some of our questions, Rocky?" Vincent asked.

"No, sir. I'm all yours," Rocky said as he laid his copy of the Salem Newspaper aside.

THE ROCKY RACCOON REVIVAL

* * *

Vincent and Blanche were not only satisfied with the answers Rocky provided to their questions, but they also rededicated their lives to Jesus Christ that very night. Vincent even offered to do a story about Rocky.

"That's not necessary, sir. I really don't do any of this for the publicity."

"Look, son. I respect your compassion and knowledge of the living God, but trust me, the newspaperman when I say that your testimony will make a big difference in a lot of people's lives. If you really want the revival we spoke of, word needs to get out about what God's been doing here in New England."

"I guess you're right about that."

"Of course I am! I'll do my best to clean up Salem's image too. For starters, consider the paper's witch retired. I can use that space for something else, like a daily Scripture reading."

"That sounds great, Vincent. I just have one last question for you,"

"What is it, son?"

"How do I get back to my car without being eaten?"

The Fallen Angel

Rocky arrived at Tuttle Hall and found the guys all gathered together in the lounge praying, prompting them to immediately stand up to greet him.

"Are you okay?' Chip asked.

"Yeah, guys, I'm fine, thanks. I didn't know we had a scheduled prayer meeting tonight. I'm really sorry I missed it."

"No, Rocky. It wasn't scheduled. We were praying for *you*," said Jim.

"Thanks, but why?"

"I can't really explain it," Chip said, "but I just felt like you were in a great deal of danger, no matter what I did I couldn't shake the feeling. So I tried to look for you, and when I couldn't find you, we got together to pray for you."

"Clearly we were wrong, but better safe than sorry," Steven said.

"No. I think Chip was right, and I really do believe that I may owe my life to you all tonight."

"What do you mean?" Jim asked.

"Well, if you remember, we went to Brubaker's today after church, and we got into that whole debate over the Salem newspaper's insistence of using a witch on its cover. Anyway, I decided to do something about it tonight. I drove to visit the owner of the paper, Vincent Armstrong, and went to his front door...."

"I can't believe you went!" said Rick. "Did he try to shoot you?"

"No, but I'm happy to see your healthy pessimism is alive and well, my friend. When I got there, the storm had already taken down a lot of trees around their estate, including one that covered a BEWARE OF DOG sign. Apparently, they have trained killer attack dogs on their property. Trust me, this place is worth millions! Well, I got up to the main door, rang the bell, and Mr. Armstrong let me in, amazed that I wasn't mauled to death. He then explained that, in a vague sense, they were actually expecting me."

"What do you mean 'expecting' you? Did you call ahead of time?" Chip asked.

"No, they said that they prayed to God for some sort of sign to rededicate their lives to Christ. Then here I come telling them that God wanted me to come and talk to them."

"That's fantastic!" said Rick.

"It's weird though, because, in a sense, I was really going there to tell them that all I wanted them to do was remove the witch from his newspaper."

"You know, Rocky, God will use you and work through you as He sees fit," Chip said. "Just like all of us here, there may be 25 reasons why we decided to come to Easton, but the main point is we're here because God wanted us to be here. You may have gone there tonight to discuss the theological or historical reasons on why they should change their front cover, but God had something much grander in mind."

"You're right. Though, on a minor note, I would like to

mention that the witch will be replaced by Scripture passages starting tomorrow morning."

"That's awesome! You're a one-man revival, Rock," said Steven.

"No, I'm with a one God revival."

* * *

Rocky went to his room where he spent the next half-hour praying and praising God. "Lord," he whispered, "I know that I am not the cause of revival, but I am sure happy to have seen some miraculous things happen. Thank You."

Rocky slept well that night but was up again in a few short hours for his morning prayer time, jogging, and of course, breakfast shift.

* * *

The cafeteria was abuzz with discussion and laughter during lunch Monday. Rocky had never seen it quite so alive. He also unavoidably found himself in the spotlight all day.

"Great job, Rocky!" he heard from numerous people. He received many invitations to join several tables for lunch at the end of his shift. One surprising invite came from the clique, as Meredith and Martin congratulated Rocky on his many recent endeavors. Even more surprising was that Tom was now dining alone at another table.

With everyone making some sort of comment or compliment to Rocky, the typically fast-paced food line was now moving as quickly as a glacier.

"Man, if you don't stop with all this super-Christian stuff our shift is never going to end!" Sam joked.

During his break, Rocky opted to sit with the clique, given that this opportunity had never presented itself. He sat down right next to Meredith and across from Martin.

"What's wrong with Tom?" Rocky asked.

"You are," Martin said.

"He's a pretty proud guy, Rocky," Meredith said. "But he's not a bad guy."

"I've seen bad, and Tom's definitely not bad," Rocky said.

"When have *you* seen bad?" Martin said with an unbelieving grin.

"This morning when I looked in the mirror."

"Yeah, right! You're the seminary's new poster child."

"Not by choice, to be sure. I admire guys like you, Jim, and Tom. You all really know your stuff. I'm rather envious to be honest."

"Jealous?" Martin replied. "Buddy, all you have to do is enroll. Trust me, I think you'd be a sure thing. Anyway, none of us pay tuition here at Easton."

"Really?"

"Yeah," Meredith answered. "Some very rich and generous person donated something like $400 million to a dozen ministries and to Easton Seminary."

"Who did that?"

"No one knows?" Martin said. "Dr. Casper may know. The point of the donation was to allow a generation of future pastors and missionaries a chance to go to seminary debt free."

"You forgot Christian counselors!" said Meredith.

"Oh yeah. Everyone here, including the professors and staff are rewarded with this donation. Frankly, this gift made it possible for most of these people to be here, including you."

"Well, if I ever meet the donor, I'll be sure to thank him," Rocky said as he took his first bite of lunch.

"Put in a good word for me too," said Martin. "With your reputation, I imagine that the donor already knows all about you."

After eating, Rocky took his tray, cleared off his trash, and then took the rest of garbage out to the dumpster. Rocky walked back inside and looked up at the clock as his shift was coming to an end. He saw a small crowd of students coming his way, and he started to walk away to avoid them but stopped, sighed, and turned around to politely talk rather than pursue the quiet time that he treasured.

*   *   *

Later that evening during dinner, Rocky was able to join another new table for fellowship and dinner. Though he wasn't thrilled with the praise directed his way, he was happy to know everyone on campus a little better now. Another motive for sitting there was that Tom was sitting alone at the table next to them.

As he sat down to join Eric, Dave, Greg and Dan, he was shocked to hear the topic of conversation.

"Hey, look at this one, guys!" Eric howled.

"What's hers say?" Greg asked

Eric read: "My name is Angel. I'm a 21-year-old beauty who is 5'7", 120 pounds, with brunette hair and hazel eyes. I am a full service independent escort. Come join me for an erotic evening, filled with a striptease, nude non-therapeutic massage, kissing, cuddling, hot tubs, and making a man feel vibrant and alive again. All of Angel's heavenly attention is focused on YOU! I'll give you anything your little heart desires."

"At least it's theological." Dan laughed.

"How much is *this one* charging?" David asked.

Eric kept reading, "It looks like two hours are going to cost $350, gentlemen. Hey, that's more than I paid per credit hour at University of Michigan!"

"Yeah," Dan said, "if you went to Michigan in the 1970s maybe."

Rocky sat there stunned as these students were reading classified ads for escorts just to make fun of them.

"Hey, Rocky," Greg said, "You're from Ohio. What do you think of Michigan?"

Rocky looked up, unaware that the ridicule of Angel, and others like her was over, and that the discussion was now on college football.

"I'm an Ohio State Buckeyes fan, so naturally I root against Michigan. Their school is incredible though. There's no shame in graduating from there, right, Eric?"

"You got that right, pal!" Eric said.

"Hey, guys, we need to get going and finish our study group before the football game comes on tonight," said Dave.

"Sorry, Rocky, we've got to run. You're welcome to join us up in Polaris Hall for the game," Eric said.

"I'm not really into the NFL these days. Anyhow, I have an errand or two I want to get done tonight."

"Okay, your loss, Rocky, cause tonight is the Miami Dolphins' night!" said Eric.

"There he goes again, living back in the 1970s!" Dan said with a laugh.

As the guys left, Rocky found himself sitting alone, with Tom still enjoying the solitude at his own table. Rocky turned around to nod a hello, but Tom lowered his head to avoid the silent acknowledgement.

Rocky got up and threw his garbage away. Tom watched as Rocky made a deliberate effort to pick up the classifieds that the students were reading aloud and place it in his back pocket before returning back to the kitchen to complete his shift with Sam.

* * *

Tom waited outside of the cafeteria as Rocky finished his shift, and kept a low profile in the lobby. He quickly positioned himself under the stairwell when Rocky came out of the dining room. He watched Rocky lock the cafeteria doors behind him and then walk over to the mailroom with the classified ads still in his back pocket. Tom, a graduate of Stanford University's psychology program, observed his subject.

* * *

Rocky walked into the mailroom and went to the archaic payphone. Tom peered around the corner and listened in on what Rocky believed to be a private phone call.

"Hello, Angel? Hi, I read your ad this evening and would love to meet with you tonight."

Tom leaned in more, barely visible to Rocky, had he possessed the inclination or instinct to look in Tom's direction. Rocky listened carefully to the girl's instructions.

"That sounds great! I know the hotel you're talking about. Let's meet there at 9:00 then. Okay, I'm looking forward to meeting you too, Angel."

Rocky hung up the phone and Tom ducked behind the doors between the mailroom and the lobby. As Rocky walked right by, Tom rediscovered his smile.

* * *

89

THE ROCKY RACCOON REVIVAL

Rocky pulled into the Hewson Hotel; unaware that Tom's truck was trailing behind him. Tom pulled up to the entrance, and saw Rocky walk into the hotel lobby and approach a girl fitting the description he heard the other guys read at dinner.

* * *

"You must be Angel."

"Hi, baby. You must be, Michael. You're cuter than I expected. I rarely get a hottie. My lucky night!"

"Thanks, but please, call me Rocky."

"Honey, I'll call you whatever you want tonight.".

"Great. Let's go down to the lounge."

"Don't you want to go to your room now, sweetie? The clock is running."

Rocky pulled out his wallet and discretely gave her the agreed upon payment.

"*Please*, join me in the lounge, Angel."

* * *

Tom waited outside in his truck for three hours, frequently checking the classified ad to verify Angel's fee. Finally, he saw them both walk to Rocky's car and drive away. Tom followed them to a 24-hour greasy spoon restaurant where they shared a meal, and later witnessed Rocky drop her off back at her car still parked at the hotel.

* * *

Rocky gave Angel a hug goodbye and helped her into her car.

90

He then drove back to Tuttle Hall. Following his prayer time and devotions, he crawled into bed ready to fall asleep.

* * *

Following his morning routine for his physical and spiritual well-being, Rocky made his way to the cafeteria for another morning of making coffee and watching friends dart to class with bagels in their mouths.

As Rocky walked into the cafeteria, Sam walked up to him and said, "Dr. Casper wants you to go to his office *immediately*."

"It's not because I'm late again, is it?"

"No, Rocky. The man seemed genuinely upset this morning. You'd best be on your way to see him."

"Okay, if you think you can handle this crowd yourself!" He joked, as he looked around the empty cafeteria. "You'd think people this age would know the value of a good breakfast."

"I'll see you when you get back, Rocky."

* * *

Rocky couldn't understand why Dr. Casper was apparently so upset. He walked into the office and found Dr. Casper sharing a conversation with the seminary's vice president, Dr. Paul Williams; the dean of students, Dr. Mary Griggy; and Tom.

Dr. Casper looked up and said, "Good morning, Rocky. Please have a seat."

"Good morning," Rocky said as he sat down in the plush chair.

"Did you have a good night last night?" Dr. Casper asked.

"Yes, sir. It was one of the best I've had since I've been here."

91

"I see. Would you care to share with us what you did last night?"

"Not especially. Frankly, sir, I'd rather not discuss it in front of everyone here. Is it possible to just talk one-on-one?"

"We're here to discuss a serious charge made against you, Rocky, and it's standard operating procedure to have the vice-president and the dean of students present," Dr. Casper replied.

"And Tom?"

"He's a witness to the alleged offense," said Dr. Casper.

"What offense? What am I accused of doing?"

"It's been verified that you contacted a female escort by the name of Angel, met her at the Hewson Hotel on Route 95 for three hours, and later had dinner with her."

"Well yeah, I know that. I was there."

"You don't deny the accusation then?" Dr. Casper said with a frown.

"If the accusation is that I met with a girl who was in desperate need of the Gospel message of Jesus Christ, then I am guilty as charged. If the accusation is that I had any sexual relations with her, then I'm innocent."

"Rocky...if what you're saying is true...you exercised truly poor judgment. I admire your eagerness to share the Gospel, *but* this was not a good way to go about it."

"Jesus associated with prostitutes and others shunned by society."

With all eyes now on Dr. Casper, he sat back in his chair, took off his glasses, and looked as though he was about to reply, but then paused and started to wipe his glasses.

"With all due respect, Dr. Casper, the Pharisees condemned Jesus' methods and teachings which declared that the same sinners they despised were nearer to God than they in fact were. Angel showed true repentance last night, and arguably

92

appreciates God's goodness this morning more than most people on this campus."

"I understand your point, and I'm sorry; but you have to acknowledge how it must've looked to Tom who observed it all."

"Well, you can twist perception, but reality doesn't budge. I did not have any sexual liaison with that girl. I paid for the first hour of her company and took that time to publicly talk about Jesus in the hotel's lounge. The next two hours, she and I had a very good discussion about the Gospel and what it meant to accept Jesus. We then shared a nice dinner together in fellowship. Yeah, that first hour took every penny to my name, but she gave it back to me later. Even if she hadn't, it would have been worth it, because she now has a mansion waiting for her in Heaven."

Dr. Casper looked around the room to his colleagues and Tom. "Thank you all for your time this morning. I apologize for any inconvenience this may have caused to your morning routine. I'd like to have a word with Rocky alone now, please."

"What is this?" Tom said. "I cannot believe for one second that you are all going to condone this man spending time and money with a *prostitute* in a hotel! He's perverting Scripture around to justify his behavior!"

"Tom, I hear what you're saying," said Dr. Casper, "but Rocky told us what happened, and though I personally disagree with his judgment and unorthodox approach, he didn't do anything deserving termination."

Dr. Williams and Dr. Griggy shared a smile with Rocky on their way out, and Tom swiftly walked out the door. Dr. Casper stood up and sat down on the edge of his desk.

"I'm sorry. I truly am, Rocky. I don't entirely know why Tom happened to see you last night. Something tells me that it didn't happen by chance. However, I am still concerned about you seeing an escort."

"I was in the cafeteria last night and overheard some of the students making fun of the escorts in the classified ads. I was mad that they looked down upon them as fallen angels with no value instead of having pity and compassion for them."

"Fair enough…but I'm not attacking your motives. My issue is your reckless decision to be with an escort in a hotel."

"And you think, given my past in Vegas, that I might slip and backslide into that lifestyle again?"

"Yes, I do. Not because I don't trust you or your intentions. You have endured and overcome so much, but Satan can still tempt you with all the things he used to use back when he held you firmly in his grasp. Temptation, unlike opportunities, will always give you a second chance. Even after Jesus was victorious following the third temptation recorded in Luke 4, we see Satan's plan in verse 13, 'And when the devil had finished every temptation, he departed from Him until an opportune time.' Don't give him another opportunity."

Rocky nodded in agreement and brushed back some hair that had fallen out of place in front of his eyes.

"I'm sorry about the things I said earlier, Dr. Casper. I was out of line. Bob would have said the same things you just told me. I'll make a point to apologize to Dr. Williams and Dr. Griggy, too."

"That's fine, and I appreciate that. Trust me, given everything you've done for Easton, you're forgiven! Remember what I said though. Your past is still a foothold for the devil. Paul wrote in 1 Corinthians to be on alert, stand firm in the faith, and act like men. Yet, regarding sexual temptation, he instructed us to flee. Think about why that is."

Rocky nodded and started to leave but then turned to face

94

Dr. Casper. "Jesus said, 'The person who hears my words and does them is like the wise man who built his house on the rock.' He didn't say, 'The person who hears my words and thinks about them' or 'The person who hears my words and agrees with them.' Jesus wants us to hear *and* act, and that's what I did, sir. I'll be mindful of my past but not a slave to it. I've been forgiven, and I now want to serve the Lord."

Rocky then excused himself and went back to work with Sam in the cafeteria.

Lesson Learned

Sam gave Rocky a break after the lunch rush, so he grabbed some food and walked over to join Chip, Jim, Steven, and Rick. As he set his tray on the table, he discovered four grimly focused seminary students quietly skimming through their notebooks.

"Who died?" Rocky asked.

Jim looked up and answered, "We're about to die. Dr. Havaich's New Testament class is absolutely killing us this semester."

"I don't know what this guy's problem is," Steven said. "He seems to have absolutely no concept of the real world. He's one of those ivory tower types who you always complain about. This guy is all about the head and nothing about the heart."

"He's right, Rock. There's no love in this class," said Chip. "I've taken honors courses at Yale that weren't this difficult."

"Just out of curiosity, how does Tom do in this class?" Rocky asked.

"As usual, the guy has a perfect grade," Rick said. "Say what you will about Tom, but he's a great student. I'd be amazed if he's not back here in a few years teaching."

"Look," said Jim, "I don't wish to sound rude, because we all love you, man. But we really need to study now. Dr. Havaich is testing us today, and it's a long shot if any of us are going to pass."

"Don't sweat it. Best of luck to you all."

The four of them all looked up at Rocky as if he were joking, and then went about their mad routine of preparing for Dr. Havaich's test.

* * *

Rocky decided to sit in on Dr. Havaich's class today. Even though Dr. Havaich was administering a test, Rocky wanted to observe the infamous professor. Dr. Havaich only knew Rocky as an acquaintance in the cafeteria, but gave him an ever so slight nod of acknowledgment.

Rocky looked around and watched his friend Becky pulling her hair back, seemingly trying to rip an answer from out of her head. Chip, though he was very competent in biblical Greek, was clearly struggling. Even Tom didn't seem like the confident biblical virtuoso that he was used to seeing.

Dr. Havaich sat at the front of the class, seemingly oblivious to the pain he was inflicting upon his students. That or he was quietly relishing it. Dr. Havaich was a middle-aged balding man who wore thick glasses and always wore loose fitting black shirts, perhaps to conceal that he spent more time in his office studying than he did working out in the gym.

* * *

The period was about to conclude, and some of the students, looking as though they were defeated after a valiant battle, turned in their paperwork confident that they should have absolutely no reason to feel confident. About a minute before the bell was to ring, Dr. Havaich announced that the tests were to be turned in immediately. Rocky found it disheartening to hear the collective sound of moaning, sighing, and pencils falling from paralyzed hands, tired and cramped from a heroic effort to appease Dr. Havaich.

He sat quietly as many of his friends and acquaintances walked by him, shaking their heads as though they had just received horrible news from the Mayo Clinic. As the last students were handing in their work and leaving, Rocky got up and headed down to Dr. Havaich, who watched him walk all the way down from his distant seat.

"Mr. Raccoon. To what do I owe the privilege of your presence in my classroom today?"

"I wanted to see firsthand what everyone was talking about. You've got quite the reputation, Dr. Havaich."

Dr. Havaich gave a broad, proud smile upon hearing this. "So, I imagine you heard a lot of complaining in the lunchroom today."

"I did, and I must admit, I didn't like what I heard."

"Oh, really? And what didn't you like, Mr. Raccoon?"

"This isn't exactly how Jesus taught. He taught that love was the greatest commandment of them all. He taught using simple parables that were understood by the masses, or at least explained them later to those who still had questions."

"And you think I'm not being a very good Christian, being so rough on these students, huh?" Dr. Havaich asked without raising his tone or exposing a single bead of sweat on his balding forehead.

"Kierkegaard once said that there are two types of Christians, those who imitate Jesus, and those who are content to speak about Him. I think that you are doing a great disservice to a room full of compassionate Christians by entrapping them in an ivory tower."

"Wow. You're harsher than my students," he said as he started to pack up his paperwork and the students' tests.

"Look, I know theology is important, but I don't think that we should try to debate someone into Heaven when someone else can turn around and debate them right back out of it. Theology is good, but personal experience is better."

Dr. Havaich snapped his briefcase shut and then leaned forward on it, looking Rocky directly in the eye. "Do you feel better now? Is it out of your system? Did you speak your peace? I must say I'm rather disappointed, Rocky. I've heard so much about you and find myself now questioning how much of it is really true."

Rocky tried to reply but then shut his mouth and looked down at the floor.

"Medical school is probably the hardest school there is, though I know a few lawyers who would argue otherwise. Why do you think medical school is so hard, Rocky?"

"Because people's lives are on the line, and you want someone who knows what he's doing."

"Right. Now, why do you think I would make my classes here at Easton Seminary so difficult?"

Rocky's eyes grew wide and his mouth formed a perfect O shape.

"You make your seminary classes difficult because people's souls are on the line."

"Exactly. We seem to believe that medical school should thoroughly train people to take care of people's physical health but neglect the fact that seminary is preparing people to tend to the eternal spiritual health of others. Only Jesus saves. However, He uses each of us in many different ways to help others find salvation. Jesus is the Shepherd and the lost are the sheep. We're called, if you will, to be sheepdogs. We don't save the lost sheep but direct them to the caring and loving arms of the Shepherd. Do you see what I'm talking about?"

Rocky, feeling rather sheepish himself nodded. "I'm truly sorry for coming into your classroom today to judge and condemn you. I'm also sorry that I assumed that you didn't care, or didn't do anything to contribute to the Gospel. Obviously, you do a lot, including preparing those who are called to go out into the world. You really opened my eyes today, Dr. Havaich."

Dr. Havaich stood straight up, put on his sport jacket, and extended his hand to Rocky and shook Rocky's hand. "Don't sweat it. Anyway, from what I hear, you're teaching my students quite a bit yourself this year. Keep up the good work, Mr. Raccoon."

Rocky smiled, not wishing to argue with this man anymore today.

* * *

As Rocky exited Dr. Havaich's classroom, he saw Chip in the lobby standing by the vending machine, which seemed to be upsetting him.

"Pop machine take your money?" Rocky asked.

"Yes, and it's called *soda* around here."

"If you admit that it's pop, maybe it'll give you your money back. So...how'd the test go?"

"It was fine. I think I will get a B on it. In any other class I'd be disappointed with that grade, but in Havaich's, I consider it an accomplishment."

"That Dr. Havaich is quite a guy," Rocky said.

"Yeah. We get on his case sometimes, but he really does help

100

us. The guy is a bona fide genius."

"Yes he is," said Rocky.

"I saw that you went down to talk to him. How did it go?"

"I learned a few things from him myself today."

"Well, if you enjoyed debating him, I'm sure that you'll have a good time tomorrow night."

"What's tomorrow night?" Rocky asked.

"You wanted to know the next time I was going to see Simon in Cambridge. I'm going tomorrow with Becky and Steven. Are you still wanting to go to Café Veritas?"

"Yes, I'm very excited to meet Simon. The man is a legend in these parts."

"Some say the same thing about you, Rocky."

Simon

Rocky stayed up late preparing for a possible encounter with Simon, but he still woke up early and had his devotional time, followed by a morning jog in the cool New England autumn air. The family of deer living on campus no longer feared him but seemingly accepted him as part of their own morning routine.

Rocky ran up the stairs of Tuttle Hall and found Chip already awake, reading his Bible in the common room.

"Good morning, Chip. I'm not used to seeing anyone else up this early. Is there another book sale I didn't know about?"

Chip looked tense, and his wide eyes met Rocky's.

"I'm scared," Chip said just above a whisper.

"Simon?"

Chip nodded as Rocky sat down across from him.

"I don't know what it is about Simon. The guy's brilliant. I don't mean brilliant simply because he's at Harvard. I mean this guy's intelligence is off the charts. I can state a strong case, and he dissects everything like a master surgeon."

"I think you're right."

Chip couldn't help but chuckle, "Thanks, Rock. That's a real confidence booster."

102

"I don't think debating this guy is going to change his mind. The reason for unbelief is never an inadequate hypothesis. The atheist's problem is not always a soft head but sometimes a hard heart. I think some people must understand before they believe, and then there are others who have to believe before they understand."

"I hear what you're saying, but I've tried to help him understand."

"Perhaps you're focusing so much on his I.Q. that you've dismissed the possibility that he needs to believe before he understands. You gotta know how to let the heart lead the head as well as vice versa."

Chip looked at him and sat quietly for a moment. "Rocky, even if you could reach him, it's a very hostile atmosphere. The café is filled with people who militantly follow Simon, and even if he'd start to sway, they'll coax him back with peer pressure."

"Or...they may *follow* their leader."

Chip got up, closed his Bible, and went to his room to get ready for the day. Rocky went up to get a shower and to change the strings on his guitar. It was open-mic night at Café Veritas.

* * *

Rocky was on the lunch line serving food to Easton's students. As usual, he greeted everyone by name with a smile. Tom did not return Rocky's greeting or make eye contact while asking for the spaghetti.

"Tom," said Rocky as he dished out Tom's lunch, "why don't you join Chip, Becky, Steven, and me tonight at Café Veritas? We could sure use you down there with Simon."

"I can't make it tonight," Tom replied as he reached for his plate and walked away.

103

Rocky looked over at Sam and shook his head. Sam replied simply with a slight shrug of his shoulders.

As lunch was coming to a close, Rocky took his break with his friends from Tuttle Hall.

"I heard your invite to Tom," said Jim. "That was nice of you to ask."

"I only wish he would come," said Rocky.

"I think he's got too much to lose," Steven said. "He's top dog here and doesn't see any benefit to putting his belt on the line against 'Simon the Great.'"

"I'd like to see what he could do with Simon though," said Rocky. "Maybe he'd be effective."

"Frankly, Rock, I'm more interested to see what *you'd* do with Simon," said Steven.

"I'm going there to perform a song I wrote last night, inspired by Dr. Havaich, and then wait for him to come to me."

"What makes you think Simon will come to you?" Chip asked.

"He'll come."

* * *

Becky, Chip, and Steven dressed up, camouflaged in the aristocratic Cambridge attire of the academic intelligentsia. Steven knocked on Rocky's door to let him know that it was time to go. Rocky was tuning his guitar and then placed it in its case. He grabbed a small, beat up notebook and opened the door to greet his friends. Rocky surprised them by wearing faded, ripped jeans and an old Dickies gas station attendant jacket he over a formally white t-shirt.

"I'm ready. Let's do it!" Rocky said.

"Yeah…let's do it," Chip echoed with less enthusiasm.

THE ROCKY RACCOON REVIVAL

*   *   *

The drive down was quiet and somber. The traffic was smooth until they neared Boston, which was tantamount to Mr. Toad's infamous wild ride. Their search for a parking space led them to believe that they would sooner find the Holy Grail than a place to park. They settled for a spot a few blocks away.

Even though it was a chilly autumn evening, there were street musicians banging rhythmically on pots and pans, fast-talking magicians, folk artists plucking strings to James Taylor classics, and circus-like performers. Rocky enjoyed the shows so much that he looked disappointed when the arrived at the front door of Café Veritas.

Café Veritas did not mirror the décor or atmosphere of the other Cambridge establishments in the neighborhood. Unlike the other sites, which featured marble columns, cherry woodwork, fountains, and portraits of Harvard's elite, Café Veritas was a hole in the wall that resembled a coffeehouse from a Jack Kerouac novel. It was poorly lit, over-crowded, and housed a layer of smoke perpetually hung in the air much like the smog in Los Angeles.

It was a very busy night, and they sat down at a small table that really didn't accommodate them, but that seemed to be the case for every party in attendance. Becky and Steven went to get some drinks while Rocky and Chip saved their seats.

"So, you're really going to play tonight?"

"Yeah. I wrote a new song, and there's nothing better than an audience to tell you if it's any good or not," he said with a grin.

"Is that Chipper from Easton?" A loud voice called out.

A well-dressed, slender, young man in his early 20's approached their table. It didn't take a rocket scientist, or any other scientist in attendance that night, to recognize that this must be Simon.

Simon looked Rocky over and smirked. "Gee, Chip, I know you're a caring Christian and all, but you could have just placed the money in his cup; you didn't have to actually bring him in with you."

"Si-Simon," said Chip, "th-this is Rocky. Rocky, this is Simon."

"Rocky? Rocky Raccoon, n'est-ce pas? I have been reading about you in the media?"

"It's been a slow week for news I guess."

Simon betrayed a slight smile at Rocky's self-deprecating reply.

"Well, it's nice to meet you, Rocky. You came to the right place if you want to learn a thing or two."

"Actually, I came to sing tonight."

"Great! I'm always up for some tunes. I'll make sure they fit you in. I'm anxious to hear the great Rocky Raccoon sing."

Simon then walked over to someone holding a list.

"I'm sorry about that, Rocky," said Chip.

"Don't be. I think he just got me on the list."

Steven and Becky came back with everyone's coffee.

"This place is crazy tonight," said Steven.

"I like it this way. I wish we came down here more often," said Becky.

"It makes it hard to debate though," said Chip.

"Well, Jesus had tougher crowds than this, *and* people conspired to kill Him," said Rocky. "I think we'll be fine."

"Just look at them." Chip pointed at the sycophants surrounding and following Simon around the café. "It makes me sick to see these people just doing whatever he says and believing whatever he professes."

"Remember, win over Simon, and the rest will follow," said Rocky.

They drank their coffee, and then the music started. The first guy walked up, appearing to be someone trying to look like Bob Dylan. Unfortunately, his efforts to write and play like Dylan were equally in vain.

The next person called up looked impressive. He wore nice trendy clothes and carried a custom made Olson guitar, which must have cost around $10,000. Regretfully, he invested his parents' money in the guitar and not the lessons.

Following that act was a girl dressed like a million other nonconformists in colleges across the nation. She promised "three chords and the truth," but only delivered on the first half.

Simon walked up to the microphone and tapped on it. "It gives me great pleasure to introduce to you a man who captures the essence of Easton Theological Seminary...its janitor, Rocky Raccoon!"

The crowd, as always, took its cue from Simon and started to laugh. Rocky didn't appear to mind though as he was now a featured performer instead of background noise like those who had played before him.

"Hi. I'm Rocky, and here's a song I wrote just last night. I'd like to dedicate this song to Simon."

Simon stood against the wall with an amused look on his face.

Rocky didn't have a custom made guitar costing thousands. Instead, he held an old black guitar that looked as though it had seen combat in Korea. Rocky started to bang on the wood of the guitar in a rhythmic pattern until the audience responded, keeping the beat by clapping or banging on the tables with their hands and coffee mugs. He started to play some power chords that reverberated throughout the café, and then played a quick riff followed by some harmonic taps on the fret board. He started to sing:

Only Jesus Saves! Only Jesus Saves!

I'm Jesus' Sheepdog
I'm the Savior's Sheepdog
I'm the Shepherd's Sheepdog

Scripture teaches there's only one way,
That's through Jesus, love and obey.
We cannot save a single one,
We point lost sheep to the Son!

Only Jesus Saves! Only Jesus Saves!

I'm Jesus' Sheepdog
I'm the Savior's Sheepdog
I'm the Shepherd's Sheepdog

I love you with all my heart,
Most I can do is give you a start.
Turn to Him, let Him do the rest
Accept Him in, you're saved and blessed!

Only Jesus Saves! Only Jesus Saves!

I'm Jesus' Sheepdog
I'm the Savior's Sheepdog
I'm the Sheppard's Sheepdog

Rocky finished with a lightning quick riff and a harmonic tap

108

that chimed throughout Café Veritas.

Rocky's table cheered, but the crowd remained silent until they noticed Simon start to clap. Even if some didn't like the song's message, everyone there appreciated his musicianship.

Simon walked up to the microphone and said, "To be honest, that was pretty good, Rocky. *However*, this is Café Veritas not Park Street Church. If you want truth, my friends, you will not find it in the Gospels. If anyone disagrees, then prove *me* wrong right here, right now!"

Chip was about to stand up, but Rocky, who already had a microphone in front of him replied, "I accept that challenge, Simon."

"Do I want to debate a man who cleans toilets for a living?" Simon asked rhetorically to the amusement of those in attendance.

"You're right. I do deal with a lot of crap for a living. Perhaps that gives me an unfair advantage."

Simon offered a sly smile, like someone who knew something that everyone else didn't. He appeared to appreciate Rocky's chutzpah and seemed eager to face this new colorful opponent.

Rocky surveyed Café Veritas. He noticed that the ad hoc debate effectively concluded open-mic night, and that they were now were now the center of attention.

Rocky v. Simon

"Rocky, we do things pretty informally around here," Simon said. "We'll share in a dialogue, and either one of us can interject whenever we feel like it, instead of waiting twenty minutes after the point has already been forgotten, just to keep things simple. Agreed?"

"Fair enough. To start, we know that Christianity is both historical, hence verifiable, yet it's never been disproved. Let's keep it simple as you say. If Christ rose from the dead, we know with absolute certainty that God exists. We even know what He's like, and how we can come to know Him on a personal level."

"True, my friend. However, if Christ did not rise from the dead, as you believe, then Christianity is nothing more than an interesting museum piece."

"Of course. I argue that if Christ rose from the dead, nothing else matters. If He did not, then nothing matters."

"I agree with the first half of that statement, but find your dismal outlook on life if Jesus isn't who He says He is a crime against the goodness of man."

"Ah, yes. I apologize. You're quite right. Man is essentially

110

good. It's only his behavior that tends to let him down."

A few in the audience chuckled at Rocky's observation, which left Simon slightly red faced.

"Then it all comes down to whether or not Jesus rose from the dead," Simon said. "I'll concede that if He did, I will not only gladly change my mind, but my whole way of life. Reason dictates that I'd be a fool not to. However, Christianity, to its credit, puts it all on the line. If it's proven that Jesus didn't rise from the dead, then you must acknowledge that Christianity is completely false."

"But of course. Even its most effective preacher, the Apostle Paul agreed with your premise."

One of Simon's sycophant yelled, "Hey! Let's not confine this to just Christianity since all religions are basically the same anyway!"

Simon's head noticeably dropped and Rocky turned to face the heckler. "So you believe that all religions are basically the same?"

"They are!" said the heckler.

"I see. Well, most do believe in ideas such as goodness and love. They just disagree on trivial matters such as creation, sin, heaven, hell, God, and salvation."

The audience laughed at the heckler's expense, and Rocky gained some unexpected momentum. Simon stood up, motioned for the crowd to settle down, and signaled for Rocky to start.

Rocky stood up and said, "If we're going to debate, I really need to know where you stand. Please, Simon, tell me what kind of God you don't believe in. More than likely, I don't believe in that God either."

Simon smiled.

"I will concede that Jesus was a good moral teacher, Rocky. Arguably one of the best philosophers ever, in fact, but I just

111

don't think that He was God. That's not a knock against Him though, as no one else is God either."

"How do you respond to the historical account of His bodily resurrection then? That's a pretty impressive trick for a simple philosopher. Or maybe He really was a clever conman Who was not only able to arrange a virgin birth, but also planned on being taken to another country while He was an infant, all to fulfill prophesy. I ask you, how does one do all that, *and* resurrect Himself from the dead if He isn't who He said He was?"

"Christians are *always* on safe ground when it comes to discussing the resurrection of Jesus," Simon said. "You basically say, 'Prove the resurrection never happened,' and then make conditions that limit me to only the accounts found in the New Testament written by the very people trying to persuade others that the resurrection really happened. The argument always ends up that I have to produce some 2,000-year-old corpse to disprove the resurrection, which is an impossibility given that there are no non-Christian records of Jesus' burial."

Rocky nodded. "I want to look at it from your point of view then. You say Jesus didn't rise from the grave and is, in fact, still dead somewhere other than where he was laid to rest on Good Friday."

"Yes, like my hero Socrates, he's dead. Food for worms," he said and then made an obnoxious sucking sound to create an image of worms eating flesh for his adoring audience.

Rocky pulled out his notebook from his back pocket and quickly looked it over.

"Simon, there's only so many possible scenarios for what happened on Easter morning. First, Jesus rose from the dead, as believed by Christians worldwide. Second, Jesus didn't rise from the dead, but the apostles were deceivers who pulled off an incredible conspiracy. Third, Jesus didn't rise, but His followers later created myths about Him. Fourth, the apostles themselves were somehow deceived, perhaps by hallucinations. Last, Jesus didn't actually die from his wounds, but merely lost consciousness and was mistakenly determined to be dead. Are these topics of discussion agreeable with you, Simon?"

"Yes, but let's skip over the premise that Jesus actually rose from the dead, and focus only on the last four."

"That's fine, as I said I want to look at it from your point of view. However, to be intellectually honest, I'd like to go by the standards of the great thinker and writer, Sir Arthur Conan Doyle, who wrote, 'Once you eliminate the impossible, whatever remains, no matter how improbable, must be the truth.'"

Simon appeared to appreciate the reference to the author of the legendary Sherlock Holmes, the master detective who could solve the most confounding mysteries. Simon simply nodded his head to indicate that he agreed with the standard set by Doyle.

"First," said Rocky, "I'd like to focus on the accusation that the disciples deceived everyone by some conspiracy, where they actually made up the resurrection, perhaps even going so far as to steal the body of Jesus to do so. Let's cut to the chase. What advantage or reward did the so-called conspirators derive from their lie?"

"What advantage did they derive from it? For starters, it *obviously* helped to create Christianity. Without it, Christianity is an obscure footnote in history. Secondly, and not as well known is that before he met Jesus, Peter was a fisherman on the Sea of Galilee. This was a dangerous, thankless, low-paying job. According to 1 Corinthians 9:4, after he met Jesus and preached about the resurrection, Peter and the other apostles and their wives were supported by the early Christians. Paul says that this was only right, and that he himself could have had that privilege, but he chose not to. In 2 Corinthians 2:17, Paul complains about people who peddle the Word of God for money. He could only have been talking about his fellow Christian preachers. Acts makes clear that the early Christians sold their land and houses and gave the money to the apostles for them to do with as they wished. Peter would have had more money than a Galilean fisherman could ever dream of making."

"I find your theory to be very creative and surprisingly pragmatic. 'What's in it for me?' is a powerful and timeless motivator, but I don't think that you're taking this particular scenario to its logical conclusion. The consequence of discipleship was death, not growing fat and wealthy. A happy ending was not an option. I fail to see how the disciples gained any advantage whatsoever from the resurrection. They were persecuted, hated, imprisoned, tortured, exiled, beheaded, crucified, boiled alive, roasted, disemboweled, and fed to lions. Please help me to see the perks of this conspiracy again."

"What can I say? If you've ever had money, you'd know that it could make you do some pretty crazy things. People rob banks for money, fully aware of the consequences if they get caught. As you already alluded, power, prestige, and possessions are powerful motivators, and I know that even Christian pastors teach on this, so I am sure that money and authority could have been corrupting unless the disciples were all perfect."

"Perhaps you'd be willing to die a horrible death for money, Simon, but...."

"No I'm not the type since I *already* have money."

The crowd laughed and applauded Simon's response.

Rocky smiled. "I guess you wouldn't die for money, and I believe that the historical record of the disciples and their ministries demonstrates that they didn't either."

"Well, perhaps I am giving these simple, superstitious illiterates too much credit. Maybe these fishermen just came up with a whopper of a *fish story* and everybody bought into it."

"If this is a conspiracy, then these 'simple, superstitious illiterate fishermen,' as you put it, with little to no intellect, created one of the most creative and clever enduring stories in all of history. Did they not? This story rivals anything written by Shakespeare or Dickens! Can you imagine a handful of uneducated fishermen coming up with the mother of all fish stories, so convincing that it has changed the lives of *billions* on a personal level, and helped to create and destroy empires? Even more incredible and unlikely is that these men created a lie, and then were willing to *die* for it. Your hero, Socrates, died for the truth; would you die for something that you knew was a lie?"

"No, of course I wouldn't die for a lie. Maybe they just convinced themselves. If you say a lie enough times, you start to believe it."

"But does that sound *reasonable* to you?"

"It doesn't prove that Jesus rose from the dead."

"You certainly haven't disproved it either, my friend. I'd like to point out that the contemporaries of the disciples could not prove that the resurrection was a lie either. The Pharisees during that time could have produced a body if Jesus was still in His tomb, but they didn't. Likewise, if He wasn't in His tomb, how'd He get out with Roman soldiers guarding it?"

"I think that your reasoning is flawed on this matter as it presupposes an interest in Christianity which first-century non-Christians may not have had. Because of Christianity's status in the 21st century as a major world religion, it is easy to forget that Christianity in the first-century was not the center of attention in religion. For almost the entire first-century Christianity went unnoticed by most people in the Roman Empire and was viewed as a tiny, odd, antisocial, irreligious sect, drawing its followers from the lower strata of society. First-century Romans had about

115

as much interest in refuting Christian claims as 20th century skeptics had in refuting the misguided claims of Charles Manson. They simply didn't care to refute it. As for the Pharisees, Jewish sources do not even mention the resurrection, much less attempt to refute it. This hardly suggests that Jewish leaders were actively engaged in attempting to refute the resurrection story but failed in their efforts. Of course, it is possible that the Jews wanted to keep the resurrection story quiet precisely because they couldn't refute it, but in order for your argument to have any weight, you have the burden of proof to show that that mere possibility is probably what happened."

"You make some good points, Simon, but to say that the life and crucifixion of Jesus had no importance in Jerusalem seems at odds with the historical facts that He was the focal point of the Jewish leaders and that He was dealt with personally by Pontius Pilate, the Roman governor. I'll concede that Christianity wasn't a major religion back then and was even misunderstood and ignored by many, but the interest in Jesus and the following claims of His resurrection cannot be denied."

"Again, you're citing Christian accounts of these events, which of course insist upon the vital importance of Jesus."

"Okay, then, let's look at the historical record. If it was a conspiracy or an effort to create some sort of myth, then the enemies of Christ could have exposed the lie eventually. Most conspiracies are, after all, eventually exposed. However, it is a historical fact that no one ever confessed, freely or under duress, bribed or tortured, that the story of the resurrection was a lie."

"Wait a second, Rocky. I know for a fact that many Christians broke under pressure, and sometimes torture, to deny Christ and worship Caesar."

"True. You're exactly right! However, in spite of all that, no one ever let the proverbial 'cat out of the bag,' if you will, revealing the resurrection as a fake. No Christian believes that the resurrection was a conspiracy, or else they wouldn't have become Christians in the first place. The disciples and many Christians since then became courageous and fearless men and women. Why? Their leader overcame death, and they could too! If it were all a big lie, how would it then transform lives? "

"Lies can transform lives too. Hitler's lies transformed the lives of millions. You may be able to name a million people who believe it, but that doesn't make it true. If a million people believe a lie, a lie is still a lie. You're building your case on texts written by those who may have helped create this myth."

"I agree with you that you don't find truth by counting noses. I do not agree with there being any fault to the New Testament texts however. Most biographies rely upon research, sometimes several years after the event. The New Testament was written by people who were either there, or had access to the apostles who were. These were eyewitness accounts."

"But look at the sources! Also, these books were written about twenty years after the fact. That's hardly *timely*."

"Several historical texts were written several years after the fact, yet academia cites them as reliable. The earliest copies of Caesar's *Gallic Wars* date 1,000 years after it was written, and the first complete copy of the *Odyssey* by Homer dates 2,200 years after it was written. Alexander the Great's biography was written 500 years after his death. About 500 years after that, people started to add myths to his biography."

"That's my point," Simon said. "Over time, the story of Jesus grew and grew. Now, Jesus is said to be Lord. Can you imagine a movement today claiming that a soldier in World War II rose physically from the dead, but when you asked for proof, all they offered you were a mere handful of anonymous religious tracts written in the 1980's? Would it be even remotely reasonable to believe such a thing on such feeble evidence? I think not! What about alien bodies recovered from a crashed flying saucer in Roswell, New Mexico? Many people sincerely believe that legend today, yet this is the modern age, with ample evidence against it in print that is easily accessible to anyone, and this legend began only thirty years after the event."

"Let's say I decide to write a biography on John Lennon," said Rocky. "I could embellish it and make claims that he never made, like he was God and was raised from the dead. However, as soon as I publish it, people who were alive when he was could point out those lies. Likewise, Buddha and Muhammad did not perform any miracles, but later traditions hundreds of years later ascribe miracles to them. You see, at least three generations must die out in order to create this myth; otherwise eyewitnesses who were there could prove it to be false. The Gospels have been dated to the first-century, and people were still alive who could refute those claims. However, those closest to Jesus embraced and supported the accounts of His life. Anyhow, regarding your accusation that people added to the New Testament over the years, there are about five thousand copies of original and virtually identical copies of the early New Testament. Nothing else in ancient literature is that reliable."

Chip leaned over to Becky and said, "I've never seen anyone take on Simon quite like this. Usually Simon indulges in long diatribes, but he's up against the ropes. I only wish I had gone this route in the past with Simon."

"Simon, I don't wish to beat a dead horse, only your argument," Rocky said with a mischievous grin, and a few in the crowd responded with some cheers and whistles. "I say we should move on to one of the other areas of contention regarding the resurrection."

"Ah, yes, Rocky, I think we covered that last point very well.

Not bad for a janitor. I dare say you're smart enough to be *Harvard's* janitor."

Simon's buddies let out a few laughs, but the once strongly partisan crowd was now becoming more evenly mixed.

"Why is Rocky letting him talk that way?" Steven said to Chip and Becky.

"I've known Simon for a few years," Chip said, "and I have to believe that these two are genuinely having a good time together. I don't think Rock's offended at all. I think he's simply exchanging ribs with a buddy."

"Simon a buddy?" Steven echoed in disbelief.

"Hey, Rocky, let's discuss that one thing you said about hallucinations. That sounds like a good topic for this crowd."

"Oh yeah, sure. Another point made by the detractors of the resurrection says that Jesus wasn't raised from the dead, nor did the disciples stage a grand conspiracy. Instead, the disciples just experienced hallucinations of Jesus following His death."

"I'll be honest with you all," Simon said, "I haven't heard this one before. However, think about it. If someone thinks they're seeing a dead man walking and talking, it does seem reasonable to believe that they are hallucinating."

"You mean like an Elvis sighting?"

"Yeah, like an Elvis sighting. There are always people seeing this guy walking out of a convenience store somewhere, like Kalamazoo, Michigan." Simon laughed.

"The difference is, however, that several people saw Jesus after His death on the cross."

"There's no difference, Rocky. Many people have also claimed to have seen Elvis. People are just obsessed with those claiming to be 'the King.' Just wait till Richard Petty dies. The cycle will continue," Simon said and smiled.

"500 separate Elvis sightings could in fact be attributed to

119

hallucinations, but if 500 people, all at the *same time* see, talk to, touch, and dine with Him, then that's a whole different story."

"Let's look at Paul for a moment," Simon said as he pulled out a heavily marked up and dog-eared old pocket-sized New Testament Bible. "In 2 Corinthians 12:1-7, Paul boasts of the revelations he has received. He went up to the third heaven and heard and saw several things. In fact, nowhere in Paul's letters or in the three accounts of his conversion in Acts does Paul or Luke ever state that Paul saw a bodily Jesus. He saw a bright light and heard a voice. He saw a vision not a physical body. Getting back to the Elvis issue, even 2,000 years later, people still have visions of Jesus. Do these visions count as sightings of the physically resurrected Jesus? If not, why do Paul's visions count as sightings of the physically resurrected Jesus?"

"They don't count as a physically resurrected Jesus, as Jesus had already ascended up into Heaven, thus leaving the physical world. He can still reach people and communicate with people though."

"Well, I really do not know this argument too well, and obviously you came prepared. I'll give you this one."

"I'll take it, along with the first debate. I do want to elaborate for any of those sitting here listening that hallucinations aren't shared by several people at the exact same time. Hallucinations usually only last a few seconds or minutes, not for 40 days. Also, hallucinations don't eat, can't be touched, and if it was a hallucination, why wouldn't the Jews just produce Jesus' body and say, 'Look, here He is. Still dead!'"

"Okay, calm down, boy. Hey, waiter! No more caffeine for Rocky tonight!" Simon said to the delight of a few in the audience. "I already conceded this one to you. I also don't recall awarding the first debate to you."

"We set the standards, and you didn't disprove anything. I

offered evidence and reasoning for why the disciples wouldn't commit such a conspiracy."

"Well, let's not debate results, but let's continue to strive for the truth," said Simon.

"That's more like it. Blaise Pascal said that there were three types of people: those who seek and find God, those who seek but haven't found Him yet, and those who never seek and never find. Logically, the second category will eventually join the first. I'm encouraged by your pursuit of the truth."

Simon gave Rocky a crooked grin.

"Well," said Rocky, "we basically discussed the issues concerning deceit or mythmaking by the disciples, and we both agreed that the hallucination theory was probably the result of someone's own hallucination. Let's discuss the possibility then that Jesus didn't actually die, and thus, when He came out on Easter morning, He wasn't a resurrected dead man, but a man who had passed out on the cross, was buried alive, and then regained consciousness, later to meet with His followers to proclaim that He did indeed defeat death."

"Is it possible? Yes. I don't know if this is my favorite theory, but if the man wasn't killed, then of course that would naturally explain how He could be walking around alive."

"I don't think it is reasonable, Simon. Roman soldiers were masters of the black art of death. Roman law sentenced any soldier to the death penalty who let a capital prisoner escape in any way. The Roman soldier didn't even break His legs, a method usually incorporated to speed up the dying process. He knew that Jesus was dead."

"Again, based on Christian texts, your points are good ones. However, there are many reasons to be skeptical. Let's consider the setting, the time and place in which this story spread. This was an age of fables and wonder. Magic, miracles, and ghosts were everywhere and never doubted. People even believed that monsters were eating the moon during lunar eclipses. By modern standards, almost no one had any sort of education at all, and no media to challenge these stories with scientific facts. These were not people who were skilled or equipped to challenge the Gospel accounts. They didn't have coroners, reporters, cameras, newspapers, forensic science, or even police investigators. People back then based their judgment on the sincerity and ability of the storyteller, and the apostles were clearly gifted storytellers."

"Simon, modern medicine has stated that He died of asphyxiation based on the water that came out with the blood from Jesus' pierced heart, as specified in a detailed account of the Gospels. Also, I think it's arrogant to believe that a people from a different time and place were so ignorant. I would believe that they were ignorant or gullible if a half dead, staggering sick man who was in desperate need of a doctor stumbled in claiming a victorious resurrection. However, He came in gloriously alive and even convinced a doubting Thomas. Anyhow, how could a half dead man, without food or drink for three days, in a cold dark cave, after a massive trauma, move a two ton stone, overtake the Roman guards, stagger on pierced feet to his disciples and be convincing? Again, is this *reasonable*?"

"Why don't I believe in the resurrection, Rocky? It actually begins with a different tale. In 520 A.D., an anonymous monk recorded the life of Saint Genevieve, who had died only ten years earlier. In his account of her life, he describes how, when she ordered a cursed tree cut down, monsters sprung from it and breathed a fatal stench on several men for two hours. While she was sailing, eleven ships capsized, but after she prayed, they were righted again spontaneously. He even wrote that she cast out demons, calmed storms, miraculously created water and oil from nothing before astonished crowds, healed the blind and lame, and several people who stole things from her actually went blind. No one wrote anything to contradict or challenge these claims, and a religious man who regarded lying to be a sin wrote them, very near the time the events supposedly happened. Yet does anyone here really believe any of it? Not really. And we shouldn't."

"I think we're now debating apples to oranges, my friend."

"No we're not. As David Hume once said, why do such things not happen now? Is it a coincidence that the very time when these things no longer happen is the same time that we have the means and methods to check them in the light of science and careful investigation? I've never seen monsters spring from a tree, and I don't know anyone who has, and there are no women touring the country levitating ships. These events look like tall tales, sound like tall tales, and smell like tall tales. Odds are, they're tall tales. And there are specific reasons to disbelieve the story of Genevieve, and they are the same reasons we have to doubt the Gospel accounts of the resurrection of Jesus. The parallel is clear: the Gospels were written no sooner after the death of their main character than was the case for the account of Genevieve, and, like that account, the Gospels were also originally anonymous. Both contain fabulous miracles supposedly witnessed by numerous people. Both belong to the same genre of literature: what we call 'hagiography,' a sacred account of a holy person regarded as representing a moral and divine ideal. Such a genre has as its goal the glorification of the religion itself and of the example set by the perfect holy person represented as its central focus. Such literature was also a tool of propaganda, used to promote certain moral or religious views, and to *oppose* different points of view."

"I appreciate the story of Genevieve, it's interesting.

However, the parallel is a weak one at best. We already discussed the historical reliability of the Gospels, and I even mentioned earlier how hard it would be to lie about someone when people were still alive who remembered the person. I couldn't write a biography on John F. Kennedy, and claim that he won the Cy Young Award over Sandy Koufax without historians and baseball fans that remember these two individuals attacking my claims. The Gospel accounts, though written after His resurrection, could have been challenged by anyone who knew or knew of Jesus."

"I need more proof," Simon said as he shook his head. "It should not be lost on us that Thomas was depicted as being no less righteous for refusing to believe a wild claim without physical proof. We have as much right as he did and ought to follow his example. He got to see and feel the wounds before believing, and so should we. I haven't, so I can't be expected to believe it. And this leads me to one final reason why I don't buy the resurrection story. No wise or compassionate God would demand this from us! Such a God would not leave us so poorly informed about something so important. If we have a message for someone that is urgently vital for their survival, and we have any compassion, that compassion will compel us to communicate that message clearly and with every necessary proof, not ambiguously, or through unreliable means presenting no real evidence. Conversely, if we see something incredible, we do not attack those who don't believe us, because we don't even expect them to believe us unless we can present decisive proof."

"God has made this common knowledge. He has provided all the accounts in Scripture, and we're even debating it now," said Rocky.

"I don't think you get my point. There's a heroic story in the technology community about the man who invented elevator safety brakes. He claimed that any elevator fitted with his brakes, even if all the cables broke, would be safely and swiftly stopped by his new invention. Not one person trusted it. Did he get angry or indignant? No. He simply put himself in an elevator, ordered the cables cut, and proved to the world by risking his own life that his brakes worked. This is the very principle that has delivered us from superstition to science. Any claim can be made about a drug, but people are rightly wary of swallowing anything that hasn't been thoroughly tested and re-tested and tested again. Since I have no such proofs regarding the resurrection story, I'm not going to swallow it, and it would be cruel, even for God, to expect otherwise of me. So I can reason rightly that the God of all humankind would not appear in one tiny backwater region of the Earth, in a backward time, revealing Himself to a tiny unknown few, and then expect the billions of the rest of us to take their word for it, and not even their word, but the word of some unnamed person many times removed. I simply cannot believe that Christ is God. If He were, He'd have given me some proof, for if He is real, then I'd sincerely want to believe in Him."

"Simon, you don't truly want to believe at all. You just want to discover some fact that will satisfy your incredible intellect. Real faith is no place for intellect alone. The Truth of Who Christ is cannot be summed up as a purely rational argument. When we love someone, anyone, a thousand arguments do not make one proof nor do a thousand objections make one doubt."

"I don't want to deal with faith. I want to deal with something more objective than my feelings."

"But faith is more than feeling. Feelings can change a hundred times a day, but faith does not. I believe there are three ways to know truth: faith, feeling, and scientific reasoning. For example, a flower might really be a gift from God, beautiful, and plant cells."

"I don't want any religious dogma in my life."

"Simon, *that's* a dogma! You exclude Christianity as a way to know truth without any proof for your exclusion. That's dogmatic, my friend. You say I'm dogmatic, yet I don't exclude your precious scientific method. My faith includes your science, but your science, or should I say your faith in science alone, refuses to include my faith."

"Rocky," Simon breathed loudly into the microphone, "your thoughts are like razor blades. I can't believe that you're just a janitor. I'm not about to embrace Christianity, but you've given me a whole new respect for its validity."

Chip, Becky, and Steven were stunned by Simon's statement. Although it wasn't a declaration of defeat, Simon's supporters appeared equally shocked.

Simon turned to the audience like P.T. Barnum and asked, "So who won tonight? Was it our guest, Rocky Raccoon?"

The crowd offered a scattered applause in support of Rocky.

"Or was it yours truly, Simon the Great?" he shouted with theatrics of a megalomaniac rock star.

The crowd erupted in applause for their leader.

"Rocky, you're a good guy. You're welcome to come back here anytime," Simon offered as he reached out and shook Rocky's hand.

Rocky turned around and walked over to join his friends.

"You did great, and everyone here really knows you won," Becky said as she gave him a hug and kiss on the cheek.

"That was awesome, man," Chip said as he gave him a strong handshake and embraced him with his other arm. "Better than I've ever done."

"Thanks, I just wish I could have been more convincing."

"You were more effective than you think," Steven said. "Who

knows what seeds you planted here tonight? Anyhow, your song was great!"

"Yeah, I liked it too!" said Becky.

"Well, it's been a good night, but we really must get back to Easton. We've got a bit of a drive and a busy day tomorrow," said Chip.

"Yeah, you're right," Becky agreed. "It looks as though several others are leaving now too, even Simon and his fans."

The four of them walked outside and started down the sidewalk. Up ahead, some of Simon's supporters were laughing at an elderly man sitting on the sidewalk.

"Hey, man, get a bath!" one of them yelled.

"Then get a job!" another mocked.

"Here, man," another said throwing a wad of cash at the man, "get some better booze next time."

Simon didn't participate in the jeering of the homeless man, but he didn't say anything to stop it either.

As Becky, Steven, Chip, and Rocky approached the man, he covered himself like a boxer bracing for the knockout punch. Without saying a word, Rocky knelt down in front of the trembling man. Simon turned around and witnessed Rocky reach out to hold the man by his old dirty, coal-colored hands, and kiss them.

"Help me get him up," Rocky said to Steven.

"Where are we going with him?" Chip asked.

"I know of a nearby Alcoholics Anonymous in the area. They'll help him more than we can."

As Rocky and his friends helped the man to a local chapter of Alcoholics Anonymous, Simon excused himself from his friends and quietly walked back alone to his apartment.

Tea Time

Rocky's debate with Simon was the main topic of conversation during lunch. Rocky was greeted with a lot of praise, which seemed to embarrass him, and provoked him to act busier than he really was to avoid the limelight's hot glow.

"Can you believe that he faced Simon all by himself?" Meredith asked. "Talk about gutsy."

"Yeah, no doubt," Martin said. "I hear that he really stood his ground against Simon the Great."

"I heard that he didn't offer any original arguments but just used the same old comebacks that apologist hacks have been using for years," said Tom.

"Well at least he was there," said Meredith. "Better to be using the old reliables than to be sitting here in our pajamas doing nothing."

"I'm not wasting my time, Meredith," said Tom. "My thesis is already being considered for publishing. I plan to make an impact in this world beyond New England."

"I'm sure you will, Tom," Meredith said as she wiped her hands.

Rocky took his break after the rush and decided to join his

friends from Tuttle Hall. As he walked down the aisle between the rows of benches in the cafeteria, Rocky received a scattering of applause from everyone except Tom. Rocky smiled and playfully stood up on a chair for everyone to see and hear him.

"Thank you, but the Lord deserves your applause, not me. Please remember this, my friends. God spoke to Balaam through his ass, and He has been speaking through asses like me ever since. So please don't think too highly of me."

"Can't argue with him there," Tom said under his breath.

Rocky stepped down amidst the cheers and made his way to the table where his friends were sitting.

"Wow, what an entrance!" Jim said.

"Yeah, for a moment I thought Billy Graham had just walked in," Rick joked.

Rocky simply smiled and bowed his head to quietly say grace.

President Casper walked into the cafeteria and found his way to Rocky. It wasn't uncommon for the professors to join the students on occasion for lunch and conversation, but President Casper almost never came down during lunch.

"Good afternoon, gentlemen," said Dr. Casper. "Do you mind if I have a seat?"

"Please do," said Chip.

"Rocky, I heard about your encounter with Simon Luger. I'm really happy to hear that you and some other students had the courage to go down there."

"Thank you, Dr. Casper. Becky, Steven, Chip, and I were encouraged by what we saw and heard last night.

"Chip even told me what you did last night with that elderly gentleman. Your compassion is admirable."

"I'm just loving as I was taught to love, sir. To walk by that man and do nothing would have been a sin of neglect. I only did what someone else once did for me when I was in that position."

Dr. Casper smiled.

"I have a favor to ask you, but I wanted to be the one to ask," Dr. Casper said. "I'm hosting a dinner party tomorrow night, and I would like to have you work as our server. You'll get paid overtime for it. Can you help us out tomorrow night?"

"Yes, sir. I'd be happy to help. If I may ask, what's the occasion?"

"An old friend of mine is in town for a speaking engagement at Boston University and has made some time in his demanding schedule to accept a dinner invitation at my residence tomorrow evening."

"Great. Just let me know what time to be there and what I should wear."

"Sam will help you out with those details. There will be a few students there, including Jim, Chip, and Tom, just to name a few, so you'll feel right at home."

Dr. Casper excused himself and went back to his office to catch up on all the work that piled up in the ten minutes he'd sacrificed to visit the cafeteria. After he left the cafeteria, Rick looked over at Rocky and smirked. "Teacher's pet!"

Rocky laughed out loud and turned around to see Tom staring right at him.

*　*　*

On the night of the dinner event, Rocky showed up in black trousers, a white shirt, and a tie, all of which he had borrowed from his kind but tall and broad-shouldered friend, Jim. He looked like a boy wearing his older brother's hand-me-downs prior to being altered. Tom looked Rocky over and just shook his head.

Rocky had been by Dr. Casper's on campus residence on

numerous occasions but never had the privilege to set foot inside this beautiful Victorian house. The residence not only accommodated and housed Dr. Casper and his family, but it also provided him with a private study and an appropriate location to entertain guests.

As the students mingled and talked, Dr. Casper asked for everyone's attention and introduced Dr. Pavi Garbadawala. Dr. Garbadawala was a noted Hindu scholar from India. He was a man of short stature, lean build, and possessed a pearly white smile under his trim black mustache.

Rocky entered the kitchen and found Sam hard at work with the meal. He wore a chef's hat and sang quietly while he cooked. Rocky looked at the food and even stole a sample of the salad.

"This is really good. How'd you learn to cook since our last shift?" said Rocky.

"Comments like that, sir, will not get you dinner."

"I see that this is a vegetarian meal. That's playing it safe. Aside from cows, I'm not sure what their dietary beliefs are."

"I'm not sure either, which is why Dr. Casper gave me a specific menu to prepare. I think they can eat meat, but I think that Dr. Garba, Garba, um, Dr. Garb, I think our guest is a vegetarian," Sam said.

"I believe you pronounce it Dr. Garbadawala."

"Why don't you make your phonically gifted self useful and pour the ice water in their glasses before they sit down at the table."

"Yes, sir, I'll get to it," Rocky said as he clicked the heels of his oversized dress shoes.

Rocky walked out into the dining room and poured the water as Dr. Garbadawala and Tom were debating the problem of evil and how Hinduism and Christianity differ in their views of evil.

Dr. Casper walked out of the kitchen and announced that

131

dinner was now being served. Rocky exited the dining room, aware that he should only enter on occasion to serve additional food items and refill the guests' drinks.

He could hear the debate from the kitchen.

"Evil is an illusion, my friends," Dr. Garbadawala said. "There are no such things as good and evil thoughts. Cruelty and non-cruelty are the *same*."

"Are you saying that child abuse isn't evil then, Dr. Garbadawala?" Jim asked.

"Hinduism considers the world in which we live as a projection of God and thus unreal. Imagine if you will, a flashlight shining on the wall. The light you see on the wall is an illusion, as the source of the light is in reality on the other side of the room. The world is unreal, not because it does not exist, but because it is unstable, impermanent, unreliable, and illusory. It is unreal because it hides the truth and shows us things that lead to our ignorance. It is unreal because it changes its colors every moment. What is now is not what is next. There is always constant change. Enemies become friends, and friends become enemies. The sun and all of her planets are always changing their position in both space and time. Rivers flow, oceans shift with their currents. Even the atoms and cells in your body are always changing location, being destroyed, and recreated. The world in which we live gives us an apparent illusion of stability. It is an illusion to believe that this world is the same always, or that the people we deal with are the same all the time. The world is therefore an illusion, not because it does not exist in the physical sense, but because it is unstable, ever changing, impermanent, and most important of all never the same. Ask yourself this question: are you the same person you were a minute ago?"

"But your view denies reality," said Tom.

"No, it only denies that which is an illusion, such as evil," he said.

"Sir," said Chip, "the problem is that nobody can live if what you say is true. The universe and everything in it has a way of making its presence known in very concrete ways. I heard one Indian philosopher once say, 'Even in India, we look both ways before we cross the street, because we know it is either the bus or us.'"

Everyone at the table laughed.

"Having been sentenced to live a life of illusion, how can I ever test the truth of such a claim within that illusion?" Jim asked. "If everything, including evil is an illusion, then what does it matter what we do?"

Dr. Garbadawala straightened up in his chair and replied, "Young man, if you realize your own true divine nature, then your very nature would not allow you to do any evil deed. You would see everything as being full of God."

"I respectfully disagree, my friend," said Dr. Casper. "If God is in everything, then it stands to reason that God is in both good and evil. Then there is no absolute morality, no divine law, no divine will discriminating good and evil. Getting back to Jim's question about the illusion of child abuse. To the child, it is evil, but to the abuser in this belief system, it is perfectly fine. If we choose what is good and evil, then there are no standards. We can call the Nazis evil, but they can respectfully disagree."

"Really, my friend, good and evil are one and the same," said Dr. Garbadawala.

"By theory, Pavi, you say that once you are 'enlightened' you have transcended good and evil," said Dr. Casper.

"Yes, Peter."

"All actions, then, even evil ones, are 'enlightened'? Charles Manson went on record saying, 'If God is one, what is bad?' He then ordered the pregnant Sharon Tate and the LaBiancas butchered."

"Mr. Manson was not a Hindu, sir," said Dr. Garbadawala.

"But the same philosophy that there is no evil led to those murders. However, evil most certainly exists. The definition of evil is everything that is not as it ought to be. Evil exists, Dr. Garbadawala, because man chose and continues to choose that which ought not to be. Man tried to define his own reality, believing Satan's lie. Man continues to rebel against God. If we can make up our own definition of good and evil, then anything is permissible. The whole concept of morality is then worthless."

Rocky walked into the room with a kettle of boiling water for those drinking the Assam tea, which Dr. Casper had special ordered from India for the occasion. He continued to listen as he poured the steaming hot water into the guests' cups.

"Allow me to summarize," Dr. Garbadawala said. "Evil is an illusion, as is good. It's not real. There are no good and evil thoughts and actions. In reality, cruelty and non-cruelty are the same thing."

As Dr. Garbadawala spoke, Rocky stood behind him, and to the horror and dismay of every Easton student and its president, he held the kettle of boiling water over Dr. Garbadawala's head.

The guest of honor turned around and was terrified to find Rocky seemingly about to pour the boiling water on top of their guest's balding head. "What's are you doing?" Dr. Garbadawala shouted at Rocky.

"You said there was no difference between cruelty and non-cruelty, right?" Rocky said with an uncharacteristically cold stare.

The distinguished Indian guest quickly scooted his chair to the side, got up, and said, "Okay, now *that's* a great counterargument. If you'll allow me to sit down without getting injured, I'll be more than happy to hear what else you've got to say, young man."

"We'll be happy to talk to you some more during dessert, Dr. Garbadawala," Dr. Casper said with a nervous laugh. "First, let me have a moment with our server."

He walked past Rocky and grabbed him forcefully by the arm on the way out of the dining room. He led Rocky right into his private office and shut the door.

"What was *that*? What were you thinking, Rocky?"

"I was just applying what I learned from a Francis Schaeffer anecdote, and it worked," Rocky said with a mischievous smile.

"That's not the point, Rocky! He's our guest. I don't want guests coming to this school feeling physically threatened. It's a big deal to have a guest of his stature here to visit."

"I apologize, Dr. Casper. I thought my demonstration would hammer home the point you were trying to make. Did you see the look in his eyes? He now knows that evil and cruelty are real."

Dr. Casper rolled his eyes, sat down at his desk, and folded his hands together under his chin. He then looked up at Rocky, who now appeared to feel bad about the incident.

"Rocky, I sincerely appreciate your effort, but you need to exercise better judgment. It's just like the situation we had with that escort. You have good intentions but have to think sometimes before you act."

"Even though the results have been good both times?"

"Yes, Rocky. Angel may have been an undercover cop about to arrest you, or a temptation you weren't ready for, and may have even carried a disease. Who knows? You could have easily slipped and accidentally poured the hot water over Pavi and seriously injured him."

"I'm sorry, Dr. Casper."

"How about you say that to Pavi instead?"

"Okay. You're right. I'll go in and apologize right now."

Rocky got up and a physically shaken Dr. Casper followed him into the dining room.

"Rocky Raccoon," Dr. Garbadawala said as he sat up, "we have all had a wonderful discussion since you left. Thank you."

"I want to apologize, sir."

"Why apologize? Young man, in all of my discussions with friends and adversaries, both public and private, not one has ever taught me as much as you have with your demonstration. No, sir, I will *not* accept your apology, as you have led me to the life-shattering conclusion that my spiritual journey is not over but only now just beginning."

Rocky turned around and looked at Dr. Casper, who raised his eyebrows and gave a shrug, letting Rocky know that he was on his own. Meanwhile, Tom excused himself from the table and left for the evening.

"Thank you, sir. That's very kind of you to say," said Rocky.

"No, young man, thank you!" Dr. Garbadawala said with a wide smile.

"Well," Rocky said, "I'm going to get back to my duties. Does anyone want any tea?"

"No!" everyone said in unison, and then they all laughed.

The Visitor

"You know, after all this time and all of his exploits, we still don't really know that much about Rocky," said Meredith as she stood in the diner line. "He shares just enough to make a point, and then slams the door on his past right in your face."

"Take it easy on him," said Martin. "He's apparently done some serious things in the past and now he's repented. Dr. Casper was gracious enough to give a guy like Rocky a chance to start over. I don't recall the Apostle Paul writing vital letters all about his past. He only referenced to it when making a point."

"Look, is there anything else we can talk about?" Tom asked. "I'm really sick of hearing about St. Rocky all of the time."

"Sorry, Tom," Martin said. "I really don't know why you dislike Rocky so much."

"I don't *dislike* him. I'm just bored of the same conversation everyday, about Rocky this, and Rocky that, all right? Doesn't anything interesting ever happen here anymore?"

At that moment, an outsider entered the cafeteria and walked down the aisle between the tables toward the food line. He was instantly recognized by all and swept the words people were speaking and the air they were breathing right out of the room, creating a perfect vacuum of sound.

Rocky looked up and saw Simon. He was dressed in a designer suit, but might as well have shown up in Moses' garb, given how he split the crowd of people before him like the Red Sea.

"Can we talk?"

Rocky looked around at Sam and his co-workers still working at their respective stations. "Grab something to eat and I'll be with you in about ten minutes."

Simon nodded and stood in line for some food. He appeared amused at the fearful respect people were exhibiting toward him. He went to the salad bar and then grabbed a bottled water. After paying the clerk, he sat down alone at a table in the back of the cafeteria. He was conscious of every eye watching him, but was unflappable as always. Nothing ever seemed to rattle him. He was the heir apparent to Dean Martin's title, the "King of Cool."

* * *

"What's Simon doing here?" Jim asked Chip and Steven.

"I don't know," Chip said. "He didn't mention anything about a visit when we saw him last."

"Well, it's clear that he's come to see Rocky," Steven said.

"I wonder why," said Jim.

* * *

"Tom, you said you wanted something different and interesting. Well, it doesn't get any more interesting that this," said Martin.

"So, *that's* Simon. I think he's gorgeous," Meredith said in a flutter matching her heart.

138

"I don't see much to him myself," Tom said as he looked across the room at Simon. "I really don't think there's much substance or depth to him. He's been blessed with a lot of money and has had the best education money can buy, that's all."

"Yeah, like no one ever said that about you, Tom." Martin laughed.

"Who said that?" Tom asked.

"No one, Tom," Martin said. "It was just a joke. You really need to relax."

* * *

Rocky finished his main responsibilities, and then fixed himself a dinner. He walked over to the table where Simon was sitting and sat across from him.

"I'm glad you got the salad and not the clam chowder. I would have warned you though had you asked for it."

"Thanks. I appreciate that," Simon said as he looked around the cafeteria. "This place is smaller than I expected."

"The cafeteria?"

"No, the seminary. I always envisioned a great medieval cathedral motif with monastic halls that echo loudly with every step you take."

"I'm sorry to disappoint you, my friend."

"Don't be sorry. I like to be surprised. I'm hardly ever surprised by anything these days, so it's refreshing to find myself surprised by this place...and by *you*."

"What's even more surprising about me, Simon is that I have this obsessive compulsive disorder with the number three."

"What?"

"Yeah, anything involving numbers has to be divisible by

three. I wouldn't set my alarm clock at 8:00 for example. I'd set it for 8:01."

Simon laughed out loud. "That's surprising all right, Rocky. Remind me to give you the number of a shrink I know before I leave."

"So what brings Simon the Great up to Easton this evening?" Rocky inquired as he continued to enjoy his dinner.

"You actually."

"I'm flattered. Did you come for a rematch, or shall we arm wrestle this time?"

Simon smiled.

"It looks like you're really enjoying that sandwich, Rocky. Would you mind though if I take you out for dinner? I want to talk to you, but I don't want to talk here."

Rocky put his sandwich down and didn't question Simon's motives for wanting a change of scenery.

"Please give me about another twenty minutes to finish my list of duties in the kitchen and I'll be right with you."

"That's fine, I will just sit here on display till then," Simon said with a smirk as he noted the hundreds of eyes staring at them.

Rocky grabbed a worn out Gideon's Bible from his back pocket and handed it to Simon. "It's a bestseller, you know."

* * *

Simon read through sections of the pocket sized New Testament, waiting for Rocky to finish his job in the kitchen. He occasionally allowed his eye to wander around the room, observing the next generation of pastors, scholars, missionaries, and counselors. He started to read more from the book of Matthew when he heard a familiar voice.

140

"Simon the Great. What brings you to these parts?" Chip asked.

"Howdy, Yale Man. I'm sorry, should I not say that out loud? I don't wish to embarrass you."

"We beat you in football this year," said Chip.

"Oh yeah. I'll grant you that your scholarship behemoths are bigger than ours. Anyhow, I'm here to see Rocky."

"You came for a rematch, eh?"

"Why would I want a rematch if I won?"

"Well, that's a matter of opinion."

"Isn't everything?"

"It's good to see you, Simon. You should stop by more often."

"Actually, I will be here in two months for the big debate."

"What big debate?" Chip asked.

"Dr. Casper hasn't announced it yet? Well, I imagine he doesn't want his students to see him lose here on campus. He's debating Harvard's Dr. Illona Johnson."

"I guess I'll see you then."

"I'll see you then, Chipper."

* * *

Rocky walked over to Simon, who seemed to be engrossed in the Gideon's Bible. Simon looked up at Rocky with a smile.

"Ready, Rocky?"

"Actually, I would like to stop by my room real quick to change clothes. Not only would I not eat the clam chowder, I also don't wish to smell like it either."

"I'm a patient man. Why don't you take a shower?"

"Okay, I will. Are you enjoying the Bible?"

"Yes, I am."

141

"I told you it was a bestseller."

"Yes, but under fiction or non-fiction?"

"I can see I'm in for a good night already, Simon!"

* * *

Rocky and Simon walked into Tuttle Hall together.

"I'm surprised that you're not making any jokes about this dorm. It used to be a horse stable you know."

"Well, there's an old expression. People in glass houses shouldn't throw stones. If you've ever been in a dorm at Harvard, you'd know I have little to no room to criticize."

"So where does *all* of your dad's money go that he donates every year?"

"You've finally stumped me," said Simon.

They both walked up to the second floor and entered Rocky's room.

"Okay, I don't mean this to sound like a rude comment from some rich guy, but I've been in telephone booths bigger than this room."

"Don't sweat it. It's free, and it's home."

Simon looked around the room, which took all of a millisecond to do. He then sat down on the bed and continued to read from the Bible as Rocky went down the hallway to take a shower and got ready.

* * *

Rocky and Simon walked outside and crawled into Simon's Ferrari 458 Italia. Simon turned the engine on and then dropped the hammer on the accelerator, which allowed Rocky to imagine what it must feel like to be an astronaut during lift off in the

142

space shuttle.

"This car has good get up and go," said Rocky. "I'll have to get me one of these."

Simon laughed. "Have you ever been in a Ferrari before, Rock?"

"Only a few times. Mostly at car shows."

"I came prepared. I have the Beatles *White Album*. Wanna listen to it?"

"Can a porcupine float?"

"Simon laughed as he raised the volume of "Back In the U.S.S.R." to compete against the 600 hundred stallions stampeding under the hood.

Rocky smiled and nodded his approval, but continued to casually observe where they were going.

Rocky & Simon

After a short drive along the North Shore, Simon pulled into the driveway of an elegant restaurant overlooking the ocean. Rocky looked at himself in the side mirror and then looked back at the restaurant.

Rocky and Simon entered through the main doors and were greeted by the maitre d'. "Good evening, gentlemen. We have been expecting you."

"Thank you, Coleman," Simon said.

Rocky and Simon were led to a table with a tremendous view of the ocean and a picturesque lighthouse.

"What do you think, Rocky?"

"I am amazed they let me in here dressed like this."

"Well, ownership has its perks."

"You own this place?"

"Well, to be accurate, *Daddy* does."

"It's beautiful. I could just stare out at the Atlantic for hours, just thinking about Lindberg flying over it, the Titanic sinking, Columbus sailing it, immigrants traveling across it, and just imagining what exotic animals must be out there at any given time."

144

"You have a poet's heart."

"And a three-year-old's curiosity. Though I am enjoying your company and the view, I am curious why you came up unannounced this evening."

"You got me thinking. I'd be lying if I said you didn't."

Rocky sat up in his chair and looked him in the eyes.

"Hold on," Simon said as he lifted his hands into the air like a traffic cop, "You didn't convert me, my friend. I just want to talk. So please turn those Disney eyes of yours off for a moment, okay?"

"Fair enough. What is it?"

Simon was about to speak, but the server stopped to make his introduction. He informed them of the night's specials and then placed their napkins on their laps.

"We'll have the family label, Mortimer, 1972."

"I'm sure it's out of this world, but I cannot have any wine."

"Oh, I see someone's trying to be the designated driver tonight." Simon laughed along with Mortimer. "Look, Rocky, I'll let you take a spin in it. Please, drink up."

"Mortimer, could you please excuse us for a moment?" Rocky asked.

Mortimer acknowledged Rocky, but looked to Simon for permission to leave. Simon nodded his head, and Mortimer turned around and walked to another table.

"I apologize. I mean absolutely no disrespect, but I cannot drink a drop of alcohol."

"Oh…I'm sorry. I had no idea. Actually, I never would have guessed, given how strong a Christian you are."

"We all fall short, my friend."

"Is that why you helped out that street bum then?"

"That bum, as you say, has a name, Simon."

"I'm sorry, I chose my words poorly and out of ignorance.

You helped him out because he was a drunk?"

"You aren't the most tactful guy in the world, but yeah. I would have offered to help him anyway, but I felt both compelled and obligated to help him, given that I've been there myself."

"Do you think he'll make it?"

"Pray for him."

Simon could see that Mortimer was anxiously waiting for the okay to return to take their orders. Simon made a slight gesture with his hand, and Mortimer returned like a trained dog.

"Have you made a decision, sir?"

"Yes, we'll both have water tonight."

"Yes, sir," Mortimer replied as his perfect posture suddenly slumped downward.

"Relax, Mort, I'll still tip you the same," Simon said with a smile. "Rocky, please, order anything from the menu."

"I'll have the New York strip steak, cooked medium. I'll also have a loaded baked potato along with the house salad."

"Wow, you really are a meat and potatoes man. I'll have the Tuscany Lemon Chicken tonight, Mortimer, along with the usual."

"Very well, sir, I'll return with your water momentarily."

"So, what's on your mind?" Rocky asked again.

"I watched you closely, and though I heard the arguments you made regarding the Resurrection of Jesus, I must admit that you assisting that man on the sidewalk really touched me. I thought about everything I have in life, and yet, after I looked at you, I felt completely empty. In fact, I'm as empty as I have ever been in my life."

"That need you feel, the void in your heart, is what C.S. Lewis referred to as a Christ-shaped hole which can only be filled by Jesus. I used to try to fill it with everything under the Nevada

146

sun: alcohol, women, drugs, you name it. Perhaps you've been trying to fill that Christ shaped hole with money, or even knowledge."

"No. Trust me, I enjoy the perks of being a billionaire's only son, and my desire for knowledge has never been an effort to replace God."

"What is it then?"

"I don't know. I was hoping that maybe you could offer some insight."

"I'm glad that we're here alone instead of trying to *impress* an audience. Nothing is ever really gained by throwing mud at one another. Not only do your hands get dirty, but you also lose a lot of ground. What is your main objection against God, really?"

"I don't know. Maybe I'm angry that there's such pain and misery in this world, where evil is allowed to flourish and rule."

"You don't believe in God necessarily, but you do believe in evil. There's an inconsistency in your argument, which I'm shocked that you of all people haven't seen. How can you as an atheist know or even define evil?"

"I can see what's bad, Rock. I'm not blind. I know the Nazis were evil."

"In order to tell good from evil, you need a universal moral law. Something is good and something is evil."

"I agree. We all use a universal moral law to make the distinction between good and evil."

"Think about it, Simon. If you have a universal moral law, there must be a universal lawgiver, otherwise there truly is no universal moral law. God is that universal lawgiver. Otherwise you'd just have subjective opinions on what is right and wrong."

"Yes and no. We define our own morality. As humans, we inherently know good from evil."

"You mentioned that the Nazis were evil, but they had their

own internal value system too. They did not see themselves as evil. If we choose our own morality, Simon, who is right, you or the Nazis?"

Simon sat quietly and looked out at the bright moon illuminating the deep, black waters of the Atlantic.

"Simon, the reason most atheists know evil, but can't explain why, is because they deny God. I know that you know that if we make up our own definition of good and evil, then anything is permissible, even the Holocaust. The whole concept of morality is then worthless."

"Why would God allow evil in the first place?"

"That's a great question. I'm not an expert, and you should know that, especially given your debates with Chip, who knows volumes more than I do. I'd suggest reading C.S. Lewis' book *The Problem of Pain*. He really offers the best answer in my opinion."

"See, that's a typical Christian response, and I'm disappointed to hear you give it, Rocky. I ask many Christians tough questions, and they never seem to know what they believe or why. They simply tell me to read a book or listen to a recording."

"That's a fair criticism. I'll offer a thought or two then, based on my own understanding. I recently heard a good definition of evil. Evil is everything that is not as it ought to be. God created a perfect world, and everything He made was good. Mankind deviated from God's master plan, and everything changed for the worse, because that's what we wanted. Evil exists because man chose and continues to choose that which ought not to be. Man tried to determine his own reality and believed Satan's lies. In light of all this knowledge, we still continue to rebel against God."

"If He wanted everything to be perfect and didn't want us to rebel, why didn't he make us with the innate ability to choose right?"

"Is that free will? One of God's greatest gifts to us is freedom. He gave us the precious gift to choose. He didn't make man an automaton," Rocky said as he pulled out his pocket Gideon's Bible. "God said to Adam in Genesis 2:16, 'You are free.' He didn't put any qualifiers on it."

"Yes, He did," said Simon. "He told Adam not to eat from the tree of good and evil."

"That's where you're only partially right. He did tell Adam and Eve not to eat from that tree, but He still gave them the *freedom* to do what He just told them not to do. Adam was *free*."

"God should have made man free but programmed him to always do what is right. Then we could have the world that your hero John Lennon imagined."

"Simon, that would be a contradiction, and I think you know that. Even God cannot do the impossible. He has defined reality and cannot contradict it. He cannot make a round square or tell a lie. He gave man freedom, and that's a good thing."

"In the meantime, however, there is still evil, and there's supposedly an all-powerful and loving God who just sits idly by while it all happens," Simon said.

"Eventually, God will eliminate all evil. There will be justice. You are wrong about God. Even now, He protects and assists us against evil."

"Well, I must say, you do a pretty good job without C.S. Lewis on my nightstand," Simon said with a smile.

"Thanks. I do, however, want to suggest reading the first three chapters and the last three chapters of the Bible to seek out more answers on the problem of evil."

Simon nodded.

Mortimer returned with their water, and Simon and Rocky

both sat back in their chairs like boxers returning to their respective corners after a well fought round.

* * *

Simon placed his crumpled napkin on top of his plate while Rocky took his last bite of steak.

"In theory, Rock, Christianity sounds wonderful. However, how do you explain all the corruption and murder done in the name of Jesus? More people have died in the name of Jesus than in any other name in history."

"Ah, a historical debate. Here's where I can actually be more helpful to you. To answer your question, even one person killed in the name of Christ is one too many. However, to be accurate, more people died in the name of 20th century atheism, especially under Stalin, Hitler, and Mao Tse-Tung, than all previous centuries combined. The number of people killed by atheists absolutely dwarfs the number of people killed by those professing to be Christians. In fact, the term 'genocide' was not even coined till the 20th century. I once read that 170 million people died at the hands of these atheist states, whereas 30,000 died during the Inquisition."

"As an atheist, I'm not sure I like being included in with the likes of Hitler, Stalin, and Mao Tse-Tung."

"I wouldn't either. Hitler killed around thirteen million people, Stalin killed 40 million, and Mao Tse-Tung killed about 72 million people. That's not good company to be keeping. Now you know how I feel when others try to associate me with the Inquisition and the Crusades."

"I wouldn't classify Hitler as an atheist but rather as a neo-pagan," said Simon.

"Fair enough, but he still didn't kill in the name of Christ."

150

"How do you look at the Inquisition and the Crusades then as a Christian? How could Christians do such things?"

"I don't defend the Inquisition at all. It predates the Protestant Reformation, and Protestants like me were often on the receiving end of being tortured and killed for our beliefs. The mistake made by those in charge of the Inquisition was that they forgot that you should hate the sin and love the sinner. Unfortunately, they hated both."

"And the Crusades?"

"I'm not going to defend the Crusades either, but please remember, terrible things happened on both sides. The Muslims initiated the Crusades when they captured the Holy Land and killed Christians, who in turn sought to forcefully reclaim it. No, I don't defend it. I do know that the real issue, on the Christian side anyway, is an issue of nominal Christianity versus true Christianity."

"How so?"

"True Christianity means that one's heart is transformed by Christ, and that you seek to live a life that is truly Christ-like. Nominal Christians are usually people who profess Christianity but don't embrace it in their hearts and live it, and perhaps never believe it to begin with. They may be Christians because it's advantageous for one reason or another, or because their parents or country professes Christianity."

"Again, my friend, you speak well, and I understand your points and actually find myself hard pressed to dispute your arguments. However, I still feel empty inside. My mind is telling me, 'Simon, you may want to look into Jesus,' but my heart is fighting it."

"May I ask who some of your philosophical heroes are, Simon?"

"Sure, Socrates, of course. I'm also a fan of Bertrand Russell,

151

Voltaire, Nietzsche, David Hume, just to name a few."

"You listed some biggies, that's for sure. With the exception of Socrates, they are all pretty outspoken atheists, are they not?"

"Yeah, though now that you bring up Socrates, I have to cite one major reason for my disbelief. How could a man like Socrates be sentenced to hell for not believing in or accepting Jesus as his Savior? Socrates never had a chance to ever hear the name Jesus, as he predates Jesus by four-hundred years."

"Generally speaking, Simon, it's difficult at best to know of another person's eternal fate. Dante proposed that he was in limbo, or the porch of hell, so as not to experience the torment but be denied the pleasures of heaven. We don't always know what is in someone's heart, or what he or she may or may not believe. With that being said, if I had to guess, and that's all I can offer, I would say that Socrates is probably in Heaven."

"How can you say that? It goes against your whole belief system. It's like you're saying that just to make me feel better."

"I can see how it may look as though I'm contradicting the Gospel message, but I'm not. Jesus said, 'I am the Way, the Truth, and the Life. No one comes to the Father except through Me.'"

"Socrates may have arguably taught many themes similar to Christianity but he never accepted Christ so, therefore, he's in hell."

"Why did Socrates die?"

"In short," said Simon, "because he loved the Truth, and he died for it."

"And *Who* said that He was the *Truth*?"

Simon sat still and kept quiet.

"Look, Simon, God is a just God. He's not going to condemn every generation prior to Jesus to hell if they didn't know His name. Moses and Elijah never knew His name either, but we know from the Transfiguration that they are now with the Lord. I don't know for sure, but I think it's entirely possible that Socrates may be in heaven."

"So everyone born before Jesus is in heaven?"

"No, I didn't say that. As I said, God is a just God. People who acknowledged God through early Scripture, nature, personal experience, and so on, have a lot better chance than those who lived and served themselves and Satan. Again, I'm not a theologian, but I will answer your question with an honest guess. I'd suggest asking someone like Chip or Dr. Casper. It's a wonderful question, and I hope that I offered you a good reply."

"Yes, you did actually. Thank you."

"Now, getting back to the others you mentioned. What was Bertrand Russell's quote on religious people?"

Simon looked noticeably uncomfortable and then said, "Religion is simply a crutch for weak people, who can't bear to face up to reality."

"Ah, that's what I thought. He not only sees us as weak, but as adults who believe in another kind of Santa Claus."

"Something like that," Simon replied.

"I'm very familiar with Voltaire, so let me ask you about Nietzsche, do you agree with his comment that 'God is dead'?"

"If you would have asked me that a couple days ago, I would not have hesitated. Now, I'm not so sure," Simon said as he took a sip of water.

"I agree with him, in part."

"What? Really? How?"

"He understood that the death of God meant the destruction of all meaning and value in life. Now, I don't think that we must believe in God in order to live a moral life. I think that a person can recognize objective moral values without believing in God. I think that Nietzsche correctly reasoned that if God doesn't exist,

153

then neither do objective moral values? These men you cite all wanted to live lives pursuing their earthly desires that conflicted with God."

"Does it really matter?"

"I think so. Life cannot be lived without meaning and hope, Simon. Nietzsche spent the last years of his life as a raving madman. He was clinically insane. Voltaire didn't fair much better. I recall reading that during his last hours the man cried out, 'O Christ, O Lord Jesus. I must die abandoned by God and man.' His condition was so bad that no one came to visit him. His nurse said that she would not watch another infidel die for all the wealth of Europe."

"That's kind of thin."

"Is it? Bertrand Russell lived an absolutely decadent, adulterous life. In his mind, he created a world without a God so that his conscience wouldn't drive him mad. I think Russell had it backward. I think that atheism is the crutch for the immoral."

"Are you saying that I'm like all my heroes, because they were immoral hedonists? Thanks a lot, Rocky."

"No, I am going on a completely different path with this. Tell me, Simon, what is your relationship with your father like?"

"That certainly is a completely different path, right out of leftfield by the Green Monster!" He laughed. "What's my *dad* got to do with anything?"

"Perhaps nothing. What's it like to be the son of such a man?" Rocky asked with his elbows now on the table and his chin resting in the palms of both hands.

Simon smiled, let out a faint chuckle, and said, "My father and I are not exactly close, to say the very least. On some level, I'm a disappointment to him. He wanted me to become the next great billionaire entrepreneur in a long line of businessmen. After Mom died when I was young, he raised me on all the

154

classics, like Machiavelli and Sun-Tzu. He taught me to not simply do good things, like you, but to do great things, like him. Because of him, I sought to win his approval in his arena and even studied the likes of Alexander the Great."

"Why Alexander the Great?"

"He conquered the known world before he was thirty. Every man should have goals, Rocky," he said with a grin. "My father, however, practically abandoned me for my whole childhood, leaving me in the care of trained professionals and scholars to tutor me. So consequently, I never discovered his taste for blood in the business arena. I, instead, lost myself in philosophy so that I could better understand the world, instead of simply trying to take it over like my father. That's about all I can offer you. If you keep up with the business newspapers and money magazines then…then you probably know him about as well as I do. The bastard only let me go to Harvard if I agreed to major in business. Fortunately, he allowed me to also pursue philosophy as long as I maintained perfect grades."

"I'm sorry, Simon."

"It's okay. I'll outlive the man and try to do some good with his money. To be honest, he gives me everything, but I feel nothing but emptiness."

"That because he didn't give you *everything.* I hesitate to play psychotherapist with you, but I think that the relationship with your father has impacted your relationship with your Heavenly Father."

"I'm intrigued to see where this is going. Far as I can tell, we're still out in leftfield on this one."

"Okay, let's do this systematically," he said as he pulled out a small notebook from his other back pocket and read from it. "Voltaire rejected his father and took the name Voltaire instead of his family name. Another atheist of note, Sigmund Freud, had

155

no respect for his father because of his passive nature in the face of anti-Semitism. He admired others, instead, for their courage. America's most famous atheist, Madalyn Murray O'Hair, tried to kill her father with a ten-inch butcher knife. David Hume's father died when Hume was two years old. Bertrand Russell lost his father when he was only four. Nietzsche's father also died when he was four years old."

"Wait a second," Simon said as his brilliant mind, perhaps for the first time ever, desperately tried to keep up with his thoughts. "Are you saying that I'm an atheist, or these people were atheists, because of their relationship with their biological fathers?"

"I don't know. I thought and prayed about you quite a bit after our debate in Cambridge, and I felt strangely and suddenly compelled to research this with you in mind."

"Are you saying that God told you to tell me this, Rock?"

"I don't know that. Maybe He did, maybe He didn't. I don't know. Even with my success with drug and alcohol rehab, I am not one to place much stock in the inexact science of psychology. But I do believe that it's something to consider though."

"What other proof is there though? Is it limited to atheists?"

"I don't know. Some have definitely embraced their Heavenly Father in spite of their missing or abusive earthly father. Look at it this way. Some say there is a crisis in America, and it's found primarily in the family. Why? Single parent families are usually families without a father."

"I have never told anyone this before, but I truly feel like I am an orphan. My friends at Harvard envy the father I have, because they only know him as rich and successful. However, when my mom died, he disappeared entirely from my life, and I was alone and lonely."

156

"Your Father in Heaven will never leave you, and He's always ready to welcome you back with open arms, my friend. In fact, He'll run and meet you half way. Your Abba loves you and will never abandon you, in good times or bad."

"Abba," Simon repeated. "Doesn't that literally translate into 'daddy'?"

"Yes."

Mortimer walked over to the table and asked, "Would you care for any dessert or coffee, gentlemen?"

Simon, who now had his head lowered, slowly raised it up to reveal his tear-filled eyes.

"Mortimer, I don't think I need anything else to fill me. I have just found God."

Simon the Great

Simon drove his Ferrari to the side entrance of Tuttle Hall. Rocky undid his seatbelt and shook Simon's hand.

"Thanks for a great dinner and conversation, Simon."

Simon was too choked up to speak and took a brief moment to compose himself.

"My words are truly inadequate to the burden of my heart. All I can say is thank *you*, Rocky Raccoon. Tonight I'm a new man."

"You're welcome, my friend. Even though you might resist it, I still foresee that you will indeed be 'Simon the Great.'"

"How do you mean?"

"God's worked through many people throughout history. Look at how God used Alexander the Great."

"Go on."

"Alexander set out to conquer the world, and, in the process, spread the Greek language and culture across the known world. Paul wrote in Galatians, 'In the fullness of time God sent His Son.' Part of that fullness was the universal language that Paul used to spread the Gospel. Had Alexander the Great not spread the Greek language, then it would have been much harder, if not

158

impossible, to teach and spread the Gospel around a multicultural Mediterranean world as Paul did."

"I see. So you think I'm going to take over the world after all!" Simon laughed.

"No, I meant to say, I foresee revival in New England following in *your* footsteps."

"What? I'm the newest Christian on the planet, Rocky! How can God use me, a college student?"

"God can use anyone, even the *great* ones. Anyhow, for the record, every major spiritual revival in our nation's history started on a college campus."

Simon sat quietly.

"Thanks again for dinner, and drive safely in this thing!"

"You have a good night, Rocky. Be good."

"You have a good night, Simon. Be God's."

Rocky carefully shut the door of the Ferrari, which was more of a work of art than an automobile, and Simon drove off listening to the Beatles' song *Rocky Raccoon.*

* * *

Rocky could not help but notice several dozen faces peeking out the windows of the small dorm. When he walked through the door and up the stairs, he was greeted by what seemed to him to be the entire campus.

Everyone wanted to know what had happened. Did Rocky engage Simon in another battle of wits? Did Simon threaten him? Did Rocky use another unorthodox method of spreading the Gospel? Did Simon convert Rocky?

Jim worked his way to the front of the record setting crowd in Tuttle Hall. "So, what happened?"

Everyone stood quietly, listening to every breath that he

exhaled before answering what was on everyone's mind.

"Hi, everyone. It was a good night, and the Lord was especially good tonight."

The crowd rustled and drew in closer. They continued to whisper among themselves, guessing what had happened until being shushed by those wanting an immediate answer.

"What happened with Simon?" Becky asked.

"We had a long talk that covered many topics of conversation. I followed the message God placed upon my heart, and Simon responded to the Gospel message. All the angels in Heaven above are rejoicing tonight, as Simon's now saved!"

The room erupted with cheers, clapping, and people offering their praise to God for what everyone there considered to be a miracle.

"So, what finally made him change his mind?" Martin yelled from the back.

The crowd composed itself to hear the answer to this billion-dollar question.

"I really can't say for sure what argument, if any, really won him over. It wasn't a matter of changing his mind, as much as it was a matter of changing his heart."

The crowd again started to celebrate. One of the Malaysian students suggested that everyone go to the chapel for an impromptu praise and worship service, which led to the rest of the campus being notified.

* * *

Tom was quietly completing his reading in preparation for his upcoming exams when Martin burst through the door with the excitement of a new father announcing to those in the waiting room that he just had a baby boy. Tom remained quiet and slowly looked up at Martin.

"He did it! He did it!"

Tom didn't need any more information than that. He understood what his hyperventilating roommate was trying to convey.

"Great. Technically, though, *God* did it," said Tom.

"Well, of course! That's why we're having a praise and worship service right now in the chapel! Come on, take a break and join us! This is a true Christmas miracle!"

"Thanks for the invite, but I really do want to finish my studies."

Martin just looked at Tom dumbfounded.

Tom raised his head up from his book and without looking at Martin and replied, "I can feel your look. I'll take time tonight in my prayers to thank God for Simon accepting Christ. That's wonderful news. It *really* is. God will be just as happy to hear it from me here as he would in the chapel, okay?"

"Tom, are you really all right?"

"I wish people would stop asking me that. I haven't changed a bit, Martin. I'm the *same* guy I've always been. That's why I'm going to be valedictorian of our class."

"Well, there's talk of a revival in New England, and I think it's started here on campus. You may be the same, but the rest of us have changed," Martin said and then left the room to join the others in the chapel.

* * *

Word spread quickly throughout the seminary, and even some of the professors and staff joined the celebration service. Rocky was pleased to discover that the subject and object of the

161

praise was Jesus Christ. Revival had indeed spread throughout the seminary. The dam that once held back the waters of revival in New England was now broken, and how can anyone but God stop the rushing waters of faith, hope, and love?

Wonderful Christmastime

Rocky wanted to do something a little different this year to celebrate the birth of Jesus. He had secretly made arrangements for the occasion, and about three-dozen students and some professors accepted Rocky's invitation. Many of those attending were Rocky's close friends, although some came just to see what the unorthodox Rocky Raccoon would do next.

"What's he up to?" Steven asked.

"Rocky? I really don't know. He's the most unpredictable person I've ever met," said Adam.

"Maybe he got his new buddy Simon to fly us all out to Bethlehem," Chip joked.

"He's probably just sharing a family tradition with us. Everybody celebrates Christmas a little differently than everyone else," Jim said.

Rocky walked into the common room of Tuttle to join his friends.

"So, Rocky, any clues as to where we're going or what to expect?" Steven asked.

"Sure. Please wear old shoes or boots."

"That's it?" Jim questioned. "That's our only clue?"

"It's more of a suggestion than a clue really," Rocky said with a smile.

"Anything else?" Rick asked.

"Bring a Bible if you'd like. I'll have mine with me if you need to borrow it."

"Now I'm intrigued," Rick said.

"Only now?" Rocky asked. "I'm disappointed."

*   *   *

Most students left to go home to be with family, but many decided to stay one more night to participate in Rocky Raccoon's Christmas event. Some confessed to one another that it was a matter of curiosity that led them to participate, while others wanted to share the occasion with Rocky, who had touched them so deeply this first semester. One surprising but welcome guest was Simon.

Rocky appointed eight people to drive, and a caravan of cars followed behind Rocky and Simon. The thirty-minute trip led them all into a rural region of Massachusetts.

The caravan pulled into the Brock family farm. It was an old farm, with a vast amount of snow-covered land decorated with snowmobile and deer tracks. Simon stopped his Hummer in front of the house, and all the other cars behind him stopped and parked. The farmer who owned the land greeted Rocky.

Rocky waited for everyone to gather together before making his introduction. Many of the guests were quietly looking around the farm and exchanging glances at each other.

Rocky stepped forward. "I want to thank you all for coming. I'm happy to introduce to you the man who has so graciously allowed for us to be here today. This is Ed Brock, farmer and country parson."

"I'm glad you all could come," said Ed. "Rocky's been very special to me and my family these past few months. I welcome you all in the name of Jesus and request that you all please make yourselves at home."

"When did Rocky come up here?" Jim whispered to Rick.

"Who knows? He's always out doing something. I guess this is one of the places he visited while he wasn't working at Easton."

* * *

Rocky led everyone to the stables, and then waited until everyone was inside.

"I can see why you wanted us to wear old shoes today!" said Jim.

Rocky smiled.

A few made some grumbling sounds as they stepped in dung, and others started to noticeably regret postponing their trip home to visit family.

Rocky pulled out his trusty pocket sized Gideon's Bible and read from Luke 2:4-7: "So Joseph also went up from the town of Nazareth in Galilee to Judea, to Bethlehem the town of David, because he belonged to the house and line of David. He went there to register with Mary, who was pledged to be married to him and was expecting a child. While they were there, the time came for the baby to be born, and she gave birth to her firstborn, a son. She wrapped Him in cloths and placed Him in a manger, because there was no room in for them in the inn."

Some of the guests nodded in agreement, affirming the message and its messenger.

"Rocky and I were talking one day about Jesus and the manner in which He came down here to Earth," said Edward.

165

"Rocky started to get all sentimental on me, talking about such songs as *Away in a Manger* and *Silent Night,* and the fifth generation farmer in me couldn't help but laugh. He wondered why I was laughing, and I apologized and brought him out here, just as we are all now to see firsthand what a stable is *really* like. I want you to see, touch, hear, and smell what it is like to be in a stable. It's a tribute to Mary and Joseph, who surely were humbled by their situation. Jesus was brought into this world in the fulfillment of prophecy, but there is nothing glamorous at all about this, folks."

Dr. Casper looked around at the inspired ad hoc bible study group and smiled.

"The Son of God, the King of Kings, the Lord of Lords, was born in a place not too much different from this," the country parson said. "It's the greatest moment in human history, but one that cannot be fully appreciated or understood till you witness the setting for yourselves. Even though I own this stable and keep it orderly, I for one cannot imagine the burden of having to deliver a child into this environment, nor can I honestly say that I would've had the humility and dignity that Mary and Joseph must have had that blessed night."

Rocky walked over to a trough where some cows were feeding and said, "Jesus was wrapped in rags and placed in a manger like this. I do not say this to take away from that holy night but to make it even more real and, in a sense, more holy. We are here to celebrate the birth of our Savior, and I invite you all to sing with me."

For the next half-hour, everyone in attendance reverently sang familiar Christmas hymns that were suddenly new and fresh to them all.

*   *   *

When the caravan arrived back at Tuttle Hall, Rocky received several invitations to spend Christmas with the families of those in attendance.

"You're more than welcome to join me. My family already knows all about you," Chip said.

"I appreciate the invite, Chip, but I really must decline."

"Why don't you come down with me to the Cape? My dad isn't even in town this year," said Simon.

"I'm sorry, Simon, but I really feel called to go back to the downtown jail in Boston."

"But why now?" Rick asked.

"Now is when they need Jesus the most."

Dr. Casper walked up and patted Rocky on the shoulder, "I am sorry to hear that you will not be returning to Canton for Christmas break. I'm sure Bob would've loved to have seen you."

"I regret that I won't be going home, but I cannot miss this opportunity to reach out to these men. I'll call Bob before I leave for Boston."

"He'll like that. Do you need a ride downtown?"

"No, not this time. The lieutenant told me that I could park my car there for a couple weeks."

"You're one of a kind, Rocky," Dr. Casper said.

"I think one of me is all you can take."

Professor Raccoon

The initial paparazzi reports of Simon's volunteer work in downtown soup kitchens during the Christmas season were met with both skepticism and cynicism. Although Simon was Boston royalty, much like a member of the Kennedy family, some media pundits challenged his newfound faith. However, the Harvard debate phenom was always prepared to give an answer to everyone and anyone who asked him to give a reason for his faith in Jesus, and Simon the Great never left any doubt in the minds of the viewers and the overmatched interviewers who won these debates.

Rocky read through the *Boston Globe* as he waited in the police station for his ride. He smiled as he read the front-page story on Simon, who some now dubbed the "Postmodern-Day Apostle." Rocky couldn't help but notice that his own efforts were also featured, as the paper wrote yet another piece about his two week stint in the downtown jail.

* * *

The students and faculty were uncharacteristically excited to return to Easton Theological Seminary following Christmas break. The energy in the cafeteria was palpable. Rocky's immense popularity made it more difficult than ever to do his job, but he enjoyed catching up with his friends. He made a point to sit down for a moment at the table that used to be unofficially reserved for the Korean students, but now, like most every other table in the cafeteria, was occupied by a diverse blend of the student body. He exchanged vacation stories and shared some laughs before heading back to his duties.

Rocky sat down to eat after the lunch rush. He really enjoyed talking to the foreign students who had never experienced snow and arctic cold. Although very well read in history, he truly received an education from those students who came from a land of real poverty and knew what it really meant to be persecuted for their beliefs. He had known what it is to be poor, but his heart broke when he was told about *real* poverty, where parents cut off the hand or foot of one of their own children to make them more effective beggars, so that they will have a better opportunity to survive. His eyes were opened to the needs of the missionary field that consumed Rick and other Easton students.

He excused himself after his meal and fellowship, as he needed to get back to work. After he threw away his own trash, an Easton student named Karen approached him on his way back to the kitchen.

"Rocky! Can I talk to you for a sec?"

Rocky looked up to see Sam and his co-workers sitting around telling jokes while eating lunch, so he smiled and answered, "Certainly. What can I do for you, Karen?"

"As you may or may not know, The Sophia Way is hosting a huge feminist revival cult meeting in Boston next week, and I'd like for you to come with me."

Rocky seemed genuinely caught off guard.

"You won't be the only guy there if that's what you're thinking," she said with a grin.

"I'm really intrigued by this organization, The Sophia Way. I've only done a little bit of reading on them, but I was really disturbed by what I had learned."

"I've been following this organization for about five years, dedicating a lot time researching it for my master's thesis, and let assure you that you've probably only seen the tip of the iceberg. These radical feminist theologians have completely distorted and rewritten the Bible and have all but eliminated the contributions of Paul. They do and say things at these so-called revivals that will not only shock you but make you feel sad for those who blindly follow."

Karen then handed him a Sophia Way flyer for the revival, which stated:

The Ancient Mothers are calling YOU to celebrate the sacred feminine Goddess in the Land of Enchantment . . . With art, dance, ritual and song — Honor the Goddess within each woman. Tell YOUR Herstory with art, voice, dance, and ritual. Meditate. Create art with your symbolic Goddess language... Dance at the Temple of the Living Goddess. Walk a Hopi labyrinth . . . Connect as a sacred circle with very special women for mutual transformation. Share the magic and The Sophia Way!!!

Rocky looked up at Karen. "I don't know what I can offer you, but I'll be happy to go with you."

"Great! For starters, you could offer me a ride. My car doesn't do snow too well."

"I'd be happy to drive down with you. I'm anxious to see what's in store for us down there?"

"Well, a lot of the leadership of The Sophia Way will recognize me, but you, on the other hand, will probably be welcomed in with open arms, as they think every man in attendance is some progressive freethinker who agrees with them."

"Great. It's nice to be wanted."

"So, you'll pick me up next Saturday at noon?"

"Noon works. I'll have Sam cover for me."

"Oh, you work. I'm so sorry."

"It's not a problem, Karen. I'll talk to Sam. Anyhow, we don't see a whole lot of action on the weekend anyway."

* * *

Rocky sat in on Dr. Samuels's evangelism class following lunch. As was his custom, he chose a seat in the back corner to covertly observe the class.

"Rocky," Dr. Samuels suddenly said in the midst of his lecture. "You've done quite a bit of evangelism since you arrived, and from what I know about you, I'm sure you've done quite a bit more that none of us here even know about."

Rocky sat wide-eyed and shrugged his shoulders. He sat back in his seat as though he were trying to hide in the corner.

"Do you have any advice to offer, Rocky?"

"I'm no expert, Dr. Samuels, but I think that the most important thing in the world is to know that you're loved. I like to seek people who are usually neglected by others, whether it is the homeless, gays, immigrants, elderly, the sick and dying, orphans, mentally challenged, addicts, convicts, or what have you. They all want to be loved, and I offer them my love, and then a love far greater than my own, the love of Jesus."

A student in the class raised her hand and asked Rocky, "How do you deal with those who won't listen?"

"The Bible is pretty clear that if you make the effort, and if they are non-responsive, that you should dust off your sandals and move on to another. I don't get too mad if someone doesn't listen well though. Even Jesus experienced this in His ministry."

"Could you elaborate on that?" Dr. Samuels asked.

"Sure," Rocky answered, as he fumbled to open his abused pocket Bible. "Look at Mark 10:15, where He clearly states that anyone who will not receive the kingdom of God like a little child will never enter it. He then gets up, and a rich young man immediately approaches Him and asks a completely ridiculous question, 'Good teacher, what must I do to have eternal life?' Jesus had just answered that question! But the arrogant man either wasn't listening or just didn't like the answer he had heard. So I figure, if they didn't always listen to Jesus, then I won't feel too bad if they don't always listen to me."

Another hand was raised, and this student asked Rocky, "What should you try to avoid when evangelizing?"

Rocky, appearing to look uncomfortable, looked over at Dr. Samuels, and the noted evangelist nodded his head and smiled.

"For me, personally, the main thing to do is to love," said Rocky. "It's the greatest commandant. I do think that it's a tragic mistake to not be yourself. You should never try to project the *perfect* image, as though you have no problems. It's simply an illusion. No one is *always* joyful and in control. Be honest. If we project some phony pious image that we're flawless, then it will distance us from seekers who know that they are sinners, who don't have it all together and in control. I've had a lot of success reaching some hurting people simply by being honest and admitting that I have bad days too, and have battled some pretty nasty addictions, such as alcoholism. After one of these talks, I actually had a woman accept Christ just so she could pray for me!"

The class laughed.

A student then asked, "Maybe you can help us with a project

172

we've been working on."

"I'll be happy to try."

"Great! We're planning a youth rally in Beverly. We really need to tell these kids about Jesus so that they'll stop smoking, doing drugs, and getting pregnant."

"And?" Rocky asked.

"That's about it I suppose," the student replied.

"Well," Rocky said as he now stood up and scratched his head, "I'm concerned about those vices and teen pregnancy too...they certainly are a problem to be sure...but the root cause of all our sins is our alienation from God. Maybe instead of telling these kids about Jesus to help to get them to stop certain types of harmful behavior, I respectfully suggest that you tell these kids about Jesus because Jesus wants them to know about Him."

"You're absolutely right, Rocky," said Dr. Samuels. "I guess we were all trying to place the proverbial cart in front of the equally proverbially horse."

"I have a question for Rocky," Martin said. "You have a nickname that is related to the Beatles, who aren't exactly the most popular band in Christendom, especially after John Lennon said that they were better than Jesus. How do you deal with this apparent contradiction when you're evangelizing?"

"To be honest, it's never come up till now. The nickname is relatively new, though I have worn Beatles shirts on occasion. I think that there are some things to be learned in terms of evangelism as it pertains to the Beatles. First though, let me clarify that John Lennon did not say that they, the Beatles, were better than Jesus. In an interview in England, where Beatlemania was taking the country by storm, he commented that to the kids of England, the Beatles were more popular than Jesus. He didn't say that to boast, but instead, to point out that the priorities of the kids were not as they should be. If I told you that TV, smart phones, popular music, video games, or social networking websites were more popular to kids today than Jesus, you'd probably agree with me. Our conclusion, logically, would be, or *should* be, that we'd better do a better job teaching kids about Jesus. Unfortunately, the reaction in the so-called Bible Belt was not to say, 'You know, John Lennon is right. Kids do like the Beatles more than Jesus. We should do something to build up Jesus more.' Instead, they burned Beatles memorabilia and broke their records."

"What does this have to do with evangelism, Rocky?" Martin asked.

"We know from interviews that John Lennon was really hurting during this time in his life. He had worldwide fame, fortune, a wife, and child. Yet, he still felt empty. Ravi Zacharias said it best, 'Meaninglessness does not come from being weary of pain, meaninglessness comes from being weary of pleasure.' At this time, he wrote a song called *Help!* which was a literal cry for help. It starts off with him yelling 'Help!' He then goes on to talk about how he didn't need anyone's help when he was younger, but only when he had grown older and successful. He concludes begging the question, 'Won't you please, please, help me?'

"Here was a man publicly begging for help *and* who was reportedly seeking God. When he arrived at the Dallas airport, angry Christians were there to protest him. They were not there to love him or offer him the Gospel message that he may have been seeking but, instead, were there to condemn him. If Lennon knew anything about Christianity and the love of Christ, he probably left there very confused and appalled. After all, where was the love?" Rocky asked rhetorically as he looked out at the students.

174

"Do you think he would have become a Christian had they met him with open arms?" Meredith asked.

"Regretfully, we'll never know for sure. The opportunity was missed. Keep this in mind though, Lennon did continue to search for spiritual help and understanding, but it did not come from the Christian church. Instead, he and the other Beatles were introduced to another religion, Transcendental Meditation. It was a minor religion in England, but its association with the Beatles caused it to grow worldwide, including 90,000 followers of the Maharishi Mahesh Yogi in England. Imagine what would have, or could have happened had those Christians in the Bible Belt approached Lennon with the love of Jesus instead of with their own hate. How much impact would the Beatles, who defined and shaped the popular culture of the 1960s, have had if they had become Christians? Even more important than their contribution to the world is the salvation of these four great musicians. This is just one example why I think we should approach people with the love of Christ while teaching the Gospel of Grace."

Steven raised his hand and said, "Rocky, I completely agree with you regarding the Beatles. You pointed out the mistakes of those Christians in the Bible Belt during the 1960s, but what mistakes have you made in your ministry?"

"I apologize if I came off too harsh against those Christians. The Lennon quote that set off the explosive response was taken out of context, so I can understand why those people were initially upset. A follow-up interview clarified John's points, so I don't know why some Christian ministries persisted in their persecution of Lennon, even after his assassination. As for me, my best friend in Canton, as all good friends do, continuously points out my flaws. Pastor Bob sometimes calls me 'Brother Teresa,' and it is *never* meant as a compliment. After an especially busy time in my life, when I was living up to that nickname, he pulled me aside and told me to stop trying to look and sound like a saint. He said it would make it a lot easier on everybody!"

The class laughed.

Dr. Samuels looked up at the clock and asked, "Do you have any concluding remarks you'd like to make, Rocky?"

"Let me say this. Throughout the Bible, God used fragile people to accomplish His goals. He doesn't always pick the holiest or most devout person, so please don't fall for the lie that we have to be perfect in order to preach and teach the Gospel. Look at me! Keep your eyes on Jesus, and remember that the greatest commandment is to love."

"I know I put you on the spot today, Rocky, but you don't realize what a treat it was to have you in our class today. Thank you for contributing so much today."

The class gave Rocky a warm round of applause. As he was walking out, Dr. Samuels gave him a big smile. He stepped out into the hallway, and then heard the sound of footsteps approaching him. Martin and Meredith walked up to him as class let out.

"You did a great job today," Meredith said.

"You really did, Rock," said Martin. "Would it be okay if we join you next time you go out into the community and see what you do firsthand?"

"To be honest, it would be rather awkward to have you just *observing* me. If, however, you want to help, then you're more than welcome."

"Okay," Meredith answered for them both.

"Great, then tomorrow afternoon you're going to meet some dear friends of mine," said Rocky.

"All right then! We're looking forward to it," Martin said.

"Me, too. Please be sure to invite Tom," said Rocky.

Martin paused, looked at the floor, and then glanced up at Rocky. "I'll invite him, but I really doubt he's going to go."

Rocky let out a sigh and wiped his hair back from his eyes. "Does he really hate me that much?"

"He doesn't *hate* you," Meredith said. "I think he's just confused as to what his role on this campus is now that you're here."

"Why?"

"If you're asking me," she replied, "I'd say that you're like Peter, the fisherman called by Jesus to preach, and he's like Paul, the brilliant scholar who is also called to preach. You two are both needed but have different roles. You seem to know and accept your role, but he's still struggling to find his. Give him time, he'll come around."

"I sure hope so, Meredith," Rocky said.

"Incidentally, where are we going tomorrow?" Martin asked.

"Some place special."

Special Calling

Rocky woke up early to read his devotions. He prayed for the revival and continued to pray for all of those people he had met along the way, like Adam and Simon. He also prayed for blessings for the time he would be spending with Meredith and Martin.

During lunch, Martin and Meredith were busy telling everyone that they were going out with Rocky. Many were envious and others regretted never having thought of asking Rocky to go out with him. Meredith and Martin both promised to report back to everyone what they learned.

Tom sat at the table in quiet disbelief.

* * *

Following lunch, Martin and Meredith met Rocky and went out to his car.

"So now are you going to tell us where we're going?" Martin asked.

"Some place special."

"You really enjoy being cryptic don't you?" Martin said.

178

"How is it that you can be so transparent and enigmatic at the same time?" Meredith asked.

"Just doing my best to be Christlike."

* * *

Rocky pulled into the driveway of a modest ranch home with a one-car garage. Rocky knocked on the front door and was met by a smiling middle-aged woman.

"Meredith, Martin, this is Ursula. Ursula, allow me to introduce you to Meredith and Martin. They're two of Easton's finest students."

Ursula extended her hand and greeted Tom and Meredith, "It's very nice to meet you, and we're happy that you could come with Rocky today."

"It's our pleasure, ma'am," said Martin.

"Rocky! Rocky! Rocky! Rocky! Rocky!" A short, stocky man with Down syndrome ecstatically yelled as he pranced over to give him a crushing bear hug.

"It's good to see you too, Eddie! Check out those muscles!" Rocky said playfully.

Eddie raised both arms up to show off his biceps and said, "Muscleman!"

"Rocky! Summer?" Dayton said.

"Hi, Dayton. No, it's winter."

"Winter?"

"Yes, it's cold out there!" Rocky said as he acted cold.

"Snow flurries?" Dayton asked.

"Not today, unless you heard something I didn't." Rocky said.

"The carpet is blue, Rocky! Blue!" Dayton announced with great excitement.

179

"Yes, Dayton, it is blue," said Rocky.

Eddie was content to get a high five from Martin but gave Meredith a hug and kiss on the cheek. She didn't know how to respond, other than to offer a slightly nervous laugh.

"And this guy here is Josh," said Rocky.

"Hi there, Josh," Martin said.

Josh appeared to look right through Martin as if he weren't there.

"He's severely autistic, Martin, so don't expect much of a conversation with him. He does like to play ball though," Rocky said as he tossed one of Josh's tennis balls to Martin. "He'll play catch with you."

"Okay," said Martin. "Are you ready, Josh? Catch."

Josh didn't appear to be looking, and, after Martin released the ball, he feared that he was going to hit Josh right in the face, but Josh caught the ball.

Rocky looked over at his shocked friend. "I told you he was good. Perhaps he could've been a New York Yankee."

"What would he be?" Ursula asked.

"Oh, yeah, sorry. He'd be a Boston Red Sox star of course," he said with a grin.

"That's better." She laughed.

"Rocky, spring?" Dayton asked.

"What is it out there, Dayton?"

"Winter!"

"That's right!"

"Carpet blue, Rocky! Carpet blue!"

"Yes, Dayton, the carpet is blue."

Martin continued to play catch with Josh. Ursula, Meredith and Eddie retreated to the kitchen to prepare dinner. Meredith still seemed a bit uncomfortable, but she liked Ursula and was happy to help her out. Eddie stood in the kitchen rocking back and forth while watching the women prepare his dinner.

"You weren't kidding," Martin said. "Josh has magic hands. He would have been a shortstop had he not been, well, had he not been autistic."

"Perhaps. He's fine though," said Rocky. "He loves to play ball, and he *loves* coffee. If he has either one or both, he's happy."

"Rocky, carpet blue!" Dayton yelled.

"Yes, it is blue!"

"Winter, Rocky? Winter?"

"Yes, Dayton, it's winter."

"Snow flurries!"

"I hope not!" Rocky laughed. "I have to drive in that, mister!"

Dayton laughed out loud, and then yelled, "Carpet blue!"

"I saw that! It's nice," Rocky said to Dayton's satisfaction.

"So, what do you do with these guys? Is this basically it?" Martin asked.

"No, I usually take them someplace like Logan Airport. Dayton loves to watch the planes, and Josh and Eddie are content to go for a car ride, providing I remember to stop and get Eddie something to eat and get Josh his coffee."

"Jet!" Dayton yelled.

"Not today, buddy. The roads are pretty bad today, but next time we'll go to the airport."

"Okay. Carpet blue!"

Martin looked at Rocky for his response, given that this discussion had gone on several times since they arrived. Rocky stood up, looked at the carpet as though he had never seen it, and again acknowledged that it was indeed blue.

Ursula and Meredith notified the house that dinner was ready. It was a simple meal tonight, hamburgers and French fries. Josh, as usual, went right for his coffee, and Eddie was anxious to eat. Dayton looked out the window and told everyone that it was winter. Rocky said grace, and they all dined together.

*   *   *

"Thank you for having us over," Rocky said. "I'll be by next week and take them to the airport, okay?"

"They'd like that, babe. Thanks for stopping by and for bringing Meredith and Martin. We hope to see you all again."

"It was a lot of fun," said Martin.

The three of them walked out to the car and sat in it while it warmed up.

"Thanks for bringing us. You really opened our eyes today," Meredith said.

"Great, what did it teach you?" Rocky asked.

"It taught me how fortunate I am to not be developmentally disabled. We've all been really blessed."

"I agree with Meredith," Martin said. "You really did open our eyes to how lucky we are to be normal."

"Lucky?" Rocky asked.

"Yeah, well, I guess I should say *blessed*, not lucky," said Martin.

"Let me ask you this, Martin," said Rocky. "Have you ever had a bad day?"

"Of course I have."

"What about you, Meredith?" Have you ever had a bad day?"

"Who hasn't?"

"Dayton, Eddie, and Josh. They almost never have a bad day. They don't get stressed out or concerned about simple things, or even major things. They get pleasure and happiness from the simplest things and are always ready to receive love and give it back unconditionally."

"I see…then this was a test?" Martin asked.

"No, not at all. I never thought about it until just now. I always thought about how I was serving the least of these brothers when I worked with them, feeling good about myself. Now, I see that they're the ones who are ministering to me all along."

"Is it a blessing though," Meredith asked, "to be a broken record all your life?"

"You mean Dayton?"

"Yes! Doesn't that drive you crazy to have the same conversation over and over and over again?" Martin asked.

"No."

"Oh, come on now, Rocky, how could it not?" Meredith asked.

"If someone were just yanking my chain, then I'd get frustrated, if not mad after a while. For Dayton, however, each time he mentions the blue carpet, he's just as excited about it as he was the first day that that carpet was installed a year ago. He is a man who experiences joy that most never find in this busy, stressful world, simply by seeing a jet airplane in the sky. To be honest, I'm glad I'm not developmentally disabled, but I don't see these guys as cursed either."

"Thanks for taking us, Rocky. I'm sorry if we came off judgmental. They really are sweet guys. I just wish that they could experience more in life than what they do," Meredith said.

"I know," said Rocky. "It's give and take, and even if they don't know they're living in a fallen world, they're still affected by it."

Rocky put his car in reverse and backed out into the street and headed home to Easton.

Karen

Rocky drove his car to the main entrance of the women's dorm Saturday morning to pick up Karen, whom he had promised to accompany at The Sophia Way revival meeting in downtown Boston. Though he knew every woman in this dorm, he had never actually been inside of it. Like every male student at Easton, he knew that these devout Christian women would all make wonderful wives, but he was also aware that many of these women were focused on their personal pursuit and professional service for the Lord. Consequently, one of the odd dynamics of seminary life is that there are about six men to every woman, yet hardly anyone dated. The exception, however, tended to go to the extreme, with the lightning-fast courtship and engagement known by seminary students as "ring by spring."

Rocky knocked on the front door and was greeted by an attractive young lady.

"Well, good morning, Rocky Raccoon."

"Good morning, Darla. Is Karen all ready to go?"

"To be perfectly honest with you, I'm not really sure, but you're more than welcome to come on inside out of the cold."

Darla led Rocky to the common room, where they both sat

184

down together side-by-side on a sofa.

"I heard that you were accepted into a Ph.D. program at Harvard. Congratulations."

"Why, thank you, Rocky," she said as she patted his leg. "That's so sweet of you to say. I'll be pursuing my Ph.D. in Old Testament studies," she said as she scooted closer to him on the sofa.

"That's great, Darla, really," he replied as he casually repositioned himself on the sofa to reclaim some personal space.

"I heard through the grapevine that you and Karen were going downtown to The Sophia Way revival meeting."

Rocky nodded and looked up at the antique grandfather clock, and then checked his wristwatch.

"So…are you and Karen *dating*?"

"Karen and me? Oh, no. I don't really know her all that well."

"Really," Darla replied as she once again scooted over closer to Rocky, who was now in danger of falling off of the sofa if he attempted to reposition himself again. "This might go against tradition, or dating protocol, but would you like to join me and some of my friends dancing tomorrow night?"

"Well…to be honest, Darla, I really don't dance," Rocky said as he was looking around for Karen.

"Please tell me that you don't dance for theological reasons. After all, David danced!" said the Harvard bound Old Testament scholar.

"No, it's not theological at all. Anyhow, David danced in his underwear. How far do you really want to take this line of thinking?"

"Oh, Rocky," she said as she placed her hand on his leg and laughed. "You're such a character. Now really, do you want to go out tomorrow night?"

"I tend to go to bed pretty early Sunday evening. Wait a

second, didn't Steven already try to ask you out for Sunday, but you were too busy focusing on your studies? He's still available tomorrow night. Why don't you ask him?"

Darla feigned a soft laugh and got up off of the sofa. "Let me see what's keeping Karen."

"Thanks, Darla."

* * *

Karen walked into the common room where Rocky was waiting.

"Hello, Karen. Today's a nice day to hang out with some radical feminists," he said as he stood up to greet her.

"Don't laugh, Rocky. I've been to several of these, and you have no idea what you're in for today."

"I'm always up for something different."

"Then today's your lucky day."

* * *

Rocky opened the passenger door for Karen and closed it for her once she was inside his car.

"I noticed your KEAGGY license plates. Are you a big fan of Phil Keaggy?"

"He's the best," he replied. "And he's the last person to tell you that, too, which earned my respect."

"I've seen him a couple of times at Christian music festivals and must admit that he's the best guitarist I've ever seen."

"Do you play?"

"I do, actually. I am a member of the praise and worship music team at my church."

"Great. I'll have to stop by there sometime and check it out."

186

"If you do, I'll earn high marks from the church." She laughed.

Rocky looked at her confused.

"Don't give me that look, Rocky. You know that you're even more popular than Dr. Casper, who was voted one of the top preachers of his generation, along with Billy Graham I might add. Well, that was before you came into the picture."

"So…what can you tell me about The Sophia Way, other than it's the theme of your future Ph.D. dissertation."

"I never know where to start."

"Why don't you start at the beginning?"

"Let me warn you, most people usually avoid me after these conversations."

"I won't avoid you. Anyway, I fancy myself a pretty good student of history. Please, Karen, *dazzle* me with all of this information in your brilliant mind."

"Okay. Since you asked for it. Historically, there have been three phases of the feminist movement. What many call First-Wave feminism took place at the end of the 19th century. Feminism at this time focused on gaining basic human rights for women. Second-Wave feminism fought to establish equal rights and on the job economic equality for women. The current form of feminism, Third-Wave feminism, isn't really an engaged social movement like those efforts of the past, but is instead an ideologically driven effort. This current strand of feminism deals with gender issues and control issues over their bodies, such as abortion and birth control, as well as issues of homosexuality and divorce. Now, this Third-Wave feminism, which teaches women to define their own reality, is involved in radical feminist spirituality, focusing on the worship of Sophia."

"I know Sophia is supposed to be God in their belief system, but I don't know how they picked that name out exactly," Rocky said as he merged onto Route 128 South.

"Well, that's the thing," Karen replied. "It's their heretical view of God. They don't see their ideology being compatible with conventional Christianity, so they borrow just enough to justify their theology and dupe Christian women into believing that it's a Christian group. Sophia is a Greek word with a feminine gender. Greek, like German and other languages, applies a gender to its nouns, which don't necessarily have anything to do with gender."

"I seem to recall Mark Twain joking about how the German language gives a neuter gender for the German word for girl. He also mentioned that the German word for *woman* was female, but the word for *wife* was neuter."

"Exactly. Given its use in the Bible, and the fact that it means wisdom, these feminists have hijacked this word, which has a feminine gender, and used it to put a feminine face on God. That's how they came up with Sophia, who is a goddess rather than God the Father."

"I'm almost afraid to ask, but where does Jesus fit into all of this?"

"That's a good question and, in fact, the most crucial question. They don't deny His gender, but His deity and His suffering on the cross are not just minimized, but also essentially factored out of their theology. He's often referred to as 'The Prophet' and 'Child of Sophia,' as well as 'Sophia's Envoy.'"

"How do they deny His divinity?"

"They try to deconstruct and criticize sacrificial theology by denying His virgin birth, the value of the cross, and the personal salvation of someone who has faith in the risen Lord. They tend to view the cross as a phallic symbol, let alone an instrument of torture. They see it as an abuse issue."

"Abuse?"

"Rocky, you'll find today that many women in attendance are really good women, Christian women in fact, who have gone through much abuse at the hands of men. Maybe by strangers, or worse, a husband, boyfriend, or member of their family, like a father."

"Fathers 'eh? Seems like fathers are frequently the cause of belief and unbelief."

"Basically," said Karen, "many of the leaders of this movement don't see the redemptive value of the cross, but see it as divine child abuse if you will. God sent His Son to His death to satisfy God's need for justice. Many of these women, who have been victims of abuse by a man, in one form or another, don't wish to recognize the cross, or its importance, because in their eyes, they'd be embracing it as a tool of violence."

"It's tragic that these women are settling for some cult which focuses on them instead of Jesus."

"The Sophia Way can disregard Christ in their theology, because they dismiss the reality of personal sin," she replied.

"How do they view the Genesis account of the Fall?"

"They view the Fall in the Garden of Eden as an anti-woman myth. Eve is actually embraced by this group and seen as a great woman, because she sought out wisdom rather than viewing it as an act of defiance against God. The Sophia Way doesn't see a need for Christ to attain salvation but, rather, they believe that it's reached through knowledge, as well as through one's liberation."

"I can see how Eve would be the poster child for this organization."

"You haven't seen anything yet, Rocky."

189

The Sophia Way

Rocky pulled his car into the downtown garage and parked next to an SUV with a bumper sticker that read, "Women who seek only to be equal to men lack ambition." As he got out of his car, a woman in a tie-dyed shirt came up to him and asked, "Are you here for The Sophia Way Revival?"

"Yes, I am," Rocky replied with his trademark smile.

The woman then stepped forward and embraced him in a bone-crushing hug that lifted him partially off the ground. "Glad to have you here today. I wish more men were like you," she said, and then she ran to catch up with the rest of her party.

"They seem nice enough," Rocky said as he turned to look back at Karen.

"Like I told you, most of these women here are really nice and are genuinely good people. They're just seriously misguided. Some because of their feminist ideology, others because their churches haven't met their needs, and a few of these woman have definitely been involved in some sort of abuse from a man."

"I hope we can help," Rocky said as they walked together away from the larger crowd of people entering the convention

190

center rented by The Sophia Way. "What do you usually do at these things to help them out?"

"That's why I brought you. I really don't know. I usually arrive, take detailed notes, and grab their literature in order to combat them through academic journals. No one else is really doing that right now, so I'm on my own. However, I have always regretted not doing more to help these women who are here, as they may never read the Christian academic periodicals that have published my work."

"I think you have done a wonderful job, Karen, and find no dishonor in what you have accomplished at all. In fact, you're one of my heroes at the seminary. It's hard to carry the weight of the world on your shoulders. Martin Luther did what you did. He addressed the biblical and theological issues of his day, and then others followed his lead. He didn't advance the Protestant Reformation single-handedly, but he did get it started by observing the status quo, comparing it to what the Bible said, and then addressing it publicly to those who were at fault. I think you're doing a wonderful job."

"Thank you, Rocky," she replied, apparently unaccustomed to hearing any affirmation for her hard work and dedication. "It really means a lot coming from you."

Rocky gave her a smile as they walked into the convention center, now surrounded by followers and curious onlookers of The Sophia Way.

* * *

Rocky felt like a pilgrim in an unholy land. Though most everyone in attendance was nice, there was a distinct pagan atmosphere in the convention center. He couldn't help but notice that the cult's literature was in abundance and being read

191

as the Gospel truth. He was also aware that he was only one of a dozen men out of a couple thousand women. He stayed close to Karen's side. Even though he denied Darla's probing questions about his relationship with Karen, he wasn't at all afraid to let those in attendance believe that in order to avoid an awkward situation.

Rocky and Karen were among the last people to enter as the meeting started. Dr. Nicole Stockton, the leader of The Sophia Way, walked to the center stage and stood in front of a microphone waiting for the applause to cease.

"Good afternoon, ladies, and welcome to The Sophia Way Revival!" she announced in a shrill voice as the crowd cheered.

"I would also like to welcome the few good men in attendance, and I thank them for coming today to celebrate Sophia and the goddess in us all," she said to the approval of the audience.

"As you all know, the Christian church is suffering today, and that's because it's too patriarchal. The time has come to realize that we are no longer subordinate to men, which is why we are here today to destroy the patriarchal idolatry of the Christian church! As women, we must search for values above those within the Bible."

Rocky looked somberly around the room while Karen took notes like a veteran White House correspondent.

"Men created the God of Christianity and did so in their own image. By doing so, men within the church have made themselves authority figures and have legitimized the patriarchal system that has dominated women and supported the assertion that women are not made in the image of God and are therefore inferior!"

The emotionally manipulated crowd rumbled as Dr. Stockton worked herself into a furor. Rocky appeared both saddened and

192

frightened at what he was hearing.

"We in The Sophia Way are leading the cause to bring an end to God as we know it. Today we are taking the first steps to change the world, so that He will no longer fit in it! Jesus can no longer symbolize the liberation of women in a patriarchal culture that maintains a masculine image for its highest deity. Women must be able to be equal to men, and to do so, we must leave both Christ and the Bible behind!"

Rocky looked in horror at Karen, and she returned the look. The crowd started to demonstrate an uneasiness, which Dr. Stockton skillfully perceived. She cut her introduction short and called up a woman ordained in the ministry to lead those in attendance in the first of many rituals.

The Rev. Michelle Getz offered what the program listed as The Ritual of Remembrance. She stood and waited until the ushers passed out chalices of water and raisin bread to everyone in attendance. While the ushers made their way throughout the convention center, the speakers were playing traditional hymns that were familiar to anyone who had ever attended church.

After the chalices and raisin bread were distributed, Rev. Getz read, "Please raise your chalice of water, which holds the blood and tears of all women who have suffered and celebrated before us. These are the tears of joy and pain, the blood of monthly cycles and of life and death. Please drink of it."

Rocky had no intention of participating and thought that speech did not make the chalice anymore tempting for him to drink.

"The bread you now hold is made with old raisins," said Rev. Getz, "which symbolize the dried-up dreams of the sisters who came before us. The tears of our mothers watered the amaranth grain used to make the bread. Please, eat of it, and reclaim the past, so that we may enter the future and the New Creation."

193

Rev. Getz then introduced a woman who is a professor at a small liberal New England seminary. Dr. Alexis Peart was an older woman, wearing a sweater with a Native American design.

"Please pray with me," said Dr. Peart.

The crowd grew quiet and respectfully listened attentively.

"Our Universal Mother, please help us to overcome the guilt and shame we have felt for every generation due in part to the patriarchal Fall theology. We, the prophetic voices and sacred storytellers of this generation, praise the rebellion of Eve in the Garden of Eden and are ever prayerful that the phallocratic fantasy of God, as created by men, will come to an end. We thank you, Mother. Amen."

The majority of the crowd did not verbally respond to the "amen," but did not rise up in protest either. As the familiar hymns of the Christian faith were once again being played prominently over the speakers, everyone in attendance received an apple from the ushers.

"Why are we getting apples?" Rocky asked.

"You don't want to know," Karen replied.

"The Christian tradition has used the Genesis account of the Fall in a way that is harmful to women, and it is now time to rebel against it once and for all," said Dr. Peart. "At this time, you are invited to honor our mother Eve, who sought wisdom and knowledge, by biting into the apple in celebration of her and our pursuit of knowledge."

Most of the women in attendance started to bite defiantly into the apples as they sought "wisdom" by imitating Eve. Rocky and Karen, once again, did not participate in the ritual.

"Taste and see how good the fruit of the Garden of Eden really is, sisters!" Dr. Peart joyfully yelled as the PA system screeched.

"They're basically snubbing their noses at God," said Rocky.

194

THE ROCKY RACCOON REVIVAL

"They deny the existence of personal sin, and thus remove the need for a Savior," Karen replied. "They believe that they have no need for Jesus or His atoning sacrifice."

Dr. Stockton reappeared on the stage and announced the afternoon workshops that the women could attend. Karen wanted to attend the one regarding how they included their bodies when praying and celebrating. Rocky excused himself, as he was clearly overwhelmed by what he had already witnessed. Karen understood and agreed to meet him in a couple of hours for the second half of the revival meeting.

*   *   *

Rocky took a break away from the convention center and walked to a downtown fast food restaurant. He saw a homeless man sitting outside the restaurant and invited him inside the burger joint. He fed the man's body with food, but fed his spirit with the love of God through the affirmation of meal sharing.

Afterwards Rocky spent some time praying for the women at the convention, including his friend Karen, who had taken it upon herself to help these women find their way. Rocky felt overwhelmed, and unsure of what impact he could make at this convention.

Rocky returned to his seat and read some of The Sophia Way's propaganda while he waited for Karen to return from her workshop.

As he sat and read through their literature, a young woman approached wearing a sweatshirt stating, "Feminism is the radical proposition that women are human beings."

"Hi there, I'm Stacy! What's your name?"

"Rocky. It's nice to meet you, Stacy."

"It's nice to meet you, too. So, what's a guy like you doing in

195

a place like this?"

"I'm actually here with a friend from Easton Theological Seminary."

"Get out! I go to school at Bexley College, just down the road from you guys."

"Small world," Rocky replied with a grin that exposed the deep dimple on his right cheek.

"No doubt! Look, could I ask you for a favor?"

"As long as it has nothing to do with drinking anyone's sweat or blood."

She stopped, exhaled, and then placed her hands on her hips.

"Oh, you're being silly! What I need is a ride home if you don't mind. I took the train in, but it's a long ride, followed by a small hike from the station to the campus if I can't get anyone to pick me up."

Rocky smiled, as he not only understood the inconvenience of riding the train from Boston to the North Shore, but he had always had a special place in his heart for hitchhikers.

"Of course we can give you a ride, Stacy."

"Great! I met some girls down here and don't want to be rude, so is it okay if I meet you here afterward?"

"That will be fine."

"I'll see you a little later then, Rocky!"

* * *

A flow of women started to filter back into the convention center. Karen sat down next to Rocky and looked at him with a vacant stare.

"Are you okay?" he asked.

"It got pretty ugly in there."

"What happened?"

196

She paused, looked around to see if anyone was eavesdropping. "They provided an open mic for people to voice their feelings, and I decided that it was as good a time as any to speak out against The Sophia Way."

"How'd that go?"

"It got ugly. Dr. Stockton happened to be in attendance, and I guess she feared that I was making an impact, so she pulled the plug on my microphone, and I was escorted off the stage."

"You sound more like a rock star than a theologian. Perhaps I should call you Bono for now on."

"Thanks…I think. The good thing is that I may have gotten through to some of the ladies. I noticed a few of them leaving afterward."

"Well, by the looks of it, round two is about to begin," he said.

"What did you do while I was gone?"

"I made arrangements to drive a Bexley student home with us. It shouldn't be but five minutes out of our way."

"That's no problem at all, Rocky."

* * *

Dr. Stockton now returned to the podium.

"I pray that you all grew today and came to know the goddess better. Now, it is time to celebrate just how good it is to be in our bodies as we celebrate communion."

Rocky looked perplexed. "What does communion have to do with *our* bodies?"

"Not your body, the female body," she whispered. "They've even taken Christ out of communion."

"Whose blood and body are they taking then?"

"Just watch."

197

The ushers again distributed the necessary items for the rituals being performed. Rocky was surprised to find that he had received both milk and honey from the trays being passed throughout the crowd.

"Bless the goddess Sophia, who gives us vision and wisdom within," Dr. Stockton chanted. "The ritual of milk and honey is an ancient Christian tradition which was intended to heal the bitterness of the human heart."

Karen leaned over to Rocky and said, "As usual, they offer only a fraction of the truth. The ritual of milk and honey was definitely not part of the early Christian tradition."

"Please repeat after me," said Dr. Stockton. "Milk of our breasts and nectar between our thighs, we now meditate on the body we share with Sophia, and pray that she lets her milk and honey flow as she did during creation."

Rocky placed the milk and honey given to him on the floor beneath his chair, as did Karen. He looked around and saw Stacy participating in this act of heresy.

"This is definitely equating Sophia with God," Rocky said.

"No doubt about it. She is being proclaimed the creator."

Following this ceremony, Dr. Stockton announced the final ritual of the day, which was referred to as "Raising the Body."

"The Spirit has been associated with maleness for far too long, which has led to only males receiving affirmation while females receive rejection," said Dr. Stockton. "For those of you who brought spices as indicated in the invitation packets, please anoint yourselves and your sisters."

Rocky looked over at Karen.

"It's their attempted connection to Mark 16:1 where the women anointed Jesus' body. They don't see themselves anointing the dead though, but instead they're commissioning each other to continue to raise the body."

Rocky just stared.

Dr. Stockton stood quiet at the podium, staring down the audience until it was silent.

"There are some among us who have declared us heretics, and our rituals heresy. Let me state for the record that we did not use the name of Jesus, nor have we done anything in the name of the Father, and of the Son, and of the Holy Spirit."

"No kidding," said Rocky.

"Go now, sisters, and go in the love, peace, and courage of Sophia. Amen."

Following Dr. Stockton's benediction, those in attendance were led in the singing of many familiar church hymns and then were dismissed.

* * *

Stacy joined Rocky and Karen as planned following the conference.

"I really do appreciate the ride," Stacy said as she sat down in the passenger seat next to Rocky. "I wish I could have come with some of my friends from Bexley, but they wouldn't come."

Rocky looked back at Karen in the rearview mirror, waiting to see who would reply.

"So, why didn't anyone come with you, Stacy?" Rocky asked.

"They all think that The Sophia Way is some sort of cult or something. They just don't get it."

"You don't consider the Sophia Way's rituals to be pagan?" Karen asked.

"I don't think it's pagan at all. All the rituals are based on the Bible, you know. I'm sure that some of these rituals do look like pagan rituals, but the Bible itself grew out of pagan rituals."

"I think that's the real danger of this organization," Rocky replied. "They seem to borrow just enough language and imagery from the Bible that their Christian audience doesn't seem to struggle with it."

"That's not true," Stacy said. "Look at Sophia. She comes straight from the Bible, after all."

Rocky looked again in his rearview mirror at the resident expert in the backseat.

"Again, as Rocky said, they're using just enough of the Bible to legitimize their theology," Karen explained. "The book of Proverbs and a couple of the non-canonical writings do reference a personified female figure of wisdom, however none of these writings ever state that Sophia is an actual person. At most, Sophia is a literary device, whereas Jesus is a real person. There is no female goddess figure in Scripture. God possesses wisdom, and we are to seek this wisdom by walking in the way of the Lord."

"I'm getting confused," Stacy said as she slumped back in her seat.

"If it's any consolation," said Rocky, "this is confusing stuff. The Sophia Way uses Biblical language and imagery in such a way that the average layperson can easily mistake what they're saying as being true. The Sophia Way, from what I could gather, avoids critical thinking and debate over these issues by their non-stop time of worship and rituals."

"Maybe so, but the Church is still guilty of male dominance and abuse. If you remove Sophia from the equation, that leaves us with God as a male, thus proclaiming that male is God."

"Perhaps you're not seeing it, but this matter of semantics is insignificant to what happens when they take Jesus and the cross out of it all," Karen replied.

"I agree with Karen," Rocky said as he carefully drove through the New England winter. "That raising the body ritual

200

leaves Jesus lying dead in His tomb, making Him, at most, just another martyr in the Christian cause."

Stacy sat back quietly. Rocky and Karen both saw that she was thinking things through and chose to let their silence be their compassion.

For the remainder of the car ride, the three of them remained quiet and listened to *Sergeant Pepper's Lonely Hearts Club Band*. Rocky carefully steered his car up the main entrance of Bexley College. It was a beautiful campus, a true winter wonderland that many city college students would never know or experience.

As Rocky parked his car, he noticed that Stacy was weeping. Her tears soon exploded into a flood of emotions like a volcano unable to withstand the pressure from the earth's core. She undid her seatbelt and flung herself around Rocky and hugged him as she cried uncontrollably. Karen, who was sitting in the backseat, placed her hand on Stacy's head and gently massaged it as Rocky held Stacy.

After a few minutes, Stacy straightened up in the passenger seat.

"I'm so sorry, you guys. You were nice enough to offer me a ride home in this weather, and here I am bawling like a baby."

"Please don't apologize, Stacy," said Rocky. "We were happy to give you a ride. Are you okay?"

"No, I'm not. I have lived with hatred for my father for all of my life, and it wasn't till this very moment that I realized how he had not only robbed me of my innocence, but of my relationship with God. He was terribly abusive to me."

"I'm so sorry, Stacy," Rocky replied.

"I tried to tell my family about it when I was young, but they accused me of lying, and that was the end of it. Over the years, I became like a frog in a kettle. You know the story, place a frog in a kettle of boiling water, and he'll quickly try to escape. Throw a frog into cool water set to boil, and the frog will soon die unknowingly. I just stayed there in that house and slowly began to die as all my childhood friends began to live. I kept going to church, but only to keep up appearances, not to honor another Father."

"God is the perfect Father, Stacy. He's not like your abusive father. When I look into your eyes, I see a little girl who was not loved enough. God wants to love you, and He does."

Stacy reached for the door handle to exit the car.

"Do you want to know what one of the most scandalous things was that Jesus did during His ministry?" Rocky asked.

Stacy took her hand off the car door handle and turned to face Rocky.

"What did He do?"

"He astonished the Jewish community by calling God 'Father.' He took it a step further in fact. Jesus, the One who taught that we must receive the Kingdom of God like a little child, Himself called God 'Daddy' when He called Him 'Abba.'"

"Daddy?" she softly echoed Rocky's words to the amazement of Karen sitting in the backseat.

"Yes, 'Daddy.' I think we'll discover someday that Heaven is filled with toddlers and not the likes of the Pharisees who had a distorted image of God as some remote Bookkeeper Who was constantly snooping around after sinners and nailing us if our accounts were not in order. God is Jesus' Daddy, and He's your Daddy, too, Stacy. He will not fall short like your dad did but will always be with you, guide you, protect you, and love you. You have been so courageous for so many years, Stacy. Now it's time to have the courage to accept His acceptance. That's true faith."

Time seemed to stand still at that moment as Stacy found herself the prodigal returning to her Heavenly Father. Like the father of the prodigal son, she saw with her accepting eyes God running to meet her halfway and holding her in a warm embrace. She now focused on Rocky sitting before her and said, "I *am* Daddy's little girl."

Rocky hugged her, and Karen leaned over the seat to join in the group hug. Sophia did not get her way today.

Coast to Coast

Tom woke up feeling great. There is a certain amount of relief and confidence a student experiences when the end of the final semester is in sight. Tom was indeed a brilliant student with a fantastic future, including his almost certain award to study abroad in Aberdeen for a year. Tom looked in the mirror and smiled.

* * *

Tom walked into his morning class a little late. He gently closed the door behind him and turned around to find his classmates were all out of their seats, gathered in a circle like kindergartners around Professor Garra as he read to them.

Tom broke into the circle of students and found Dr. Garra reading from *Time Magazine*. He quickly discovered that there was a feature article about the "Rocky Raccoon Revival." He appeared faint, and his knees temporarily buckled. He turned to take the nearest seat to support his crashing ego. He no longer focused on the words coming from Dr. Garra's mouth, and stared blankly as his mind raced like a gazelle facing certain death from a charging lion.

Tom slowly regained his composure and found the necessary strength in his legs to flee the scene of the crime against his pride.

* * *

Rocky overslept and was late for his breakfast shift. He walked into the cafeteria to work and was met with a reception worthy of a dashing leading man on the red carpet at the Oscars. He was shocked and confused. Sam came up and hugged him while those standing in line cheered and applauded him.

"What's going on, Sam?"

"Your story is in *Time Magazine*, Rock."

Rocky was speechless, as the room continued to cheer.

"I'd like to read that article during my break," Rocky said.

"We have already purchased a handful of copies," said Sam. "The Rocky Raccoon Revival has gone coast to coast, baby!"

Rocky went about his job, receiving many congratulatory words and encouragement from everyone whom he served during breakfast. Rocky really didn't even know how to respond given that he was apparently the only person who hadn't read the article yet.

Finally, once his shift was over, Rocky decided to forego breakfast and, instead sat alone at a table to read the article that had set the seminary aflame.

* * *

TIME MAGAZINE, **Salem, Massachusetts (Jan. 19) by David Eisinger**

The winds of change have taken a surprising course, as spiritual

205

revival has once again swept across New England, the birthplace of the nation's most vital spiritual awakenings. New England is now in the midst of what has been called "The Rocky Raccoon Revival."

The revival is aptly named after an employee of Easton Theological Seminary, Michael Sinclair, who is better known in his community as Rocky Raccoon. Rocky first gained notoriety by voluntarily going to jail in downtown Boston to minister to those incarcerated. Rocky downplays his own role in this revival, but many credit him as the catalyst, prompting many to not only serve and love others, but he has also been instrumental in organizing and encouraging widespread prayer.

Pastor Marvin Beculhimer of the Ipswich Baptist Church commented, "In all the years I have been a pastor, I have never witnessed such a burden and expectancy for revival in New England as I do at this moment among Christians." He cautioned that, "A revival such as this impacts society with godliness, justice, conviction, righteousness, and peace, which, of course, is not always welcome."

Welcome or not, the Rocky Raccoon Revival has seemingly arrived according to many residents along the North Shore. There have been numerous reports already attributed to this revival. Two young people visited a woman in Peabody who had been paralyzed and bedridden for five years, who got up and joined them for tea after they prayed for her. Two teenage girls, weeping after leaving a revival meeting in Brighton encountered two medical students who mocked their faith. Upon hearing the girls' testimonies, the two students were convicted and knelt asking for prayer. Two elderly men in Rockport visited a man in a coma, crippled with liver damage from years of alcohol abuse. The two men prayed for him, and the patient was healed. Salem's most recognized Satanist, who was befriended by Rocky Raccoon, is now the heart and voice of revival in a town that has wrestled with its history and identity for so many years. Members of a Southside gang attended a revival meeting in downtown Boston with the intent of disrupting it, but were instead convicted by God and repented. All were converted, and one of them now teaches Sunday school. Simon Luger, one of Harvard's most brilliant and outspoken students, as well as son of multibillionaire Blaine W. Luger III, has become a high profile Christian convert after an encounter with Rocky Raccoon and has since led a crusade in Cambridge reminiscent of the efforts of Jonathan Edwards.

Dr. Illona Johnson, a Harvard University professor of philosophy, who is scheduled to debate Dr. Peter Casper, evangelist and president of Easton Theological Seminary next week, has dismissed many of these accounts as "undocumented, unverifiable, and unbelievable."

"It's wishful thinking," she concluded. "Is God allowing these minor 'miracles' to take place as He lets the rest of the world continue to go to hell? That doesn't make any sense to me. If there is a God, He's either all-powerful but not good, or good but not all-powerful, otherwise these miracles would occur more often, and the evil in the world would simply cease to exist. As it stands, beyond these alleged isolated instances being highlighted by the media, the other news stories give testimony to a world without a God."

Historically, America has experienced four significant spiritual revivals. The first and most famous, the Great Awakening, took place in the mid 1700s, led by Jonathan Edwards (1703-1764) and a twenty three year old itinerant preacher from England, John Whitefield (1714-1770). The Great Awakening witnessed 50,000 converts to Christianity (out of 250,000 colonists). Edwards, the author of *Sinners In the Hands of an Angry God,* commented that revivals had been criticized as scaring people with hell and damnation, but he noticed the biggest changes occur when he insisted upon the "compassions of a dying Savior, the plentiful provisions of the Gospel, and the free offers of divine grace to needy distressed sinners."

Some Christians wonder if God will bring about a revival. A cursory glance at our society indicates that revival may already be taking place. Christian music outsells jazz and classical music combined. Many religious books have broken into mainstream publishing. It is not uncommon to hear politicians pronounce their faith, which is politically expedient given that 96% of Americans believe in God.

Conversely, many indicators point to a spiritual decline. Church membership is dwindling, and though 96% of Americans say that they believe in God, 58% say that religion's influence in our postmodern society is waning.

When asked if the Rocky Raccoon Revival was indeed the real

THE ROCKY RACCOON REVIVAL

McCoy, Dr. Volker Carlsson, a professor of Christian History at Yale, replied, "I do not know Rocky Raccoon personally, but as it pertains to the revival that bears his name, spiritual awakenings, whether Biblical or in church history, tend to share many similar patterns. If you compare the Rocky Raccoon Revival to those revivals of the past, you will see that it shares many of the same common elements of those that preceded it. Rocky could very easily be compared to those early Christians who were accused of 'turning the world upside down' by the civil authorities in Acts 17:6. I'd say we have a revival on our hands, and I only see it getting bigger as the story continues to spread."

Clash of the Titans

The big day had finally arrived. Typically, a debate between Dr. Peter Casper and Dr. Illona Johnson would draw a respectable crowd, mostly of Easton and Harvard students. The event, hosted by Easton Theological Seminary, was now in the national spotlight courtesy of the Rocky Raccoon Revival. The audience now included many curious onlookers, people seeking the truth, new converts, rabid atheists, and several representatives of the local and national media.

Rocky sat in his dorm room alone. He heard a knock on his door and called out for his visitor to enter.

"Why aren't you ready yet?" Jim asked.

"I don't want to go."

"Why not? Do you realize that all of this media attention and interest from the general public is on account of your revival?"

"*Please*...I'm no more responsible for this than I am for the sun rising and setting today."

"Whether you like it or not, the Rocky Raccoon Revival was born through you. For whatever reason, God chose to work in you and through you in ways that you and I will never quite comprehend, and I think you know that."

Rocky looked up and nodded. He was keenly aware of his role in the revival that bore his name.

"Then why don't you want to go? The press will certainly want to talk to you."

"Swell. You want to know why I'm not going? I hate these things, Jim. It might come as a surprise to you, given my debate with Simon, but I hate these kinds of events."

"Why?" Jim asked. "This is a great opportunity to reach a lot of people to help them understand more about God and know that He truly does exist."

"On some level, I agree. I do believe that there are reasonable arguments to be made proving the existence of God. Some people tonight may very well be convinced and believe in Him. However, no one has ever been debated into heaven. There has to be a personal relationship with God. There needs to be faith."

"Faith and one's intelligence are not mutually exclusive."

"I know. However, if you can debate someone into believing in God, then what's to stop someone else from debating them out of their belief in God?"

"This coming from the guy who converted Simon through debate?"

"Simon confided in me that our debate had no immediate impact on his belief system."

"What did then?"

"Simon basically knew every single argument that I or any other Christian was going to throw at him. In fact, I bet that you and I could guess Dr. Casper and Dr. Johnson's main points in tonight's debate. They'll use the same old arguments that they have both used in the past and will use the same arguments that Christian and atheist scholars have used for centuries. This debate is no more than academia's equivalent to pro wrestling, with a choreographed predetermined performance. Dr. Casper will probably utilize the argument from design, the first cause argument, the argument from conscience, and probably Pascal's Wager; whereas Dr. Johnson will focus on the problem of evil, evolution, and use the same old counter arguments that we always hear. Those atheists who attend tonight's debate will leave confident that their side won. Same with the Christians."

"What about those who are neither?" Jim asked.

"They may decide tonight, but another convincing argument may sway their newfound belief."

"So, if it wasn't the debate, what did you do to convince Simon?"

"He saw me help out an alcoholic."

"When did this happen?"

"After our first encounter, Simon declared himself the victor of our debate and left with his followers to celebrate elsewhere. Simon said he witnessed my efforts to help a homeless man on the street. He later told me that he had heard the Gospel message all his life but never believed or understood it till he saw that one act of compassion. After that, he wanted to talk to me, and we discussed the Gospel."

"I see your point, but this is still on national television and will be covered by all the newspapers. God is in the headlines, and people are genuinely seeking Him and longing for Him. I think that this debate is a good thing."

"Let's hope so," Jim and Rocky heard a voice say accompanied by a knock on the partially open door.

"It's good to see you, Simon," said Rocky.

"Why wouldn't this debate be a good thing?" Jim asked Simon.

"Dr. Johnson is approaching this debate differently than she has in the past. Dr. Johnson and Dr. Casper are friends and usually have a nice, clean, cordial debate, but she's out for blood tonight."

"Why the change in attitude?" Jim asked.

"If you're an atheist, especially a high profile atheist, and are about to be thrust into the national spotlight in a debate on God's existence while also trying to discredit a spiritual revival that's running wild in your own backyard, you'd do everything in your power to win, too," Simon said.

"Rocky doesn't want to attend the debate," said Jim.

"What? Rocky, you *have to* attend. I know that you've never been comfortable with the Rocky Raccoon Revival label, but I think you should really see this as an opportunity. Trust me, no one thinks that you are claiming to be the Second Coming, all right? They do, however, see you as the face and heart of this revival."

"It's God's revival, not mine."

"No kidding, Sherlock. Everybody knows that," Simon said as he playfully slapped Rocky on the back of the head. "Now get dressed and come down and be happy that God is the national focus tonight. Even if this revival is the real deal, it won't last forever. Now is a time of *action*, Rocky."

Rocky reluctantly nodded in agreement.

* * *

Rocky entered the seminary's main auditorium in the Lewis Center, along with Simon, Adam, and his buddies from Tuttle Hall. The atmosphere resembled an Ohio State Buckeyes and the Michigan Wolverines football game more than it did an academic debate about God. He appeared shocked by the number of cameras and reporters, let alone the presence of a crowd that could not possibly be accommodated by the confines of this modest auditorium.

212

THE ROCKY RACCOON REVIVAL

Legions of reporters and photographers besieged Rocky once word had spread that he had arrived. His friends promised to save him a seat, and Rocky was now left alone to answer reporters' questions about everything from his own conversion to what flavor he would be if he were a lollipop. Rocky handled the media with the same wit and charm that endeared the American public to the Beatles upon their arrival in New York City. Even Rocky's fashion sense, his trademark torn faded blue jeans, white t-shirt, and sandals captured the imagination of the media. He was the most reluctant member of Andy Warhol's fifteen-minute club.

Rocky accommodated every member of the media, prayerfully optimistic that his testimony would touch the hearts of the TV audience, and that Dr. Casper would reach their minds. Rocky joined his friends who managed to get good seats, saving one for him on the aisle.

*   *   *

Dr. Paul Williams, vice-president of Easton Theological Seminary, was serving as the emcee. Though Dr. Williams was a noteworthy scholar and popular author, he nervously approached the center stage, very much aware that he was being televised around the nation and the rest of the free world on some of the cable news networks.

"Good evening, ladies and gentlemen, and thank you for your interest in tonight's debate between Easton Theological Seminary President, Dr. Peter Casper, and Harvard University Professor of philosophy, Dr. Illona Johnson. My name is Dr. Paul Williams, and tonight you will be treated to a thoughtful and challenging discussion on a topic that has confounded and empowered mankind for thousands of years. Does God exist?

213

Tonight, you will hear two different points of view offering their reasons and evidence to support one belief system over the other. Tonight's format will provide each side an opportunity to state his and her case, and respond to his or her opponent's argument. In the final analysis, it is up to you, the audience both here and at home to decide; but decide you must, for if you choose not to decide, then you still have made a choice. Our guest, Dr. Johnson, has graciously opted to allow Dr. Casper to start the debate, as he is arguing in the affirmative, that God does indeed exist. Without any further ado, I give you Dr. Peter Casper."

The mixed applause for Dr. Casper betrayed a very partisan audience in attendance. He was truly one of the shining stars of Christendom, not only in academia, but also in ministry. Some have declared him heir to both C.S. Lewis and Dr. Billy Graham, though his humble response to such comparisons was reminiscent of Mother Teresa.

"Thank you, ladies and gentlemen, for your kind welcome. Tonight we will be discussing the existence of God. For the purposes of this debate, I will define God as the eternal uncaused Cause of all else that exists. God is a personal, moral, and intelligent being Who is unlimited in all His attributes. God is separate from His creation, but He is also involved with it. In short, I will argue that the God of Theism exists. It should be emphasized from the onset that one cannot scientifically prove or disprove the existence of God. However, it is certainly permissible to study the character of the universe and question, 'What does it reasonably suggest: an intelligent Creator or a self-caused universe?' There are many arguments for the existence of God. They're like roads, starting from different points, but all leading to the same goal."

Dr. Casper paused, leaned forward on the podium as he often

214

did in class, and said, "President Calvin Coolidge reportedly won a bet once. A young woman said, 'I'll bet I can make you say three words.' Coolidge simply replied, 'You lost.' He was known as a man of few words," Dr. Casper said, smiling. "I think I can do President Coolidge one better tonight. The question being discussed tonight is, 'Does God Exist?' Ladies and gentlemen, I can do that in one word. Yes. I will expand upon that however. There are at least a dozen or so good arguments to prove the existence of God. I'd like to go through just a few of them tonight. I will focus on the argument from design, the first cause argument, the argument from conscience, the argument from desire, and lastly, I'd like to close discussing Pascal's Wager."

Rocky looked over at Jim and grinned. Jim cracked a smile.

"Firstly, there must be a universal designer. Though most atheists will of course deny this, everyone admits it in practice. For example, if you were to see the letters 'S.O.S.' on a beach, your first thought would not be, 'The waves and wind must have produced it.' No, you'd think a *person* did it. If you found a hut on that same island, your first inclination would not be to assume that it arrived by chance, but, rather, someone *created* it. There may indeed be a one in a trillion chance that 'S.O.S.' could be written in the sand by wind and waves, but who would honestly and sincerely assume a one in a trillion explanation? We immediately infer a designer whenever we see design. Some atheists have put my faith to shame, honestly refuting Christian claims of design by explaining that if you had a million monkeys in front of a million typewriters banging on the keyboards, that one monkey would eventually produce Shakespeare's *Hamlet* by chance. However, when one reads *Hamlet*, one does not assume that it came from a monkey. Why then does the atheist use this implausible and incredible explanation for the universe? Is it possible that design just happens by chance, without a designer?

Well, according to a bumper sticker on a car I saw this weekend, you know what just happens."

The audience laughed. Dr. Casper was a brilliant scholar, but his charm is what has won the hearts and minds of so many.

"Clearly, the reason for this flawed logic is that it's the atheist's only chance to remain an atheist. You might say we need a psychological explanation of the atheist more than we need a logical explanation of the universe. We have a logical explanation for the universe, and the atheist doesn't like it. It's called God."

Rocky started thumbing through the program, nodding along with the familiar arguments.

Dr. Casper spoke of the Anthropic Principle, which states that the universe was specifically designed from the beginning for human life. He noted several mind blowing statistics from Nobel Prize astrophysicists, including the vital importance of the Big Bang. If the temperature of the primordial fireball that followed the Big Bang had been even a trillionth of a degree hotter or colder, then carbon, the basis of all life, would not have developed. He noted the distance from the sun, the earth's tilt, and issues involving just the right amount of cosmic rays that led to the hemoglobin molecule. He then cited the oft-quoted Sir Fred Hoyle, who once stated, "The current scenario of the origin of life is about as likely as a tornado passing through a junkyard beside Boeing Airplane Company accidentally producing a 747 airplane."

Dr. Casper smiled, as he received the reaction from the audience he expected.

"When discussing design, inevitably, someone asks, 'Doesn't evolution explain everything without a divine designer?' Please allow me to answer a question with a question. Could something as complex as the human brain come from no design? This

216

explanation violates the principle of causality, which states that you cannot get more from the effect than you do from the sum total of its causes. Put simply, if there is human intelligence, there must be intelligence in its cause, God. A universe ruled only by blind chance would have no intelligence, therefore, there must be a cause for human intelligence that transcends the universe."

As Dr. Casper spoke, Rocky's mind began to wander, and he thought about his first theological conversation.

* * *

Michael and his grandfather took a walk one summer day along a shallow creek lined with trees. It was a windy day, which seemingly kept the deerflies at bay and also caused Michael's Chicago Cubs ball cap to fly off his head halfway along the creek.

"Grandpa."

"Yes."

"I know you believe in God, but how do you *really* know? You can't see Him. I believe in Santa Claus, but I have seen him at the mall with Mom and Dad."

His grandpa smiled. He walked a few steps with Michael in silence and then stopped and pointed up at a bird.

"Do you see that?"

"I see a bird," Michael replied.

"Birds do not plant or harvest any food, but God feeds them. If there was no God, we wouldn't have any birds."

Michael didn't seem entirely satisfied with that answer.

"They eat *birdseed*, Grandpa!" said Michael, as only a six-year-old can.

"But where does it come from?"

217

"I don't know. God?"

His grandpa nodded.

"But why can't we see God? Wouldn't everyone believe in Him if they could see Him?"

His grandpa knelt down beside his inquisitive grandson and said, "Okay, let's look for God."

Michael's eyes grew the size of golf balls, as he didn't think anyone could actually see God. He knew, though, that if anyone could, his grandpa could.

"Where is He?" Michael whispered, as if he might scare God away the same way one might startle a rabbit.

"Look at that leaf," said his grandpa as he pointed.

"Which leaf? The one on that long twig?"

"That's the one. Do you see it moving?"

"Yes!" Michael yelled out, no longer afraid of scaring off the Master of the universe.

"God is just like the wind, Michael. Have you ever seen the wind?"

"No."

"But you do know that the wind is there right?"

"Yes, Grandpa."

"How do you know that?"

"I can see what the wind moves. I can see it blow leaves, and I see it make waves in the creek."

"God is the same way. You can't see Him, but you can see what He does. Never forget that, Michael, because someday someone may try to make you believe that there is no God."

Michael smiled and then looked up at his grandfather, whom he loved and admired so very much.

"Thanks, Grandpa. Could you now explain to me how Santa Claus gets all the kids in the world their presents in one night?"

His grandpa betrayed a nervous crooked grin and took a few

steps before getting into another one of life's lessons.

* * *

Dr. Casper had skillfully articulated a strong case for the existence of God. He now was concluding his opening statement.

"Blaise Pascal didn't believe that one could prove or disprove the existence of God. Instead, he addressed the skeptics who, like many of you perhaps, do not believe that there are any arguments for the existence of God."

"Suppose for a moment that someone you love lay dying in the hospital, and the doctor offered to try a new experimental drug that he could not guarantee. He can state with certainty, though, that this miracle drug offered a 50/50 chance of saving your loved one's life? Wouldn't it be reasonable to try it, even if it were expensive? What if it were given for free? Wouldn't it be unreasonable to decline?"

The Socratic teacher paused to give his audience a chance to truly ponder the question.

"To the mothers and fathers, I ask you, if you hear a report that the school was on fire and that your children were still inside, would you ignore that report since it could be either true or false? No, you would take a moment and call home or run to the school, just in case the report is true."

"Let me now appeal to our own self interests. Suppose there is a winning sweepstakes ticket worth ten million dollars, and that there are only two tickets left, knowing that one of them is the winning ticket, and the other is worth nothing, wouldn't it be a good investment to spend a dollar on a good chance of winning ten million dollars?"

The audience seemingly understood the arguments, and many

219

nodded their heads in agreement.

"In each example," said Dr. Casper, "no reasonable person is ever truly in doubt. Pascal argues that believing in God is much like these examples. It is the fool who does not bet on God, even if there is no proof or guarantee that your bet will win. Pascal wrote that 'either God is or He is not, but to which view shall we be inclined? Reason cannot decide this question. Infinite chaos separates us, at the far end of an infinite distance, death, a coin is being spun that will come down heads or tails. God or no God. How then will you wager?'"

The audience started to rumble and murmur as they discussed the concept with their neighbor.

"If God does not exist, then obviously it doesn't matter how you wager, as there is nothing to win or lose then after death. However, if God does indeed exist, your only chance of having eternal happiness is to believe, and your one and only chance of losing it is to refuse to believe. As Pascal reasoned, I'd be much more concerned about being mistaken and then finding out that Christianity is true, than be mistaken and believe that it is true. If you believe too much, you neither win nor lose eternal happiness, but if you believe too little, you risk losing everything. What is the cost? What must be given in order to wager that God does exist? Whatever it is, it's only finite, and it is most reasonable to wager something finite in order to win infinite happiness in Heaven.

"In closing, an atheist once went to a noted priest and demanded him to prove the existence of God. The priest refused, and the angry atheist got up to leave. The priest called after him, 'But how can you be sure that there is no God?' The atheist later wrote that 40 years after that encounter, he is still an atheist but the priest's question haunted him every day for the rest of his life. Pascal's Wager has that chilling power."

220

THE ROCKY RACCOON REVIVAL

Dr. Casper sat down to a warm applause by those in attendance.

*   *   *

Dr. Illona Johnson walked to the podium like a woman on a mission. She was highly respected, and her face was as familiar to the general public as Dr. Casper's. Like Dr. Casper, she carried no notes, as she was a battle-scarred veteran of such debates and author of several books on the topic.

"The telescope was invented in 1608 by a Dutch lens grinder named Hans Lippershay. One day, Lippershay, quite by accident, discovered that by putting lenses at both ends of a tube and then putting the tube up to his eye, he could view distant things 'close up.' He called this device a 'looker,' and he thought it would be useful in warfare. Conversely, Galileo got a looker, improved upon it a little, and then used it himself to challenge prevailing ideas held by the Church about the solar system. This lecture is dedicated to the spirit of Galileo."

"Thank you, Dr. Casper and Easton Theological Seminary for welcoming me back to debate the existence of God. As Woody Allen once said, 'To *you* I'm an atheist. To God I'm the Loyal Opposition.'"

The crowd laughed, and her legion of fans and students were vocally supportive.

"With all due respect to my good and dear friend, Dr. Casper, I am reminded of a joke. A biology class student conducted an experiment on what would happen to a grasshopper if its legs were taken off. He pulled off one of its legs and yelled, 'Hop!' and the grasshopper hopped. Then he took another leg and yelled, 'Hop!' and the grasshopper hopped. Then he took all of its legs and yelled, 'Hop!' but the insect did not hop. He yelled

221

again, but the insect still did not hop. So he came to the conclusion that when all the legs of a grasshopper are removed, it will become deaf."

The crowd again laughed as Dr. Johnson was cleverly winning the audience over through her personality.

"Dr. Casper, like the biology student, takes information and facts, and somehow arrives at misguided conclusions. Tonight, I'm going to offer a few arguments, including the most damning one of them all, the problem of evil. I will also counter all of Dr. Casper's attempts to prove the existence of God."

Simon leaned over to Rocky and said, "I told you that she was going to be a little nasty tonight."

"Let me first start by clarifying what it is that we are talking about tonight and what my position on the matter truly is. I also wish to address the methods of science and its limits. Science cannot investigate negative statements, and you cannot prove negative statements. There is no way that I know of as a philosopher to prove the inexistence of something, unless you can define that something by positive statements. So, for example, you can't ask me to come up with a proof of the inexistence of God without clarifying what you mean by God—it's completely impossible. Dr. Casper was kind enough to share his definition of God, which can best be summed up as the Christian God of the Bible. With that in mind, I offer my first argument.

"The first argument of note, and perhaps the only one necessary, is the problem of evil. It's simple enough. If there is an all-powerful and all-good God of the universe, why does He allow evil to exist? I have never heard a satisfactory answer."

Rocky leaned over to Simon. "This is her strongest argument. Dr. Casper could give 30 convincing arguments for God's existence, but this one argument is a tough one to overcome."

222

"I will quote Bertrand Russell, who stated it as well as I ever could, 'If I had ten billion years and this is all I could come up with, the universe as it is, I should be ashamed of myself.' Being born and raised on the west coast, I can envision a better world than one with earthquakes!"

She took a drink as she waited for the audience's laughter to subside.

"Likewise, I can imagine a world better off without blizzards, murders, tornados, AIDS, and rapists. So, it begs the question asked a moment ago, how does this all-powerful and all-good God allow us to be in this mess down here on earth? And please spare me with the stock Christian answer, 'The devil did it,' as the devil is a creation of God, so it still falls back upon God. This argument for my money is airtight, unless one wants to argue that creation had unintended consequences that didn't go the way God had wanted; but that road leads one to believing that this is God's personal failure, which no Christian in this room would ever accept either."

The crowd was uneasy, and Rocky noticed the reporters in attendance taking notes at a lightning pace, as each was eager to report that Nietzsche was right after all. God is dead.

Dr. Johnson looked over the audience, turned to look Dr. Casper in the eye, and continued with her assault.

"Dr. Casper argued at length that it is astonishingly unlikely that life could have arisen by chance and cites one impressive statistic after another to support his case. He then concludes, and some of you naively bought into it, that there must be a God who was the cause and designer of the universe."

"For those of you who are not familiar with probability estimates, please allow me to explain. These estimates are valid only under certain assumptions. The probability estimates to which Dr. Casper refers seem to be based on the classical theory of probability: the ratio of the possibilities favorable to life to all possibilities. However, this theory can only be applied if one has good reason to suppose that the possibilities are equally likely. As it is though, we have no reason to make this assumption in this particular case. Conversely, the frequency theory of probability cannot apply either. On this theory, probability is the frequency in which a type of event occurs within a class of events. For example, in the case of life on this planet, this might be the frequency of universes with life generated by big bangs that occur within the class of all universes generated by big bangs. However, and please correct me if I'm wrong, there only is evidence of one universe generated by the Big Bang. Given these considerations, Dr. Casper's example of a Boeing 747 created from a junkyard by a tornado is misplaced. Here there is ample evidence that the frequency of Boeing 747s brought about by tornadoes is zero."

Rocky's attention started to drift. Theory had lost its meaning to him back when he was a college student. It's one thing to believe something in theory, but another thing to believe in something when called upon to put it into practice. He then thought back to that day when his theology quickly became more real than he had ever hoped, or feared it could be.

* * *

While attending Ohio State University, prior to dropping out to move to Las Vegas, Michael worked third shift in an exclusive, all-suite hotel in Dublin, a wealthy suburb located in northwest Columbus.

Work went on as usual until that fateful cold February morning. He drove to the hotel tired that evening. Being an astronomy buff, he couldn't help but notice the red moon on the horizon. The "Bad Moon" Creedence Clearwater Revival had made famous. Not being the superstitious type, though, he ignored the phenomenon.

At 4:25 a.m., two knife-wielding thugs wearing expensive athletic apparel surprised him. They were better dressed than he was, yet the gutless assailants found it necessary to take his wallet. He played it cool, as on many a boring night he had played out this scenario in his mind. He also wanted to expedite this attack before any innocent hotel guests wandered in, thus being placed in jeopardy.

One of the armed thieves approached Michael, and took a moment to look at his Christian themed tie with the familiar fish symbol pattern. The thief threatened, "You'd better do just as we say, or else we'll send you to meet Jesus."

Ironically, the threat on Michael's life served to strengthen him. He not only knew that the worst these men could do was to send him to paradise in Heaven, but he was now reassured by the presence of Jesus with him during this trial.

They proceeded to tie him up with duct tape and throw him down to the ground. The tape wasn't so bad, except when they tied his hands behind his back; they made it a point to wrap up his thumbs. He was quickly losing his circulation, though their next move might have eliminated any concern for circulation.

Lying face down on the ground, with his head by the hotel's drop deposit safe, one of them placed his knife up against Michael's throat and gave him the option of giving them the second key or bleeding to death. Michael felt a strange sense of peace and confidence from his faith. The peace of mind that only God could give him at that moment allowed him to convince his would be murderers that he honestly did not have the key, and they instead opted to take the entire safe with them. Looking back, it's hard to say what he would have done had the key not been sitting safely on the general manager's dresser twenty miles away.

After their impressive feat of carrying the safe out to their car, they took whatever wasn't nailed down. The two men looked down on the ground where Michael was laying, and he looked up at them both and said, "I forgive you."

He didn't say it believing that they would see the error of their ways at that exact moment, but he sincerely hoped that he might be planting a seed for their eventual repentance and salvation. They left Michael in the office, and then cruelly shut the lights off. As soon as he thought it was safe, he made every effort to free himself.

He backed himself up against the safety deposit boxes not being used at the time and grabbed a key as best as he could behind his back. He thought he might be able to saw through the tape. He was unable to cut through the tape but did loosen it a bit to relieve the strain on his thumbs. He then utilized a trick he had learned from gymnastics during his childhood and stood up without the aid of his arms. He was now standing in a pitch-black office, although he knew he could navigate through it with his eyes closed.

He bent his head down and moved along till he hit the phone. He then swung his jaw hard along the receiver in order to knock it off and get a dial tone. That was the easy part. The trick was dialing the 9-1-1 in the dark with his nose. He successfully pressed his nose on the touch-tone keys and dialed 9-1-1.

His head dropped and his heart sank when he failed to get a hold of 9-1-1. It then hit him that he had to first dial a 9 first to get an outside line. He grew frustrated, but regained his composure. He said a quick prayer and pressed his nose on the 9 key twice followed by the 1 key twice. He then fell to the ground after he heard a noise that he thought might be one of the thieves checking in on him.

In just a few minutes, the office door was opened and the lights were turned on to reveal a Dublin police officer. They quickly untied Michael and sat him down in the hotel's video library to question him and file a report. In a matter of minutes, the hotel manager had arrived, as well as many of the hotel morning staff and the guests who woke up early for the complementary full breakfast buffet.

Every employee and manager who walked in after hearing the news feared that Michael would be shaken up or angry, but instead, they found him humming and singing while filling out police reports.

Many of his co-workers, hotel guests, and even some of the police officers asked how he could be in such a good mood following this experience, and he proceeded to share his testimony with them all. He told the Gospel message to about fifty people that morning who would have otherwise never heard it that day.

Michael reflected on his morning as he drove home from the police station following his visit with the department sketch artist. The day theory was challenged by practice, was the day he believed he had become a Christian man.

* * *

Rocky lifted his head and looked upon Dr. Johnson coming to her conclusion.

"Lastly, I want to comment on Pascal's Wager. I won't spend much time on it, because it doesn't deserve that much attention, and Dr. Casper is clearly offering it knowing that his other arguments have failed. Dr. Casper noted that Pascal's Wager isn't an argument for God's existence, which is correct. It does purport to provide people with good pragmatic reasons for belief. It's simple, if you do believe and God exists, you will be rewarded; and if you don't believe and He does exists, you will be punished. If there were really a good, moral God, perhaps, just maybe, God would not appreciate people believing in Him for these practical reasons. God may want people to believe in Him for reasons other than these pragmatic reasons and punish those who subscribe to this argument. Anyhow, isn't it a sin to gamble?" She asked with a mischievous grin.

"I'm sad to say, ladies and gentlemen, that if you want to achieve immortality, you'll have to achieve it by not dying, as there is no God."

With those words, she smiled for an Associated Press photographer and then walked confidently back to her seat.

* * *

The unflappable Dr. Casper approached the podium with the cool headedness of Atticus Finch and smiled to the audience, the press, and the cameras awaiting his reply and defense to Dr. Johnson's verbal siege.

"Dr. Johnson saw fit to dedicate tonight's debate to the spirit of Galileo, which is fine with me, as I earned my bachelor's degree in astronomy as an undergraduate at Arizona State University. I do take exception with the conflict between the Roman Catholic Church and Galileo being used to perpetuate the myth that Christianity is inherently at odds with science, or is anti-science. I'd like to note that history teaches that many high-ranking Catholics were on Galileo's side, including Cardinal Baronius, who wrote that the Bible teaches 'how one goes to Heaven, and not how the heavens go.' Galileo delighted in antagonizing his fellow professors, who were Aristotelians, and believed in a geo-centric solar system. It was they who mainly caused the Pope to condemn Galileo's teaching. Galileo and his Catholic supporters helped broker the final plea bargain. As you can plainly see, professors have a history of irrational actions, which continues to this day," he smiled as he looked over at Dr. Johnson with a slight nod.

"Dr. Johnson, a fellow native West Coaster, reasoned that God couldn't exist if there is evil and flaws in His creation, such as earthquakes. Earthquakes, or plate tectonic activity if you will, are in fact necessary for life to exist. Without earthquakes, nutrients essential for life on the continents would erode and collect into the oceans. Note however, that if earthquake activity were *too* great, people would not be able to populate cities. God designed, out of love, the necessary number and intensity of earthquakes to recycle life-essential nutrients back to the continents, yet not so intense that dwelling in cities becomes impossible. That is a *good* God, not an evil one.

"I believe that the law of causality, that everything that has a beginning, even the universe, is essential for proper scientific investigation in this and any related matter. I'm not alone in this view. Albert Einstein, in response to his colleagues who entertained the possibility of uncaused effects on the subatomic level stated, 'God does not play dice.' The most brilliant scientist of the 20th century saw that uncaused events would take away the underlying order of the universe necessary for true science to function."

Rocky looked around and noticed that the crowd seemed impressed with Dr. Casper's fountain of knowledge, but that he may be losing some of the audience.

"I'd like to take a moment and address Dr. Johnson's critique of Pascal's Wager. Firstly, I don't ever recall reading in Scripture that God hates gamblers. Not that I think God is satisfied with gambling, as I'm sure that He would prefer better motives for believing in Him than Pascal's Wager. At its heart, as I said before, it is a very low and selfish motive. However, God, the Loving Father, stoops to conquer," he said with a smile.

"To those who say not to wager at all, Pascal replies, you *must* wager, as you are already embarked in life. The time is now, not after it's too late. Pascal's Wager works because of the fact of death. What if a man proposes to a woman, and she says she needs time to make up her mind? The man comes back day after day, and the woman keeps offering the same reply day after day, 'Tomorrow.' There will come a time when there are no more tomorrows, and tomorrow is certainly not a guarantee for anyone. Someday 'tomorrow' and 'maybe' become 'no.' The man will die, and one does not marry a corpse. The same applies to God's marriage proposal to your soul. Saying 'maybe' and 'tomorrow' to God cannot continue indefinitely, because we do not live indefinitely. Pascal stated that you have two things to lose, the true and the good. He said that the things at stake are your reason and your will and your knowledge and happiness. Your nature has two things to shun, error and wretchedness. Since, as I have demonstrated, you must choose, choosing one over the other does not compromise your reason. If you win, you win everything. If you lose, you lose nothing, so do not hesitate then, wager that He does indeed exist!"

The crowd applauded Dr. Casper's defense of this old but reliable argument. Rocky couldn't help but notice that there was always a camera on him. He figured that Pastor Bob was watching him on TV at that exact moment. He then thought about his old friend in Las Vegas, the Franciscan Priest who literally found and delivered him from the gutter.

THE ROCKY RACCOON REVIVAL

* * *

Michael was more than a resident of Las Vegas; he had become one of its disciples, spreading the gospel of excess, indulgence, gluttony, greed, and lust. He didn't waste his time in the "family friendly" areas of Vegas. He preferred to frequent the hole in the wall establishments that focused more on his vices than those other places offering the bright neon lights that attracted tourists and gave drug users like him migraines from over stimulation.

He was a young man accustomed to having a woman at his side. He dressed in flashy attire that would have embarrassed a rock star, and he always had an illegal substance on him…or in him. Most casinos turned a blind eye, as he was a good customer. Michael, who always had a great memory for names and faces, knew almost every cocktail waitress in Vegas by name. His drinking was legendary to everyone but him, who could never recall what he had drunk after he sobered up. It wasn't unusual for him to wake up and not have any idea where he even was.

One morning he woke up with a colossal headache on the doorstep of a downtown building. He had no idea how he had arrived in such a predicament. Judging by the foul stench of the dried vomit that encrusted his beard, as well as his uncontrollable shaking after so many hours without his favorite drugs and alcohol, he knew that he had been out "having a good time."

He got up to walk home but lost his equilibrium and unceremoniously fell back down. He looked up and saw a homeless man walk by and just shake his head at him, as he was now sitting in the gutter trying to drag himself back up to the doorstep.

Michael crawled back like a beast of burden to the doorstep and pulled himself up to a sitting position on the steps. Although it wasn't at all unusual for him to wake up completely unaware of where he was or what exactly he had done, this time it really made him think. It's difficult not to internalize too much when one wakes up smelling like garbage in a gutter.

He took in the first breath that didn't nauseate him. His nose took in the scent of a wealthy woman walking by, along with her daughter and henpecked husband. The woman was bossing her husband around, clearly mad about something he had said or done, and the girl stopped and stood in front of Michael as her parents continued to walk down the sidewalk.

"Hi, mister. My name is Lauren."

Michael had to take a moment to clear his throat of whatever residue remained from the night before and replied, "My name is Michael. Nice to meet you, Lauren."

The little girl smiled, seemingly oblivious to his fallen state. The stench and sight that repulsed even him was filtered by the innocence of this little girl who was happy to have made a new friend.

"What's a nice girl like you doing in a place like this?"

Lauren didn't get a chance to answer.

"Lauren!" screamed her mother. "Don't look at such filth!"

Lauren didn't move so her mother grabbed her by the arm and then lectured, "You don't know where he's been!"

Lauren turned around and waved at Michael as she was being dragged away by her mother. Michael waved back, and then wiped his eyes as they started to well up with tears.

A man who witnessed the episode now stood over him. Michael was expecting to find a police officer ready to throw him in the drunk tank, but instead found himself looking into the blue eyes of an elderly Franciscan priest.

Michael was suddenly on his knees with his arms wrapped around the legs of the priest, crying and confessing every sin that he could possibly remember.

"Rise, my son. God loves you."

Michael tried to get to his feet but was unable to stand. The priest smiled and sat down next to him on the steps.

"God couldn't possibly love *me*, Father," Michael said. "I've done way too much. I can't hide it all from Him."

The priest listened to Michael elaborate on his sexual escapades, substance abuse problems, and greed. He built a case against himself that would make any district attorney proud. The priest simply listened to him, allowing him this opportunity to confess.

"What's your name, son?"

"Michael."

"Ah, what a wonderful name. It means he who is godly."

"That's a joke."

"It's never too late to live up to that name, Michael. God does love you."

"How could He?"

"Please allow me to let you in on a secret that should have never become a secret. There is nothing you can do to make God love you more and nothing you can do to make Him love you any less. He loves you as you are, Michael, and not as you should be."

"How?"

"Because He is God, and God is love. His love is so great, that He sent His only Son to die for you."

"Not for me, Father. I know enough about the Bible, John 3:16, to know that He did it for *everyone* in the world."

"True, but look at it this way though. Even if you were the only person in the world, He still would have died for you. You

233

are valuable in His eyes."

Michael sat still and quietly pondered what the priest had said.

"Are you able to stand?"

Michael put his feet down on the ground and was able to get himself up this time with the assistance of the priest.

"Yeah, I can make it, but not too far."

"We're just a couple blocks away from my church. We have a shower there that you can use, and then we'll grab some breakfast and coffee."

"You're a very understanding guy, Father."

"I'm a recovering alcoholic myself."

Michael couldn't conceal his genuine shock, and the priest shared his testimony with him as they walked together to the church.

Following his shower, Michael changed into a clean set of clothes given to him by the priest, and the two men sat down and shared breakfast together. Michael was nearly sober, and the light returned to his eyes.

"Do you believe in God?" the priest asked.

"I went to my grandpa's church every summer when I was a kid."

"I didn't ask you how you spent your summers as a child. I asked if you believe in God."

"I did...I do."

The priest nodded.

"I guess I gave up on God. If you would have asked me yesterday, I would have said that God gave up on me."

"You took your eyes off of Him," the priest said.

"What?"

"It's not at all uncommon. There are many in the Bible who did this, including Peter."

"You mean when he said he didn't know Jesus?"

234

"No. That was a matter of denial. Peter took his eyes off the Lord when he got out of the boat and started to walk on water. Sound familiar?"

"Yeah, I remember that. I just wasn't sure where you were going with it. He took his eyes off the Lord, and he started to sink in the water and he was about to drown."

"Michael, I listened to your testimony today, and it seems to me that you need to get rid of everything that is causing you to take your eyes off the Lord. Anything that causes you to do this needs to be cut out of your life."

"That's *a lot* to give up. I don't know if I can do it."

"I not only think you can, but I think you must. You won't be alone. God is with you. You should also make a point to find a person to hold you accountable during this time of rehabilitation."

"How about you?"

The priest shook his head. "You need to leave Vegas. I'm here for the long haul, my friend. There are many here who need Jesus. My work isn't done with you."

"I could go back to Columbus and finish college."

"Speaking as someone who had to fight similar addictions, I'd suggest going to your home church. Find someone there to be an accountability partner who can help you, and get involved with the church serving others instead of yourself. Also, you need to get into a rehabilitation program, like Alcoholics Anonymous."

"I think I might return home to Canton first and go back to church. Maybe try to find some work in the church," Michael said. "I cannot believe that I'm about to drop *everything* to follow Jesus."

"You're not the first one to do so. Actually, the first Christians did just that. Go and live up to your name, Michael.

235

But do so because you love God so much that you want to change and not because you think He'll love you more if you do change. Never forget that what Jesus did for you on the cross is sufficient."

"Thank you so very much for everything you have said and done."

"You're welcome, young man."

"By the way, what is your name?" Michael asked.

"My name is Michael," said the priest with a smile.

* * *

"There are a few dozen good proofs for the existence of God, but there is only one good proof against the existence of God, which is the argument for evil. I must admit that evil counts against God. However, if there are a couple dozen arguments that prove Him and only one that disproves, than the preponderance of evidence is on His side," said Dr. Casper.

"St. Augustine once summarized the case for and against God in two simple sentences. If there is no God, why is there good? If there is God, why is there evil? The answer to the second question, ladies and gentlemen, is a mirror. Evil is not a part of God's design, but rather, it comes from human selfishness. The origin of evil is not God, but people freely choosing sin and selfishness. Why? Not to sound glib, but we're nuts!"

The crowd chuckled at Dr. Casper's assessment.

"That's one of the meanings of what we call the doctrine of original sin. We're morally insane. However, we are also deeply sane. There's a little good in the worst of us, and a little bad in the best of us. In other words, we're human."

Rocky nodded in agreement.

236

"The worst aspect of the problem of evil is eternal evil, hell," said Dr. Casper. "Many would argue that hell contradicts a loving and omnipotent God. However, hell is the consequence of freewill. People freely choose hell for themselves; God does not cast anyone into hell against his or her will. If a person is really free to say yes to God's offer of love and spiritual marriage, then it must be possible for a person to also say no. Essentially, that is what hell is. Freewill, in turn, was created out of God's love for us. Therefore, as bizarre as it may sound, hell is a result of God's love. No sane person wants hell to exist. For that matter, no sane person wants evil to exist either. But hell is just evil eternalized. If there is evil and if there is eternity, there can be hell."

Dr. Casper looked over the audience, sensing that he may want to sum up his argument.

"The solution to evil is what Jesus did on the cross. According to the Gospels, one need only repent, believe, and seek to live a life following His commandments. It's grace that frees us, and it is truly free.

"In conclusion, ladies and gentlemen, it doesn't matter into what area of science or field of study you enter. Eventually, you will discover that there is overwhelming evidence for the God of the Bible. God promised that all who seek shall find, and He provided just enough evidence of Himself for any honest seeker.

"An atheist, however, is a person who makes the bold assertion that there is no God. I say bold because an atheist claims in an absolute manner what even Dr. Johnson believes can't be done: to prove the existence or non-existence of God. In order to make such an assertion, an atheist would have to be God Himself. In order to come to such a *dogmatic* conclusion about the non-existence of God, one would need to possess the qualities of God to confirm this belief. Even the most brilliant and widely traveled people living today could not possibly know 1/1000th of all that *could* be known. Keep in mind, ladies and gentlemen, that knowledge is now *doubling* by the years rather than by decades or centuries! Is it possible that God could very well exist outside this very limited experience of one highly intelligent human being? By *faith*, the atheist, our friend says, 'No.'

"I will close by quoting James Russell Lowell who stated, 'I challenge any skeptic to find a ten square mile spot on this planet where they can live their lives in peace and safety and decency, where womanhood is honored, where infancy and old age are revered, where they can educate their children, where the Gospel of Jesus Christ has not gone first to prepare the way. If they find such a place, then I would encourage them to emigrate [there and] proclaim their unbelief.'"

* * *

Dr. Johnson strutted up to the podium and adjusted the microphone, as Dr. Casper was nearly one foot taller than her.

"Dr. Casper's defense against evil can be easily summed up as a consequence of the Fall; and the amount of evil contained in this world is the best possible way a loving God has of persuading humans to desire His Kingdom to come to earth. I have already successfully criticized the Fall defense, fully anticipating that he would use it, because it's such a damning argument to the existence of God. Why, ladies and gentlemen, should people be persuaded to desire God's Kingdom by the existence of seemingly pointless suffering and needless premature death? I find myself in agreement with Dr. Casper, that one of the greatest obstacles to accepting God's existence is the existence of evil.

238

"Dr. Casper wants you to believe in God's design of the universe. He argued that the universe is *so* complex that it must have had a designer. He implicitly argues that, if you look long enough, you will find that there was a 'Watchmaker.' However, if you listen to what science has been saying for the last 100 years, there may be reason to believe that a watch has a watchmaker, but there is nothing to demonstrate a conscious intelligent designer of the universe. Please note that I am indeed acknowledging that the world had been 'designed.' However, I believe that natural selection, not God, should be credited. So, in this case, biological evolution is definitely a designer. But it is an unconscious designer. Evolution as a designer works mechanically. So we do agree that there is a designer. The question that remains is who or what is the designer?"

Rocky squirmed in his seat.

"One of Darwin's best arguments against the theistic position that Dr. Casper espouses was that if you really look closely at the world—and you don't even have to look that closely—you'll find out that it is not perfect at all, and therefore you can question to what extent it actually reflects a designer. For example, the so-called perfection of human beings must be questioned, as they have what can be best described as a bizarre eye structure. The eye used to be a favorite example of theists. They argued that it's the kind of structure that you really cannot explain except by design. Well, it is pretty poorly designed because we have blood vessels right in front of our retina, which means that under certain light conditions we see these funny little things flying all over the place across the visual field. Well, that's certainly not a good design. Besides that, there are organisms that are better designed. For example, squids have their blood vessels in the back of their eyes, so they actually see much better than we do. So my question to you, my good and dear friend, Dr. Casper, is

239

why are squid eyes better designed than human beings'?"

Rocky's memories of Vegas triggered thoughts of his time spent with his mentor, friend, and accountability partner, Pastor Bob. Father Mike had reintroduced God back into his life, and Pastor Bob really opened the doors for Rocky to love and serve others. Rocky's life changed when he was loved, and it grew as he loved others.

* * *

Michael drove up to the church. He was really happy to see that the building project, which more than tripled the size of the church, was nearly done. He was excited by the youth center especially, which offered young people a place to play basketball, tennis, swimming, and a variety of other sports to keep them fit and out of trouble.

He walked inside and knocked on Pastor Bob's door. Bob's door, as well as his heart, was open to everyone, especially Michael. Michael had been quite a blessing to the church. He came home rather suddenly, and, upon hearing his testimony and history in Vegas, Pastor Bob took him in. He quickly developed into his mentor, as well as serving as his accountability partner, and soon they became best friends. Michael's faith in God had grown greatly. Although he had a foundation for belief built by his grandfather, years of neglect tore down much of that structure. Bob spent a great deal of time with him, and Michael responded like a musical prodigy hearing Mozart for the first time. He studied and read all he could, but mostly, he sought opportunities to serve. He strived to serve those neglected by society, such as the elderly, sick, homeless, and developmentally disabled.

Despite all that Michael had brought to this church, Pastor

240

Bob was not surprised to learn of some jealousy within his flock. Bob knew that it was possible for a new believer to be far more grown up in the Lord than someone who has been saved for 50 years. Someone who has been a Christian for many years can still be spiritually immature. He was reminded of D.L. Moody, who, as a new convert, developed a hunger for God's Word and spent an incredible amount of time reading it. He was so willing and eager to obey it that he became a "menace" to some believers as his rapid spiritual growth embarrassed those who had been saved for years but never matured in Christ. Moody would share a new experience he had with the Lord every week, which finally drove the older saints, who felt humiliated by Moody's exemplary life, to speak to his uncle, with the hopes of quieting down his nephew. Though Michael didn't cause such extreme emotions to develop, like Moody, his vigorous spiritual health and eagerness to serve disturbed the napping of many older but spiritually immature Christians. While they were sucking their proverbial thumbs, Michael, like Moody, grew until he left them far behind. Pastor Bob marveled at how Michael grew more in just a couple years than others had in thirty.

"Bob! How are you doing?" said Michael.

"I'm doing well, my friend. What can I do for you today?"

"Actually, Bob, I came in to see what I could do for you today. I am off work today and wanted to see if I was needed anywhere."

Bob smiled. This request would have caught him off guard prior to Michael's arrival, but now he was always ready with an answer.

"I'm glad you asked. The deacons are short staffed today and could use your help in delivering food to shut-ins."

"Shut-ins?"

"Yeah, folks who can't get out for whatever reason. Perhaps

they're elderly, bedridden, sick, poor, disabled, and so on. Basically, you'll just arrive and drop off food for them. It's a nice service provided by the members of this church."

"Great. I'm in."

"Just meet with the deacons downstairs, and they'll give you your assignment."

Michael met with the deacons, who were thrilled to see him, not only because he was an extra person to help lighten the load, but also for all that he had contributed to the church. They gave him food to be delivered to Ryan Callender, a 34-year-old man in a life and death struggle with AIDS.

He finally arrived at Ryan's house after a few wrong turns. He took the food out of the back of his car and walked up the sidewalk to the front door. He knocked on the door and heard a distant voice say either "coming" or "come in." After waiting a moment, he figured that he must have heard the latter.

He walked into the home, which was decorated in rare antiques. The history buff in Michael was in awe.

"You must be a new guy," he heard a seemingly disembodied voice say.

"Ryan?"

"It's okay, you don't have to come in any further. Just leave it on the table and you can leave."

"Where are you? Are you okay?"

"I'm fine, thanks. I just wanted to give you a chance to get out without creating an awkward moment."

"Why would it be awkward? There's a lot of food here. I figured…okay, *hoped*, that you might need some help eating it."

Ryan stepped out from around a corner to see with whom he was talking.

"Hi, my name is Michael."

"Didn't they tell you? I'm HIV-positive."

"Yeah, I know. I'm really sorry to hear that," Michael said as he sat down.

"You can leave. It's quite all right. I understand, okay?"

"I really don't have any place to go right now. If you want me to leave, I will. However, I can stay for as long as you'd like."

Ryan walked closer, looked at the food, and then replied, "There is a lot of food here. It would be a shame to waste it."

"Then it's settled! I'll stay."

"Great," said Ryan who was still unsure what to make of his guest. "I was going to watch a Fred Astaire movie, if you don't mind."

"I don't mind at all. Fred's a genius, though Gene Kelly is my favorite."

"Fred's better, you know," Ryan said.

"Oh, really? Are you an expert?"

"Yeah, in fact I am. I have been a dancer for as long as I could walk. I've danced in New York, Washington, Chicago, and a few times on the west coast."

"Wow, that's impressive. However, I still like Gene Kelly better."

"Why is that?"

"It's nothing against Fred. Technically speaking, he may have actually been better than Gene in certain styles, though I think their styles are definitely unique, so it's hard to compare the ballroom style of Astaire with the street hoofer skills of Kelly."

"I can't argue with that."

"I always liked the classic films," Michael said. "For several years, James Dean was my favorite, because I related to him so much, and not in a good way. I sometimes felt like the misunderstood and unloved characters that he often times played."

"Often times? He was in *three* films, Mike."

"Yeah, I guess so." Michael chuckled. "Anyway, Gene's films are so much fun, and he's always smiling. He sings and dances in the rain, for goodness' sake. What a wonderful character!"

"You're an optimist, I see."

"Sure, why not?" Michael replied as he started to eat a roast beef sandwich.

"I used to be…until I was hit with this disease. I was extremely popular, always out with people, and loved by audiences wherever I performed."

"It's pretty lonely here, isn't it?"

"It is. No one comes to visit, and even the deacons from the church who are kind enough to deliver this food, never really stop to talk."

Michael nodded.

"I cannot even remember the last time I was physically touched by another human being. Even my doctors wear latex gloves, and the most contact they give me is with medical instruments."

Michael got up, walked over to Ryan, and gave him a strong hug. When he released his embrace, he found Ryan crying.

"Thanks, Mike," Ryan said, trying to compose himself. "I was beginning to wonder if I was even human anymore. Thank you. I have been reading the Bible the church gave to me and began to question if it was really true, since no one seemed to really show the love that Christ taught, and He hung out with lepers!"

"You're not a leper, Ryan."

"No, but I might as well be. Thank you for being different. You are a good man."

"I'm not good. I only seek to be Christ-like. I fall just as short as everyone else. If you knew me a couple of years ago, you'd be disappointed."

"No. I don't know what you did, or think you did, but even if

244

it were that bad, you're still a living testimony of what Jesus can do in a person's life. I know that I have a death sentence, and I have accepted that with confidence because I know Jesus, but I sometimes feel like I'm already dead to the world. Promise me that you'll come back and visit."

"I will. In fact, we can even take turns watching Fred and Gene movies."

"I'd like that," Ryan smiled.

*   *   *

Rocky looked up and saw that Dr. Johnson was nearing the end of her long talk.

"Dr. Casper has said repeatedly that the universe has a cause, and it has a beginning. This may very well be true, but I must qualify this statement by acknowledging that astronomers change their minds on matters such as this in every generation. Put bluntly, I wouldn't bet my life on this, but let's assume for the sake of argument that the universe had a beginning and, in fact, had some sort of cause. That does not necessarily imply that the cause was what we commonly refer to as God. It only means that there was some kind of cause that is still a mystery to us. There is nothing that dictates that the cause was conscious and had supernatural powers. So perhaps, there is a cause to the universe. Dr. Casper insists that it must therefore be a personal agent, but where did this agent come from? Why does he believe it to be personal rather than impersonal? In terms of our science, I don't think that we're that far from each other, as many scientists believe that there must have been a cause and that the cause was more than likely impersonal. I just disagree with your assessment that the cause is God. Again, going back to my opening statement, ladies and gentlemen, Dr. Casper has pulled the legs off the proverbial grasshopper in this debate and has come to the wrong conclusion. There isn't a God, and more than likely, there never was a God."

Dr. Johnson then sat down.

The emcee for the night, Dr. Paul Williams, approached the podium.

"I would like to thank both Dr. Johnson and Dr. Casper for their thoughtful participation here tonight. I'd like to remind you, though, that the night is not over yet. It is now time for the really interesting and fun part of the night, questions for our speakers. Please stand in line at the microphone on the floor and wait until you are called upon. You may address both speakers or choose to direct your question to either Dr. Casper or Dr. Johnson."

A Harvard student walked to the microphone and asked, "Dr. Casper, I have been to many of these debates discussing the existence of God. Doesn't this contradict the Christian faith?

Dr. Casper got up and approached the microphone to reply. "No, of course not. The faith held by Christians is a response to divine revelation, which means that God Himself told us about Him. He also teaches us about Him through *reason* and faith, or nature and the Bible, if you will. God, the Teacher, cannot contradict Himself, just as truth cannot contradict truth. Therefore, logically speaking, reason cannot contradict faith."

A middle-aged man from the audience spoke into the microphone, "Dr. Casper, if God is omni-benevolent, why did He create a world full of people with the hopes that they will love and worship Him? Isn't this a bit conceited, if not selfish?"

"That's an odd question. That would be like asking me, 'Professor Casper, you are a good and unselfish parent. Why then have you had three children who you have lavished such time, attention, money, and energy on all your life? Aren't you conceited or selfish?' That's a very peculiar question indeed."

The crowd enjoyed Dr. Casper's wit and sense of humor, laughing at his response.

An Easton Theological Seminary student approached the microphone. "Dr. Johnson, Dr. Casper acknowledged Einstein's support of a created and designed universe. You had no reply in your last statement. Do you deny this?"

Dr. Johnson quickly went to the podium and replied, "I will not deny that Einstein was a great physicist, but he was human and capable of error. In the judgment of the vast majority of physicists, he was indeed mistaken in this case."

Another Harvard student approached to ask a question. "Dr. Casper, if someone proved logically that God doesn't exist, would you forsake your Christian faith? Or would you have faith that the reasoning was somehow flawed?"

Dr. Casper got up and replied, "Your question has a self-contradiction built into it. If someone proved logically that God doesn't really exist, and there is nothing wrong with the proof, as well as no ambiguous term, no false premise, and no logical fallacies, then they *proved* that God doesn't exist. It stands to reason that if they prove that God doesn't exist validly, then God *doesn't* exist. Consequently, since Christianity does teach that God exists, Christianity would then be proved false. So how can anyone then have faith that the reasoning was somehow flawed? If someone proves it logically, that means that the reasoning is not flawed. If the reasoning is flawed, then they haven't proven it logically, they've only seemed to. I'd suggest taking Dr. Johnson's philosophy course next semester if you need further help with the concept of logic and proofs."

"I am one of her students," he said.

"Oh, well, then you can transfer here to Easton," Dr. Casper joked.

"Dr. Johnson, does not Jesus Christ counter your claims?" an elderly woman asked.

Dr. Johnson got up and answered, "According to Roman documents of the time, Jesus was just one among many that told people that he was a prophet and doing miracles. There were a bunch of them running around. He was just one of many. He was probably a particularly gifted one, and that's why his particular brand of religion eventually succeeded in the world. However, there were many, so why think that that particular one was special? Just because, by some historical accident, it happened to be one of the most successful world religions? As it pertains to His miracles, we can find a bunch of people who claimed to make miracles, who claimed to be prophets throughout history, including today. I think you can get the address and send e-mail to people who claim to be prophets and miracle makers. Would you believe them? Well, I don't. Not without seeing something in person myself. Of course, there are those who claim to have seen miracles in person, but then again people also claim to have been abducted by aliens or to have seen fairies around. Incidentally, even though I don't believe in UFOs and alien abductions, I think that those are much more credible than miracles."

One of Dr. Johnson's colleagues directed a question to Dr. Casper. "It seems to me that the universe must be the way it is, to be so finely tuned that is, for if it weren't, there wouldn't be any observers around to observe. So we can be shocked and amazed at the probabilities you cited, but the fact remains that it is necessarily the way it is for us to be here and to be amazed at the probabilities. And if it's necessarily so, that doesn't explain anything at all about the causality of the universe."

Dr. Casper walked to the microphone at the podium and replied, "The fallacy in that argument was first exposed by

248

Richard Swinburne a number of years ago. The analogy he developed is simple. You've been convicted of murder, and the penalty for murder is death by a firing squad. You are then blindfolded and taken out to the backcourt, and sixteen sharpshooters aim their rifles at your heart and pull their triggers, yet you survive the event. One conclusion that you could draw is, of course you survived the event; you wouldn't be here unless they all missed. Richard Swinburne's point is that this would not be the *first* response from an individual surviving such an event. He argues that your initial response would be that someone *purposed* that you be alive. Either these sixteen individuals purposely aimed away from your heart, or someone loaded their guns with blanks. That's the response you would get from the evidence, not, 'Well, golly, I wouldn't be here unless they all missed anyway, and so, let's move on with life.' No, there's a deeper question at stake."

Rocky was now at the front of the line, ready to ask a question. Bulbs from cameras were flashing throughout the room, and everyone's attention was now on Rocky.

"Dr. Johnson, you're a scholar…a scientist. I argue that the Christian faith is verifiable in the laboratory of one's life. God promises that all who seek shall find. It's a Biblical promise. You don't find Him by simply talking about Him, but you must talk to Him. If He does exists, and the Bible is His Word, then He wants to reveal Himself to us."

"Could you please get to your question," said Dr. Johnson.

"It's more of a challenge really, rather than a question. If you are an honest and sincere scientist, truly seeking to know God, then I'd suggest utilizing the scientific method in a relevant experiment, just as you would for any other study. Pray to Him, be honest, and admit that you are a skeptic, but sincerely seek Him and pray that He reveals Himself in His time and in His way. If Christianity is indeed true, He will. This prayer constitutes a scientifically fair test of the Christian hypothesis, as long as you remember that He will work on His own time and in His own way."

The room started to fill with sounds of laughter and snickering among the Harvard students.

"You're Rocky Raccoon, right?"

Rocky nodded.

"If they were going to name you after a Beatles song, they should have chosen the *Fool on the Hill.*"

Segments of the audience laughed out loud.

"There is a serious problem with the 'scientific' experiment you propose," said Dr. Johnson. "Suppose I actually do try this experiment and nothing happens right away. How long should I wait until I may conclude that the experiment has failed to reveal the existence of God? If nothing happens, am I to assume that God does not exist or that God simply hasn't gotten around to answering me yet? This idea is preposterous and naïve. If I do it, I'll be sure to ask God to give me some clear sign, like making a large deposit in my name at a Swiss bank!"

The audience again laughed along with her, but Rocky never even flinched. He simply smiled and nodded at her and went back to his seat in the midst of laughter on one side and an awkward silence by those sitting in the Easton side.

The Messenger

Rocky's room was pitch black. The residents of Tuttle Hall and many of Rocky's friends were apprehensive about visiting him. They discussed among themselves how he was humiliated in front of all of his peers as well as an international television audience.

Simon walked into Tuttle Hall and found its residents gathered together in the common room. The general consensus was that Dr. Casper had won a tough debate, but their hearts grieved for Rocky.

"She was out of line," said Steven. "It's one thing to be arrogant, if not belligerent with Dr. Casper. He's a peer. But to attack a member of the audience is reprehensible."

"She had a point, Steven," said Simon as he took a seat.

"What? You agree with what she said to Rocky?" Steven asked.

"I don't agree with the personal slam about *The Fool on the Hill*. That was a cheap shot and completely beneath someone of her character and reputation."

"What do you agree with then?" Rick asked.

"I understand the point Rocky was *trying* to make, but it was

251

poor science and she called him on it. What's she supposed to do? Wait for God to get back to her in forty years, since that's 'His time'? I appreciate Rocky's faithfulness that God does reach out to all who seek Him, but to ask someone to apply the scientific method to God is a little out there, even for our lovably unorthodox friend."

"Maybe Simon's right, guys," Jim said.

"How's that?" Chip replied.

"I do believe the biblical promise that all who seek shall find, but what Rocky said is demanding God to act now and not in His own way and time," said Jim.

"Rocky clearly stated that it would be in His time, not Dr. Johnson's," Rick said.

"This reminds me of a joke, or a modern day parable, if you will," Jim said. "Little Matt was lying in the middle of a meadow on a warm spring day. Soon, he began to think about God. 'God? Are you really there?' Matt said out loud. To his astonishment a voice came from the clouds. 'Yes, Matt? What can I do for you?'

Seizing the opportunity, Matt asked, 'God? What is a million years like to you?'

Knowing that Matt could not understand the concept of infinity, God responded in a manner to which Matt could relate, 'A million years to me, Matt, is like a minute.' 'Oh,' said Matt. 'Well, then, what's a million dollars like to you?' 'A million dollars to me, Matt, is like a penny.' 'Wow!' remarked Matt, getting an idea. 'You're so generous...can I have one of your pennies?' God replied, 'Sure thing, Matt! Just a minute.'"

"That's an old joke, Jim. Just to warn you, most of your congregation will have already heard that one," said Steven. "I see your point though."

"I almost hate to ask, but how is Tom reacting to all of this?"

Rick asked.

"Not to gossip," Simon prefaced, clearly about to do so anyway, "but I saw him walk out with some of my Cambridge colleagues. He seemed, shall we say, in good spirits."

"Just whose side is he really on?" Jim asked.

"His own," Chip replied.

"So, has anyone gone up to talk to Rocky?" Simon asked.

No one answered, but their faces indicated that they were giving Rocky some space.

Simon got up.

"Where are you going?" Steven asked.

"I'm going to go visit Rocky."

* * *

Dr. Johnson was driving back to Cambridge down historic Route 128. She was transporting five of her philosophy students back to Harvard in her Honda Odyssey minivan, which was usually reserved for her preteen twins, Emma and Jonathan. The mood on the ride home was jovial, with play-by-play recaps of the debate. They were in hysterics about the "great" Rocky Raccoon, and one of the philosophers, in the same vein as Nietzsche, declared that the Rocky Raccoon Revival was dead.

Dr. Johnson was happy that her students were so ecstatic, but she was noticeably silent. One of her more thoughtful students cared enough to ask if she was all right.

"I am. I'm sorry for being a killjoy. It's just that my mother is in a nursing home at the next exit," she confided to her student.

"Why don't you stop by for a quick visit? I'm sure your mom would love that!" Allison suggested to the dismay of her friends in the back who all wanted to go home and celebrate.

"It wouldn't do much good, Allison. She's suffered through

253

many strokes and is an invalid. She has severe brain damage and probably wouldn't even know that I was there."

"Then it will be a short visit," Allison answered. "When's the last time you came up here for a visit?"

"Back around Christmas. It kills me to see her for too long."

"I think you should go then. I don't think anyone back here will mind," she said as she glanced back at everyone daring them to object at their own risk.

"No one minds?" Dr. Johnson asked as she looked back at her students in the rearview mirror.

They collectively replied that they didn't mind, and Dr. Johnson exited off Route 128.

* * *

Simon slowly walked up to the second floor to visit Rocky. He wasn't entirely sure that he was doing the right thing but he knew that if their positions were reversed Rocky would be there for him.

He approached Rocky's door and noticed that there were no lights on. He knocked lightly on the door and waited. Nothing. Not a sound. He knocked again, and this time he heard the rustling sound of someone moving inside the room. Rocky opened the door and was met by the blinding hallway lights, causing him to put his hand up over his eyes just so he could glimpse at who was knocking at his door.

"Oh, hi, Simon."

"Hey, Rock. How are you doing?"

"Never been better. It's been a great night!"

"Really? You think so?"

"Of course it was. I was so wrong about tonight. It was a great idea. Dr. Casper was awesome."

"Yes, he was, but...what about your confrontation with Dr. Johnson?"

"Confrontation?" Rocky laughed. "I wouldn't call it that. Truth be told, Simon, I was going to go up and ask a dumb question regarding her observations on the difference between human and squid eyes. Thank God I didn't!"

"What made you change your mind?"

"I suddenly felt strangely moved to say what I said. It was as surprising and new to me as it was to everyone else, but that's how the Spirit moves. I really think people will try it. I don't think people are atheists because they tested Christianity through research, study, and prayer. They're atheists because they *want* to be, perhaps to avoid guilt. Anyway, I've been here praying since the debate that people would be moved tonight; perhaps for reasons they may not entirely know or understand, to seek God. Especially Dr. Johnson."

"Even though she insulted you?"

"Insulted? Oh, the whole *Fool On the Hill* thing? I was surprised she knew that song. It's not one of their biggies. She must be a fan," he said with a grin. "I didn't take it personally. I knew that what I was saying might sound crazy, and that people might react the same way they did to the Gospel the first time Jesus preached it. No blood, no foul. Right?"

"Very well then," Simon said. "I guess I didn't look at it that way. My pride would have gotten in the way."

"I left my pride in a gutter in Las Vegas and have never looked back."

"May I pray with you?"

"Yeah, that would be great."

Rocky lit a couple of candles, and the two spent time together praying for God to reveal Himself to those who seek His face.

255

* * *

"Great Compassion Nursing Home? Really? Your mom is a resident of a *Christian* nursing home? Now, that's ironic," said one of Dr. Johnson's students.

"This is one of the most respected nursing homes in the state, and the fact that it's a Christian nursing home gives me a little peace of mind, okay?"

"Sorry, Dr. Johnson. I didn't mean anything by it."

"It's all right. I didn't mean to jump down your throat. It's just that I love my mother, and I wanted her to receive the best care. Though Christian scholarship is not up to secular standards, they do tend to exceed the world's standards in compassion."

Dr. Johnson parked the van and then turned around to her students. "I won't be here too long, and you certainly don't have to come in. I can leave the radio on or even play a video for you if you don't mind cartoons."

The students chose to stay in the car, though Allison felt compelled to accompany Dr. Johnson since it was her prodding that prompted the visit.

"Good evening," the charge nurse greeted Dr. Johnson. "I saw you on the TV tonight."

Dr. Johnson could only offer a nod and a half smile in response.

"There's no rush, ladies, but visiting hours are almost over. Given your mother's condition, I don't think it would hurt anyone if you stayed a little later."

"Thank you, but we won't be here long," said Dr. Johnson.

"Well, you know where the room is. It's nice seeing you again, Mrs. Johnson."

Allison's ears hurt upon hearing her mentor called *Mrs.*

Johnson instead of by her professional title.

They entered the room, and Dr. Johnson walked up to her mother while Allison sat down in a chair.

"Hi, Mom. It's me, Loni. Just wanted to stop in and say 'hi.'"

Her mother was silent, comfortably lying in her bed.

"I was on television tonight. Jerry recorded it. If you want, I will bring it in next time I visit."

Her mother remained still. She hadn't spoken a coherent word in about four years, and Dr. Johnson doubted if her mom even understood what she was saying. However, she talked just in case her mom could hear her.

"I brought one of my students with me, Allison."

"Hi, Mrs. Hindman. It's nice to finally meet you."

Mrs. Hindman was stone faced. She was no longer a part of this world.

"Well, Allison, I guess we should leave. Thank you for suggesting we stop by. I do miss her, and even though she and I can't talk, it's still nice to see her. She was a great mother to me. She encouraged me to pursue education back when other girls my age were discouraged from it."

"She sounds like a great woman."

"She was," Dr. Johnson said with a sigh. "Could you give me a moment alone with her, Allison?"

"Of course, Professor."

Allison left the room and waited just outside the door. Dr. Johnson walked back over to her mother. She laid her head gently on her mom's chest.

She looked up on the wall and saw a small painting of Jesus with a cross hanging above it. She started to think about what Rocky said earlier that night, and her eyes rolled up into her head.

"God, Loni Johnson here. Look, I'm sorry, but I have a hard

257

time believing in You. If You exist, You made me this way, so You should understand. If You don't exist, then I imagine that I'm just talking to my subconscious. I'm sorry. I'm not one to pray, so maybe I'm screwing this all up. Do You exist? If You do, I certainly would want to know You. I want to not only know about You, but I want to know that my mom will be happy, or is happy. I know that if Rocky is right, You'll reply in Your own time and in Your own way, but I beg of You. Please don't take too long. I just need to know. Please."

She raised her head and looked back at her mother, who still hadn't moved. She got up and started to walk toward the door. She then turned around and said, "Good night, Mom, I love you."

As she was about to walk through the door, she heard a voice.

Dr. Johnson turned around, realizing that her mother was quietly speaking. She paused for a moment and started to talk again, though Dr. Johnson could not understand what she was saying. She quickly called for Allison who ran right into the room.

Dr. Johnson then rushed to her bedside and asked her, "Mama, who are you talking to?"

To Dr. Johnson's astonishment, her mom replied, "I'm talking to your little girl!"

Mrs. Hindman was still lying in bed but was now peacefully looking at her paralyzed left arm.

"Isn't she beautiful, Loni?"

"What little girl? Emma?" Dr. Johnson asked.

"No, Loni. Your *other* little girl, Theresa."

Dr. Johnson stumbled backward till she found a seat to sit in.

"What's wrong," Allison asked. "Who's Theresa? What's she talking about?"

Dr. Johnson put her head between her knees, took in a couple of deep breaths, and then her now pale-face looked up at Allison.

"Jerry and I have twins as you know; Emma and Jonathan. However, we had twins before Emma and Jonathan. They were born prematurely and didn't survive. Theresa lived only through the night, and her brother James was stillborn," Dr. Johnson said as she began to cry.

"How did she ever remember this?" Allison asked. "It's been years since then?"

Mrs. Hindman was still talking about Theresa and telling Dr. Johnson just how beautiful she is.

"Mama, where is she?"

"Loni," she said, "she's right here! Don't you see her? The angel brought her to me."

Mrs. Hindman's eyes were focused still at her left arm, as if little Theresa was lying right there in her arm.

"I don't see her. What does she look like?"

"She's so beautiful, Loni!" she said as she still concentrated on her left arm. "She has a bright smile on her face and has light brown hair to her shoulders with bangs."

Dr. Johnson sat next to her mother's bed, crying uncontrollably. Her mom was now apparently listening to Theresa and then she smiled.

"Mama, what did she say to you?"

Her mother looked at Loni with the sweetest smile and said, "She told me 'I love to come see you, Grandma.'"

Just then her mother's eyes went from looking at her left arm to looking at the ceiling.

"Look! The angel is coming!"

Mrs. Hindman's eyes went from her left arm and then slowly drifted up again toward the ceiling.

259

"See, Loni? The angel came and took her by the hand, and now they are going."

Dr. Johnson, who was looking at the ceiling, looked back at her mother and found that her mother had immediately returned to her invalid state of mind.

"Mama? Mama? Please answer me, Mama!"

Allison sat still, completely amazed at what she just witnessed.

"I can't believe this," was all Allison could utter.

The charge nurse rushed in to see if everything was okay, and Dr. Johnson proceeded to tell her what just happened.

"Praise God! You have just had yourself a miracle, Mrs. Johnson."

Dr. Johnson was almost in shock. She looked up at the nurse who was grinning from ear to ear. She then looked over at Allison.

"We need to go *back* to Easton. I need to talk to Rocky Raccoon!"

"Can it wait till tomorrow? I think the others want to go home. Rocky may not even be in right now," Allison replied.

"No, I *have* to talk to him *now!*"

*　*　*

Adam and Simon had left for the evening, and many of the Tuttle Hall residents were now in their rooms studying, watching TV, or turning in early for the night. Rocky continued to pray.

Jim was sitting in his rocking chair reading Karl Barth when he thought he had heard the hallway bell. The hallway bells were little hand bells hanging on a string attached to the wall by every entrance into Tuttle Hall. When a female visitor entered the men's dorm, she would ring the bell to alert the residents to her presence on the floor. Jim and others started to peek out of their

260

rooms to see who had a guest at this time of night.

Steven opened his door and found Dr. Illona Johnson and five of her students standing right in front of him. Steven, who was wearing boxers and a t-shirt, stood there stunned.

"Please excuse us, but which room is Rocky Raccoon's?" Dr. Johnson asked.

Steven couldn't speak, he simply pointed to the next room.

"Thank you, young man."

Steven managed to nod in return.

Dr. Johnson walked to Rocky's door and knocked.

Rocky opened his door to find Dr. Johnson and her ragtag band.

"Good evening, Dr. Johnson."

"You're not surprised to see me, are you?"

"Not really. I just figured that it would take a couple of days before you tried my little experiment."

"How did you know, Rocky?"

"All who seek God find Him, Doctor. I was just prayerful that God would reveal Himself to you sooner than later. In fact, Simon and I were praying all night for you."

"Your prayers *were* answered," she announced to him and to all within earshot, which was now all of the residents of Tuttle Hall, as they wanted to know what the infamous Dr. Johnson wanted with Rocky.

"What happened?" Rocky asked.

She went into detail for everyone to hear. She explained her mother's medical condition and how she hadn't spoken in years because of her strokes and subsequent brain damage. She told them about her first twins who didn't survive and her mother's description of the angel who delivered her first baby daughter to her mother. After she went through all the details, with Allison corroborating her testimony, she started to cry uncontrollably.

Rocky had seen many people who had seen the light, but these weren't the usual tears of joy that he had grown pleasantly accustomed to seeing.

"What's wrong, Dr. Johnson?"

"I felt such joy and comfort, hearing about my little girl, Rocky, and of course, discovering that God does exist," she said. "But..."

"But what?"

"But, I immediately began to wonder about my boy, James. Theresa lived through the night, but James was stillborn and never breathed once. I just can't believe that my little boy would have just been a throw-away. I was happy to hear about Theresa, but saddened about James. That's why I came here. I *have* to know, Rocky. Is my little boy in heaven with Theresa?"

Rocky stood quiet in a crowd of people waiting for his response.

"Dr. Johnson, I think we should go back to the nursing home and visit your mother."

"But visiting hours are over."

"I think we'll be okay there," he said. "First, though, I think we should all pray. Please, hold hands with your neighbor and pray with me."

Every resident of Tuttle Hall, along with Dr. Johnson and her Harvard students, prayed with Rocky regarding her first baby boy, James.

Following the prayer, Rocky excused himself for a moment to get dressed. Dr. Johnson's students were no longer in a hurry, as they were just as amazed as she was.

Word quickly spread throughout the seminary, as phone calls were made, and students were running throughout the seminary with news of the impossible. Dr. Casper received a call, and word even reached Tom and Martin's dorm within minutes.

262

THE ROCKY RACCOON REVIVAL

Rocky drove Dr. Johnson back to Great Compassion Nursing Home, and Allison drove her fellow students back to Harvard in Dr. Johnson's van.

* * *

Dr. Johnson walked through the front door of the nursing home and was greeted by the charge nurse.

"I'm sorry, Mrs. Johnson, but visiting hours are definitely over now."

Rocky walked in behind Dr. Johnson and said, "Nurse Millie! It's good to see you!"

"Rocky Raccoon! Why on earth are you here so late tonight?"

"You two know each other?" Dr. Johnson asked.

"Do I know him? He's my favorite visitor. He's always here to spend time with the residents. He talks to them, sings to them, but mostly he listens to them and prays with them. He's *always* welcome here, ma'am."

"Millie, we're here to see Mrs. Hindman. We'll be quiet, I promise."

"That's fine. We're all very excited about what happened earlier. She hasn't moved a muscle since, but we know that what God did here tonight was a miracle."

"It sure was," said Rocky.

"Well, don't waste your time gabbing with me. Go ahead and see Mrs. Hindman." She motioned to them.

Rocky and Dr. Johnson walked into the room, and she found her mother just as she had left her.

"You said she's been like this for about five years now?"

"Yes. Frankly, until tonight, I had forgotten what her voice even sounded like."

They stood by Mrs. Hindman for a while, prayed over her,

and then sat down after a while.

"I swear I'm telling you the truth."

"I believe you, Dr. Johnson."

"Please, call me Loni," she said.

Rocky smiled and nodded.

"I'd also like to apologize to you, Rocky. I said some awful things to you earlier tonight."

"That's all right. I've been called much worse in my life than a fool."

"No, it's not all right. That was on national television. I will hold a press conference tomorrow to not only apologize, but to announce that I am now a believer."

"You don't need to apologize to me on national TV, Loni, but I think it's great if you can offer your testimony as a follow up to tonight's debate."

For the next hour they talked about theology, and Rocky shared some of his testimony.

"What made you leave Ohio State University to go to Las Vegas?"

"Stupidity."

"You really don't like talking about yourself do you?"

"Not especially. It's the subject I know least about."

"Really? I don't know if I believe you. I think I understand what made you leave Las Vegas, but what caused a good Midwestern boy to go out west and become a victim of the Vegas underworld?"

"Well, if you promise to keep this just between you and me…," he paused waiting for her reply.

"Of course, Rocky."

"Well, it's like this, I…."

"Look!" Mrs. Hindman suddenly yelled out while looking up at the ceiling.

Both Rocky and Loni looked up but saw nothing.

"What are you looking at, Mama?"

"Here comes the angel with your little boy!"

"What little boy, Mama? Jonathan?"

"No, Loni! It's James!"

"Where is he?"

"Don't you see him, Loni? The angel brought him down by the hand."

"What does he look like, Mama?"

"He has curly blond hair and has the same big smile as Theresa. Don't you see him?"

"No, Mama! What's he saying to you?"

"He said 'I'm so proud of my mommy.'"

This was almost too much for Loni. Rocky stood next to Loni and held her in loving support.

Her mother looked up and said, "Here comes the angel," and proceeded to watch the angel slowly move downward.

"Please tell James that I love him, Mama."

"Your mommy loves you, James."

Mrs. Hindman's eyes started to look upward.

"Look! The angel took him by the hand, and they're going!"

Loni and Rocky both looked up at the ceiling and then looked back at her mother, who was back in her previous state of mind.

Loni turned around and hugged Rocky Raccoon.

"Thank you, Rocky," she cried.

"Don't thank me. Thank God."

"I will. I'm now a true believer."

The Stoning of Rocky Raccoon

The whole seminary was abuzz with excitement following the miraculous events of last night. Dr. Illona Johnson's acceptance of Jesus added fuel to the fire of revival in New England, and the legend of Rocky Raccoon grew in kind.

Rocky was the focus of attention all day. One could not escape the regional and national media coverage of last night's events and the morning's revelations from Dr. Johnson, as well as the ongoing New England revival that was born out of Easton Seminary and its janitor.

Tom, though he sat with Martin, Meredith, and other members of their clique during lunch, was noticeably quiet and withdrawn. He had no desire to engage in any of the talk about Rocky, so he silently and swiftly finished his lunch and got up to leave the cafeteria.

Tom approached Rocky who was picking up around the garbage and silverware trays. Everyone in the cafeteria couldn't help but notice the ensuing confrontation. Tom stopped in his tracks.

"Good morning, Tom!"

Tom did not return the greeting, but he did offer a cold stare that bore right through Rocky's soul. He then thrust his tray into Rocky's unsuspecting arms with enough force to impact his chest. Tom turned around to see that everyone witnessed the silent but rude altercation and then turned his back on their unbelieving eyes and left for his room.

Several of Rocky's friends immediately surrounded him to see if he was all right.

"I cannot believe he just did that!" said one of the Korean students.

"There was no call for that," Jim said as he looked at the door and considered going after Tom.

"I'm so sorry about that," Meredith said. "That's not really like him, Rocky."

"Yeah, right," Steven said. "Tom has *always* been selfish, but we're finally seeing what happens when the spoiled brat doesn't get his way."

"Please," Rocky said as he tried to win back some of his personal space. "Don't speak poorly of Tom."

"We're not going to stand idly by as he assaults you," said Jim.

"That wasn't an assault. I've been assaulted before, and that ain't it."

"It was still inappropriate, whatever you want to call it," Martin replied.

"I don't know why he did it. Perhaps he didn't even mean to do it so hard. Please, don't judge him by this one incident," said Rocky.

"This is hardly an isolated incident, Rocky. He's been after you now for a while. Don't you remember he almost got you thrown out of here?" Jim asked.

"I remember. I also remember that my actions looked very suspicious and that anyone of you might have thought and done the exact same thing."

"Maybe so," Jim said, "but we weren't purposely spying on you looking for it."

Rocky excused himself from any further conversation about Tom by getting back to work. He had no intention of gossiping or attacking Tom for what might have been an accident or misunderstanding.

* * *

Rocky finished his work in the cafeteria. Though he usually didn't look forward to going to Tuttle Hall for his janitorial duties following lunch, he yearned for the privacy that typically accompanied his work in the dorm. No one talks to a guy while he cleans a toilet.

Rocky made his own schedule. He decided to pursue the janitorial duties of Tuttle Hall following lunch, as most of its residents were in class at this time. Consequently, he wasn't in anyone's way, and he could then spend time with them later when it didn't conflict with his work and their school schedules.

As Rocky was in the second floor bathroom scrubbing the toilet he heard the door open and shut.

"Occupied by a janitor that reeks of bleach, enter at your own risk," said Rocky.

He turned around and found Tom standing over him, and he wasn't laughing.

"Hi, Tom. Can I help you?"

"Just shut up!" Tom screamed. "I have had it with you. You're like a cockroach. No matter what happens, you just won't go away."

"I'm sorry, Tom, but...."

Tom kicked Rocky in the chest, knocking him down.

268

"You think *you're* so smart! You're nothing! You're no one!"

Rocky was slow to get up as Tom had kicked the air right out of him. Tom promptly shoved him back onto the ground, with Rocky's head bouncing off the toilet seat.

"Who do *you* think *you* are?"

Rocky wasn't sure if this was an opportunity to speak or if Tom would just hit him again. He hadn't recovered yet from the first cheap shot but made his way to his feet and stood in front of Tom.

"Who the hell are *you*, Rocky Raccoon?" Tom yelled as he landed a hard right on Rocky's cheek.

Rocky stumbled back but stayed on his feet.

"Who do *you* think *you* are?" Tom squealed as he landed another right hook on Rocky's face, this time causing Rocky's lip to bleed.

Rocky took the blow but stayed on his feet, either unable or unwilling to fight back.

"Do *you* know who *I* am?"

Tom walloped him again with his best right hand yet. Rocky fell to one knee but defiantly got back up, refusing to even wipe the blood from his mouth and nose.

"What could *you* possibly teach *me*, you piece of trash?" Tom screamed as he delivered a devastating blow to Rocky's left ear, causing him to collapse to the floor.

Rocky didn't immediately answer Tom as he lay prone on the white floor, now marred by his own blood. He pulled himself back up to his feet with the aid of a sink and then slowly limped over to Tom.

Tom grabbed Rocky by his collar, cocked his arm back to land the knockout punch, and watched as Rocky turned his head to the left, exposing his right, pristine cheek. Tom's eyes welled up with tears as he stared at the cheek Rocky had turned and offered him. He let go of Rocky's collar and ran out of the dorm sobbing uncontrollably.

Rocky fell back to the floor where he would later be found.

The Fish Story

Rocky awoke to find himself lying on a bed in Jim's room. He looked around and found that the room was full of people.

"What's going on?" Rocky asked.

"We know what happened, Rock," Jim said. "We're going to take you to the emergency room."

Rocky sat up and replied, "I don't need to go to the ER. I do need an aspirin though. Actually, an ibuprofen and hot coffee would be perfection."

Jim looked over at Steven and nodded. Steven quickly left to fulfill Rocky's request.

"Where's Tom?" Rocky asked.

"Don't you worry about Tom. He won't bother you again," Jim said. "He's quitting."

"Quitting? Quitting Easton?"

"Yes," said Rick. "He's leaving, and, frankly, all I can say is good riddance."

"Why is he quitting?"

"Aside from the fact that he'd probably be expelled anyway for what he did to you, Martin said Tom just kept rambling on about how he wasn't supposed to be here, or in ministry for that

271

matter, after what he did to you," said Jim.

"What else did he say?" Rocky asked.

"We don't know," Jim replied. "Martin said that Tom hasn't spoken a word since. He said that Tom looked as though he were in shock."

"He should be in jail," Steven said as he returned with Rocky's coffee and ibuprofen.

Rocky started to get up out of bed.

"Where do you think you're going, Rocky? You need to rest and put some ice on that face of yours," Jim said.

"No, I have to talk to Tom before he makes the biggest mistake of his life."

* * *

Steven drove Rocky to the top of the hill to Tom's dorm. Rocky slowly stepped out of the car and walked toward the door.

"Rocky, I should come in with you," said Steven.

Rocky turned around, shook his head, and then walked inside.

There was a small crowd gathered in the hallway by Tom and Martin's room.

"Hi, Rocky! How are you feeling?" Meredith asked.

"I'm fine. It looks worse than it feels. What's going on?"

"We're concerned about Tom. This isn't like him," she answered.

"What did he say?"

"He hasn't talked to anyone since he first burst in on poor Martin who was taking an afternoon nap," she said. "Now he won't let anyone inside to talk."

Rocky walked up to the door and then looked around at the

crowd.

"Could you give me a moment? I'd like to try and talk to him," Rocky said.

The crowd moved down to the lobby in silence so that they could hear what was happening.

Rocky knocked on Tom's door.

"Go away! I don't want to talk to anyone!" Tom screamed.

"Tom, it's me, Rocky."

Rocky then heard Tom unlock and slowly open the door. Rocky did not hesitate and accepted Tom's invitation.

*   *   *

Rocky walked into Tom's room, mindful that this was his first time in there. Tom stood on the other side of the room with his back turned toward Rocky.

"Look, Rocky, I need to tell you something, but I can't say it to your face."

"Okay, Tom. Whatever you say."

"You see, Rocky, this is what I've been battling all year. You are so considerate of everyone's feelings. People see Jesus in you, Rocky. They only see a theologian in me."

"Theologians are Christians too, Tom. Some of the greatest saints have been theologians."

"Maybe so. I once received a vision that I was going to be a powerful instrument in Christ's Great Commission. Instead, I've become a monster driven by personal ambition and pride instead of compassion and serving others, as you have."

"God uses us in different ways. You have talents and gifts that I cannot even comprehend, and God will work through you in ways that you cannot even fathom."

"At one time, I would have agreed with you. Now I find

273

myself lost. I cannot believe that I attacked you like that. I'm *so* sorry, Rocky. I do not know what happened, but I have turned my back on God and now I must leave this place."

"Don't you dare leave this place, Tom. If you leave, I will leave too."

Tom turned around upon hearing this and looked Rocky in his swollen eye.

"What? Why should I stay?"

"If you leave, then you will indeed be turning your back on God."

"Rocky, I have *already* turned my back on God. All year I have been resisting and ignoring Him, even in the midst of this miraculous revival."

"God's not through with you yet, Tom. Not by a long shot! Remember Jonah? He had received very specific instructions from God to go to Nineveh. Not only did Jonah disobey God, but he also tried to flee to Tarshish, which was in the *opposite* direction! Now *that's* disobedience! In Jonah's case it took a great fish swallowing him and vomiting him up on a beach to get through to him. Despite everything that had happened, the Lord came back to Jonah after his willful act of disobedience because He wasn't done with him yet. The same God who restored Jonah to ministry wants to restore you as well."

Tom started to cry and fell to his knees in front of Rocky.

"Get up, Tom. Stand with me."

Tom looked up with his red, tear-filled eyes, stood up, and then embraced Rocky.

Rocky said nothing but just held him as Tom released his guilt, frustrations, and shame to a God who was eager to forgive.

Tom finally let go and sat down on his bed. Rocky sat down next to him.

"Tom, I forgive you, just as I know God forgives you. Now,

you need to forgive yourself."

"I don't know if I can."

"That's pride talking again. God forgave you. Let go of your pride and accept forgiveness, especially from yourself. What if Paul never forgave himself for being the ringleader in the slaughter of Christians, as well as quietly observing the stoning of Steven? He might have become pathological, but, instead, he became the greatest theologian and preacher of them all. Tom, I see Paul in you."

Tom let out a slight chuckle. "That's kind of funny actually. I always perceived you as Peter."

"Well, I guess that would track. You're Paul the scholar, I'm Peter, and Simon is Alexander the Great, who set the table for Paul's ministry. Peter needs Paul, and Paul needs Peter. *Please* don't leave. We'd all be diminished by your absence."

"Rocky, I look at you, and I see what others see in you. I might have more knowledge than you and can read in German, Hebrew, Latin, and ancient Greek, but you seem to have a relationship with God like no one I've ever known. How do I feel closer to God, Rock?"

Rocky took a moment, shrugged his shoulders, and said, "I really don't know. From my own experience, especially a few years ago in Vegas, I learned that closeness to God is about obedience and not about my feelings, which change a thousand times a day."

"What do you mean?"

"I believe that those who are obedient are closest to God. If we obey occasionally, we sometimes feel closer to God. If we disobey, we really don't have much of a chance, which I learned by spending a couple of decadently sinful years in the belly of my own giant fish, Las Vegas. Our actions do matter, but ultimately we're saved because of what Jesus did for us. Had He not gone

275

to the cross and died for us, all the water in the world wouldn't wash away our sins. Without Him, our prayers would never be heard in heaven. Had Jesus not risen from the dead, there is no way that you and I could become holy and feel close to God. The answer, as the billboard says, is Jesus Christ."

Tom nodded.

"I want to stay, Rocky. I really do."

"Great! I'll help you unpack."

"It won't be that easy. Dr. Casper is furious with me. If I stay, he'll just expel me for sure."

"Let me talk to him," said Rocky.

"With all due respect, what can you do about it?"

Rocky smiled. "Dr. Casper owes me a favor."

"That must be *some* favor."

* * *

Rocky walked into the Lewis Center and walked down through the west wing to Dr. Casper's office. His secretary notified Dr. Casper that Rocky was there to speak to him, and Rocky was immediately permitted to enter the president's office.

Dr. Casper stood up at his desk upon seeing Rocky.

"My God, look what *he* did to you!"

"I'm fine, really. It looks worse than it feels."

"I certainly hope so. As awful as it sounds, I regret that Tom withdrew before I could personally expel him."

"Tom isn't withdrawing, sir."

"Yes, he is. I have his paperwork right here."

Dr. Casper handed it to Rocky, who promptly tore it up right before his eyes.

"What are you doing?"

"I want Tom to stay here and complete his degree, and so

276

does Tom."

"I'm sorry, Rocky. As much as I respect what you have done here, I cannot grant your request."

"I'm not asking you for this favor as Rocky Raccoon, Dr. Casper, I'm asking as Michael Sinclair."

Dr. Casper sat down and motioned for Rocky to do likewise.

"I see," Dr. Casper finally spoke. "Why do you want the man who brutally attacked you to stay at Easton?"

"Because, like Jonah, he deserves a second chance. Because, like Paul, he can overcome his mistakes and strive forward in service for Christ. Because, like you, he is a brilliant scholar who can shine much light into this dark world. Because, like me, he will learn from his past and be better for it."

"Okay, Mr. Sinclair," Dr. Casper said, "I'll permit Tom to stay as a favor to you and for all you have done for us. However, Tom will be under my thumb till he graduates. He will be held to a strict zero tolerance policy. If I hear that he has even killed a fly, he's out of here. Am I clear?"

"Clear as crystal, Dr. Casper."

Unrequited Love

Tom walked through the cafeteria line, empathetic with the lepers Jesus healed throughout the Gospels. After paying for his lunch, he took a few steps out to witness a very hostile set of eyes staring at him. It was common knowledge that Tom had attacked Rocky, and it was equally well known that, by the grace of God and the forgiveness of Rocky, he was still a student. No one understood or knew Rocky's motives, but they certainly disagreed with the de facto revival leader.

"I can't believe that they didn't expel him!" Steven said.

"Apparently Rocky talked Dr. Casper out of it," Jim replied.

"Well, look at it this way," Rick said, "Rocky put the seminary back on the map and has initiated and led a revival that is taking New England and other parts of the nation and world by storm. Wouldn't you answer Rocky's request if you were Dr. Casper?"

Jim and Steven nodded in agreement with Rick's explanation.

Tom walked over to where his clique was sitting, but they continued their conversation without acknowledging that he was standing there.

Martin finally looked up at his roommate. "You're not welcome here, Tom."

Tom nodded and walked to a few more tables where he received the same treatment before he settled down at a table by himself.

Rocky witnessed the lack of Christian charity from his work post where he was serving the day's side dishes. He tossed his apron aside, grabbed a long metal ladle, and charged out to the middle of the cafeteria toward Tom. As Rocky approached him Tom shrank back. Rocky swung the metal ladle, striking the metal support pole next to his seat. He loudly banged on it till he had the attention of everyone.

"Knock it off NOW!" Rocky yelled at everyone and then paused for the longest minute to look at them all individually in the eyes.

"Either drop those stones you're casting at Tom, you *hypocrites*, or throw them at me! I've done far worse than he *ever* has, and you *know* it! You've overlooked my past! Jesus not only instructed us to forgive but even *love* our enemies! Jesus forgave Peter after denying Him when He needed him the most. He forgave Paul his past crimes against Christians and humanity, and He would have forgiven Judas had he sought it out! This ends NOW! Tom is *our brother*! What happened was between Tom and me, and I have forgiven him, and he has forgiven himself and sought the Lord's forgiveness. Are any one of you here *greater* than the Lord, or without sin yourselves? If not, then offer the same forgiveness and grace that has been given to you by Jesus' pierced, loving hands."

Tom stood up and hugged Rocky. Rocky then picked up the unrecognizable remains of his ladle, and then went back to work. Representatives from every table walked over to Tom to invite him over to share in meal fellowship.

Later that day, Tom confessed to Rocky that he didn't hear a single word that Rocky had uttered in his defense at the cafeteria. Instead, all he heard was the hymn "Amazing Grace" in his mind followed by a sudden outpouring of love from the whole seminary. Rocky smiled, as he once experienced the same phenomenon as well.

* * *

After Rocky finished with his janitorial obligations, he spent some quiet time reading the Bible. He was excited to be driving to downtown Boston to a homeless shelter later that night to help out and preach to them one on one. That moment in the gutter in Las Vegas forever moved his heart for those who must endure such an existence every day, whether it is due to alcoholism, drugs, mental illness, or simple bad luck. He knew that God loved them, and Rocky wanted to not only love those whom God loved, but love God by loving the least of His brothers.

Following dinner, Rocky finished his daily chores and headed for his car to go to downtown Boston. Driving into Boston was no easier for him than it was six months ago when he had first arrived, especially in the never-ending winter accurately forecasted by Punxsutawney Phil, the world famous groundhog meteorologist. As it pertains to parking, one will sooner find a Bostonian who actually remembers the Red Sox's 1918 World Series title than a decent parking spot. He had to settle for an out of the way parking spot in an area that reminded him of the very worst parts of Las Vegas.

He spent the evening with homeless men, many of whom had heard about Rocky Raccoon. He spoke about Jesus and of his own testimony to encourage many of the men to not only take the first step toward sobriety, but also in accepting Jesus into their hearts and lives.

"Wow, man, after hearing your story, I know God loves me," a man named John said.

"I'm glad to hear that." Rocky smiled.

"Yeah, if He loves *you*, man, then He must love me." John laughed.

"You don't know how right you are!"

Rocky treasured the ministry that God had provided for him downtown. He also grew to realize that it's impossible to judge a book by its cover. There were many homeless people who dressed so well that an outside observer might very well confuse Rocky as the one in need. Conversely, there were many students in Cambridge who dressed like they were indigent, yet they came from some of the most affluent families in the nation. No one, it seemed, was truly as he or she appeared.

* * *

The hour was growing late, and Rocky knew that it was time for him to go home. He drove west on Interstate 90 and then merged north up 95. About two miles up 95, he saw a hitchhiker walking along the side of the road in the mounds of plowed snow and salt deposits. Rocky slowed his car down and pulled off to the side. The hitchhiker eagerly stumbled up to the car and let himself in.

"Thanks, pal," the man said with a strong trace of alcohol emitted from his breath.

"No problem," Rocky replied. "I'm happy to give you a lift. I'm heading up to Beverly. Where are you going?"

"I'm heading to Rockport. I know it's late, but you don't mind going a little out of your way for me, do you, pal?"

"Of course not."

"You're a good guy. Thanks."

"My name is Rocky, what's yours?" he asked as he started to merge back into traffic.

"Rocky, 'eh? You're not a boxer or anything like that are you, pal?" He obnoxiously laughed out loud at his own joke while patting Rocky hard on the shoulder.

"No, thank God. Though I used to gamble quite a bit on boxing matches."

"Ah, I'm just teasing you. My name is Leland."

"Nice to meet you, Leland."

"Don't thank me till I get out of your car without puking my guts out." He laughed until he started coughing.

Rocky sat up straight and found that he was driving a little faster. He looked himself in the eye through the rearview mirror, sighed, and then pulled back into the right lane and slowed down.

*　*　*

Rocky was heading up 128 North and was growing increasingly uncomfortable with his inebriated passenger. Rocky looked back up into the mirror to examine his motives, but was suddenly interrupted.

"Give me your wallet," Leland abruptly demanded.

"W-wa-what?"

"You heard what I said, choir boy!" Leland screamed and became increasingly agitated.

"Look, I don't have enough in my wallet to justify the risks you're taking. Let me drop you off in Rockport, and I promise that I will not report this to the police," Rocky compromised as he pressed down on the accelerator passing by the Beverly exit and heading further north up the dark and winding road ahead.

"Listen, sucka," Leland trembled as he pulled a knife from his

282

jacket, "we do things *my* way!"

"Okay then. The wallet is in my back right pocket, take it out."

Leland reached across Rocky as he pressed the knife up against Rocky's side.

"No, Leland, it's in my *right* back pocket," Rocky said again as he drove at an increasing rate of speed.

Leland again reached across Rocky for his back left pocket and, upon finding it empty, screamed, "Don't mess with me, boy! Where is it?"

"It's in my right back pocket!"

Leland again reached across to Rocky's left back pocket and became enraged when he again found nothing.

Rocky was now getting frustrated at Leland's inability to follow directions, let alone the actual crime itself.

"Fine, I'll get it myself," Rocky said, but his movement reaching for his right back pocket confused and alarmed Leland, and, without thinking, Leland stabbed Rocky Raccoon in his side.

Rocky's body reacted to the knife's piercing penetration with a violent spasm, causing him to inadvertently jerk the steering wheel right, driving his car into the natural stonewall that lined the road along that stretch of Route 128.

The Guardian Angel

"How is he?" Simon rushed in to ask a crowd of Rocky's closest friends in the fourth floor lobby of the hospital.

Chip hugged him and said, "He's in a coma."

"What happened?" Simon asked.

"We're not entirely sure, Simon," Chip replied. "Apparently, Rocky picked up a hitchhiker. We don't really know what happened, other than Rocky was found with a knife wound in his side at the wreck."

"A carjacker?" Simon asked.

"We don't know. The man died in the crash, and Rocky is in a coma," Chip said.

"We have people all over praying for Rocky," Adam told Simon. "From what I've heard, e-mails have been sent all over the world."

Tom sat alone in his chair crying uncontrollably. Jim was seated next to him and silently prayed with him.

Dr. Casper arrived a few minutes later.

"Any improvement?" he asked.

"Nothing's changed," Rick answered.

"Word's definitely gotten out," Dr. Casper said. "Rocky is

one of tonight's major headlines in the news."

"How did they find out so fast?" Adam asked.

"Reporters listen to the police and fire scanners," said Simon.

"Well, regardless, I'm sure that Rocky is in the prayers of many people tonight," Dr. Casper assured everyone.

* * *

The hospital relaxed its visitor policy, fully aware of who Rocky Raccoon was and what he meant to so many people. His friends converted the lobby into a chapel, as they all continued to pray and support one another.

Dr. Casper was sitting in an easy chair quietly meditating when two men respectfully approached him.

"Reverend Casper?" said one of the men.

"Yes." Dr. Casper stood up to greet the men.

"Hi, my name is Matt and this is my partner Marc," he said.

"It's nice to meet you two," Dr. Casper replied.

"We're the paramedics who arrived first at the scene of the accident," said Matt.

Every bowed head in the room rose to listen in on the conversation.

"I want to thank you for a job well done. He's very special to us," said Dr. Casper.

"You're welcome, sir," Marc said, "but my partner and I wanted to share something with you as soon as we got off work."

"What is it?" Dr. Casper asked.

"When we arrived at the accident," Matt said, "we both expected the worst. We immediately knew that the passenger was dead. Unfortunately, he wasn't wearing a seatbelt. Rocky wasn't much better off though."

Dr. Casper nodded.

"Something happened, sir, and we wanted to ask you about it," Marc said.

"What is it?"

"We couldn't get him out of the car," Marc answered.

"Well, then, how did he get here?" Simon interrupted.

Matt didn't acknowledge Simon but answered the question for the benefit of Dr. Casper.

"We tried everything to get him out, and we knew we couldn't wait for the Jaws of Life to arrive because he was bleeding to death."

"That's when it happened," said Marc.

"What happened?" Dr. Casper asked.

"We don't really know. That's why we wanted to talk to you personally," Matt said. "As we worked to get Rocky out, a large black man dressed in white just came from out of nowhere. He walked up to the car, told us not to worry, and offered to help."

"Before we could reply, he went to the driver's side door, pulled everything apart like he was Superman, and gently delivered Rocky to us as if he were handing us a newborn baby," Marc said.

"We immediately took care of Rocky. And then, upon the arrival of other emergency vehicles, we finally had a chance to look around to thank this bystander, but he was gone," Matt said.

"We looked around, and it dawned on us that there were no cars around except for emergency vehicles and that we were in a section of 128 where no one would just come from out of nowhere. After delivering Rocky to the hospital, we couldn't figure out who this man was, where he came from, or how he did what he did," Marc said.

"Are you asking me if that was an angel?"

286

Matt and Marc both nodded their heads with eyes yearning for the answer. Every person in that lobby was now looking at Dr. Casper seeking confirmation of a miracle.

Dr. Casper smiled and said, "Gentlemen, based upon your testimony, I sincerely believe that an angel did indeed help you save Rocky tonight."

Everyone in the room stood in awe and amazement.

"I think this means that Rocky's going to be okay, right?" Adam asked.

"Of course it does," Simon replied. "God wouldn't spare him in such a miraculous way, only to have him die in the hospital."

Dr. Casper was noticeably silent at Simon's revelation.

Uncle Screwtape

The lobby turned chapel was reinvented yet again, this time into a motel. By early morning everyone had fallen asleep. Just a few hours before dawn, a young registered nurse gracefully tiptoed over and around many sleeping bodies to reach Dr. Casper, who was slouched in his chair asleep.

The nurse gently tapped on his shoulder. "Dr. Casper. Dr. Casper, please wake up."

Dr. Casper slowly came to and immediately sat up when he realized that it was a nurse.

"Dr. Casper, Rocky has come out of his coma," she whispered.

"Praise God. How is he doing?"

"He's pretty banged up. He lost a lot of blood. He also broke his left wrist and has a mild concussion, a punctured lung, a few broken ribs, and several contusions and cuts. His doctor is convinced that the knife wound managed to miss any major organs, but he's keeping a close eye on him."

"I see. Is he awake and alert?" Dr. Casper asked.

"He's sleeping right now. He has been transferred to ICU, which limits his visitors to only four at a time during regular

288

visiting hours," she said.

"Thank you, I'll tell the others.

* * *

Rocky awoke later that morning and found himself in a room surrounded by cards and balloons. He had no idea exactly where he was but, judging by his immediate surroundings and the tube in his chest, he quickly ascertained that he must be in a hospital.

"Good morning, Mr. Sinclair," his nurse said.

"Is it? What happened? Is Leland okay?"

"Leland? I'm sorry, do you mean the man who was in the car with you last night?"

"Yes. Leland. Is he all right?"

"His name wasn't Leland. It was Sean Cooper."

"Was?"

"He died at the scene of the accident. According to the police, he was a wanted felon, and they believe that he was trying to take your car to escape the area."

"I see."

"I must admit that I'm surprised to see that you care so much about a man who apparently tried to kill you."

"Do you believe in Jesus?"

"Well, yes, as a matter of fact, I do believe in Jesus."

"And you know that, if you were to die today, you'd go to heaven?"

"Yes, I honestly do believe that."

"Well, to answer your question, Miss, I care about him because I don't think he knew Jesus and now it's too late."

"Oh."

The nurse stood silent, turned her back to look out the window for a moment, and then left the room.

289

THE ROCKY RACCOON REVIVAL

* * *

After a visit from his doctor and several techs conducting a variety of tests on him, Rocky was allowed visitors. He took a sip of water and then heard a knock on the door, his first visitor. He eagerly looked over expecting to see his friends but was surprised to see an old face.

"Hi, Mikey," Pastor Bob said as he walked into the room.

"Bob! What are you doing here?"

"Well, I received a phone call from my old friend Pete Casper, and he told me that you were in the hospital following an incident with a hitchhiker."

"Yeah, well, I was trying to be a Good Samaritan."

Bob frowned and placed his hands on his hips.

"We've had this conversation before, Mike. Picking up hitchhikers is not a Christian obligation. In fact, it's downright dangerous."

"I pulled over to help that man because Jesus taught us to love."

"For a genius, you're sure stupid at times," Bob said. "Yes, we're taught to be like the Good Samaritan. But we're also taught that Satan is the god of this world and that we have to be discerning and mindful of his evil, otherwise we're just sheep to the slaughter. The devil is a lot more powerful if he convinces us that he doesn't exist, is he not, Michael?"

Rocky looked down, silently admitting that his mentor was right.

"Mikey, it is good to love one's enemy, as Jesus taught. Just remember that Satan can trick Christians into letting their guard down and being compromised both spiritually and physically."

There was another knock on the door. Dr. Casper, Simon,

Tom, Adam, Jim, Steven, Rick, and Chip all gathered inside the small room, much to the silent dismay of the nurse.

"Pardon the interruption, gentlemen," Dr. Casper said, smiling, "but I can't hold these guys back any longer."

"Please, come in, Pete," said Bob.

"How are you feeling, Rocky?" Jim asked.

"I feel like a mix between a crash test dummy and a pin cushion."

"Why would this happen?" Tom asked. "Why you? Why would God let this happen to you? You're the best of us."

Rocky let out a painful laugh.

"I'm far from it, Tom. Anyway, what I did last night was stupid. I shouldn't have picked up a hitchhiker without any regard for the dangers or consequences. I wasn't being a Good Samaritan; I foolishly fell into that trap of trying to be God, or playing Brother Teresa if you will. I learned a lesson the hard way, boys. Please take note, cause it hurts too much to repeat."

"You're in all the national media today, Rocky," said Rick.

"Swell."

"No, that's good news, Rocky," Steven replied. "Word of this revival and everything God has done here in New England has really captured the attention of the country. You should be happy."

"Trust me, I am. I, um, I, just…I'm sorry, but I don't feel good at all. I feel dizzy."

"I'll go get the nurse," Simon said as he quickly ran into the hallway.

"Thanks, Simon, I appreciate…," and Rocky went silent as his breathing became increasingly labored. The silence of fear was dashed by the blaring sound of alarms.   "Code Blue, room 4320 ICU, 4 Tower. Code Blue, room 4320 ICU, 4 Tower," the public address system announced.

291

Within seconds, several nurses ran into the room to tend to Rocky. One nurse put Rocky's bed flat, while another yelled for the crash cart.

Rocky's nurse looked at his petrified guests. "I'm sorry, but you all have to leave now!"

The team continued to work on Rocky, starting an IV and administering oxygen at a high level. Rocky was now unconscious and his skin was turning gray as he continued to exhibit labored breathing.

"I have a heart rhythm, but no pulse!" a nurse yelled.

"The patient's in P.E.A. Start CPR!" another nurse directed.

The doctor rushed in and joined the nurses in their organized team effort to save Rocky's life.

"Get me an intubation kit!" he ordered. "What's the patient's history?"

"He was in a car accident last night. He has a punctured left lung, broken ribs, broken left wrist, an abdominal knife wound on his right side, mild concussion, and several cuts and contusions," a nurse answered.

"By the looks of it, he threw a pulmonary embolus," the doctor diagnosed. "Where in the hell is respiratory?"

"There is no blood pressure and no pulse," a nurse confirmed.

"Give me a milligram of Epi," the doctor ordered. "Give me a milligram of atropine!"

Outside of the room, Rocky's friends huddled together praying to *the* Great Physician.

Who in the World is Michael Sinclair?

The surgeon's hands moved with fluid grace, as though experiencing déjà vu in Rocky's chest cavity. His fingers, like those of a classical pianist, were relying upon muscle memory, acting almost without the need of the surgeon's careful and conscious attention. This suited the world famous Oxford graduate just fine, as his mind was keenly aware of the ever-growing legend that lay before him. To Dr. Straczynski, Rocky Raccoon was once a figure who lived in Beatle lore, perhaps in Strawberry Fields or on Penny Lane. However, like many others in New England, Rocky Raccoon was now a household name that had come to represent a growing revival of the Christian faith in a land where many believed they had outsmarted God, or simply outgrew him, like one moved past the Easter Bunny or Santa Claus. Dr. Straczynski was also mindful of the prayer chain that started along the North Shore and had now spread throughout the nation, as well as the world, courtesy of the Internet. Many news stations from around the nation were reporting on Rocky's accident and subsequent surgery. Once again, the Gospel of Jesus Christ, which mattered most to Rocky, was seen worldwide. His name appeared along with the other prayer requests on the chalkboard at the call center in Ohio where he once worked, and it also fell off the lips of a man who Rocky would never meet, praying by his lonely bedside in a small town outside of Denver.

*   *   *

Dr. Casper and Pastor Bob stood together sharing stories about Rocky, while several others prayed together for Rocky during his surgery. Once the media reported Rocky's life threatening condition, the hospital had become swamped with many familiar and unfamiliar faces. Rocky's friends marveled at the hundreds of testimonies people gave regarding their relationship with Rocky Raccoon. They knew that he frequently left the campus to pursue his ministry but had no idea of the sheer scope of it all. Other notable appearances also included Dr. Illona Johnson and many of her students.

Some played guitar and sang songs while others chose to pray in silence. Simon was amazed at the variety of people present. People from all races, socio-economic backgrounds, sexes, education, denominations, and ages were there to pray for a young man who touched their lives forever, and for better.

A reporter from the *Boston Globe* approached Dr. Casper and Pastor Bob. She whispered something to them, and all three of them quietly excused themselves from the room to meet in private.

*   *   *

"So how did you find out?" Pastor Bob asked.

"It was only a matter of time really. Frankly, I'm amazed that I came across this before anyone else did," the reporter said. "It

294

just seemed too fantastic, that's why I came here to verify this before breaking the story."

"You know that Rocky will not like his past being front page news," Dr. Casper said.

"With all due respect to Rocky, he's now a public figure, and this story is coming out sooner or later, and I'd just as soon it be my name on the byline."

Pastor Bob nodded his head, confirmed her facts, and elaborated on some of her research just to guarantee that the story is accurate and fair.

"Thank you, gentlemen, I appreciate your cooperation and assistance," she said with a smile as she reached for her cell phone to contact her editor regarding her scoop.

Dr. Casper looked over to his old friend. "Bob, I think we should be the ones to tell Rocky's friends rather than having them learn about it in the media."

"I agree, Pete. Just make sure you offer them a seat first."

* * *

As Dr. Straczynski and his handpicked team operated on Rocky, Dr. Casper and Pastor Bob entered the crowded waiting room.

"May I have your attention, please?" Dr. Casper called out.

Those standing closest to him immediately listened, and it took only a moment for word to spread throughout the rest of the room that Dr. Peter Casper had an announcement. The room listened in nervous anticipation, expecting word on Rocky's surgery.

"Thank you for your attention," Dr. Casper said. "I want to take a moment to talk to you all. Many of you know Rocky Raccoon from Easton and, clearly, from what I can see in this lobby, he has befriended many from outside of the seminary as well. Rocky first arrived in Easton at the beginning of autumn semester. He came looking for work and an opportunity to live among and learn from the students and faculty of Easton Theological Seminary. When he wasn't working in the cafeteria or performing chores in Tuttle Hall, he was found either in the community serving and teaching others about Jesus or spending quiet time in the library or his room reading and praying. We have all heard some accounts of Rocky's life prior to coming here, especially his trials and tribulations in Las Vegas. Now, I'd like to invite his old friend from his home church in Canton, Ohio, Pastor Robert Grant, to share a little about Rocky."

Pastor Bob took a step forward and looked around the room. He was literally speechless, unable to catch his breath as he witnessed the impact his young friend had on so many lives.

"Good afternoon. Mikey, well, he may be Rocky to you, but he'll always be Mikey to me." He smiled. "He came to me with the proposition to go to Easton. He was hopeful that he could be a student but was willing to settle for a vocational position if it allowed him to be among the students and faculty of Easton. He wasn't a college graduate, and there weren't really any positions open, so I secretly told Pete, um, I mean, Dr. Casper who Michael Sinclair really is."

Everybody lurched forward to listen.

"Michael Sinclair, before he ever became Rocky Raccoon, was one of the brightest and most promising students at Ohio State University. He was an honors student and was planning to attend Cambridge University in England to pursue his Ph.D. in medieval history. To put it succinctly, he is a genius."

Simon leaned over to Chip. "No wonder a janitor held his own against me in a debate."

"What stopped him from pursuing his Ph.D.?" Dr. Johnson

296

asked.

Bob took a deep breath and then answered, "Michael had the terribly good fortune of winning the nation's largest lottery a few years ago. In the blink of an eye, he had won the billion dollar lottery I'm sure many of you read about, and I imagine several of you probably played it yourselves a few years back."

"Wait a second," Chip interrupted. "I remember that. The winner's name *was* Michael Sinclair! All this time I've been calling him Rocky, I never thought about his real name."

"Yes, the nickname certainly kept his secret for this long. Now that he's a major headline with many journalists investigating his background, the secret is about to be publicized," Bob said.

"So why is a billionaire working as a janitor of a dorm?" Steven asked.

"Well, that's the interesting part," Bob replied. "Though he was a brilliant student with a promising academic career, winning a billion dollars changed his priorities and perspective on life. He dropped out of Ohio State and moved to Las Vegas, which became his own little playground. In Las Vegas he could do anything he wanted with his bank account. Sin City lived up to its name during the time he spent there. After hitting rock bottom and rededicating his life to Jesus Christ, he came back to Canton, Ohio and we talked about his fortune. He decided that he didn't want it anymore. He saw how that money distracted him from seeking first the Kingdom of God, and how he was possessed by his possessions. He discovered a newfound freedom by giving it all away so he could serve the one Master that he truly loved."

"What did he do with his money?" Simon asked.

"Well, he gave my church a pretty healthy donation, as well as other ministries and charities. However, the bulk of his money, which was around $400 million after taxes, was divided between two seminaries handpicked by Michael. His goal was to have an entire generation of preachers, missionaries, and scholars have a free education in their pursuit to serve God and His people."

"Wait just a second," Tom interrupted. "You're telling me that the guy who cleaned the toilets and served us food in the cafeteria is the same guy who paid for our school expenses?"

"That's exactly what I'm telling you. Mike never wanted anyone to know because he didn't want to be treated any differently. I had to tell Dr. Casper that he was the same Michael Sinclair who donated all that money or else he wouldn't have been accepted to work here since there really were no openings."

Dr. Casper stepped forward. "When Michael Sinclair donated the money he had only one condition. He didn't want to place himself in a position where he could control or govern any school, but he did state in the contractual agreement that he could have veto power for one occasion at every school, just in case the school should go seriously astray in his eyes. In the case of Easton Theological Seminary, he exercised his one time veto to keep a certain student from being expelled."

"Mike never wanted anyone to know all of this, but since the media has figured it out, we wanted to be the ones to share it with you," said Pastor Bob.

The room was stunned. The pauper was, indeed, a prince.

Reckonings

Rocky awoke alone to find himself back in ICU. He was physically exhausted, and, though his body demanded more sleep, he slowly reached for the nurse's call button. A moment later a nurse entered the room.

"Hi, Mr. Sinclair, how are you feeling?"

"A-ar-are you an angel?" Rocky asked as he rubbed his eyes.

"No, sir. This is not heaven. In fact, it's closer to hell. That's why there's a nursing shortage," she joked.

"Am I going to live?"

"In my medical opinion, you're going to outlive one of those ancient sea turtles."

Rocky smiled.

"Though I really am enjoying talking with you, sweetie, you really need your rest now," she advised, only to discover that he was already asleep.

* * *

Rocky slept through the day. He woke up very thirsty and more alert the second time. His nurse came in to give him some

299

medication, check his vitals, and call to have his food delivered since he slept through dinner.

"Your friends are anxious to see you," she said as she checked his blood pressure.

"They're still here? They really should go home and get some rest."

"Oh, stop playing the martyr, silly! There's a huge crowd out there, including the press."

Rocky smiled and then drank his water.

"Please send them in when you get a chance."

"Sure thing, Rocky Raccoon." She grinned.

* * *

Tom, Simon, Jim, Rick, Chip, and Steven walked into the room.

"What? No flowers?" Rocky asked.

"Actually, ICU doesn't allow flowers," said Chip.

"Oh, shut up and come inside, guys." Rocky laughed.

"So, Rocky," Simon said, "you survive a beating, a stabbing and a car wreck, but a little clot in your lungs sends you to surgery."

"Is that what happened? I seem to find out all my medical information from you guys before I hear it from the staff."

"Yeah, well, we learned a lot of things about you today," Tom said.

Rocky slowly placed his water down on the tray.

"So how did you find out?"

"Some reporter pieced together the clues that you won that record lottery and you now work at one of the seminaries that received your generous gift."

Rocky sat as still and quiet as a defendant pleading the Fifth

300

Amendment.

"Let me be the first to say thank you," Jim said. "If it wasn't for your gift, I wouldn't be in seminary right now. I simply couldn't afford it."

"Same here, Rock," said Rick. "If I had that much student loan debt, I would have to wait several years before I could leave the country to enter the mission field."

"You have really shown me the value of Christian charity, Rocky," Tom said.

"That was really nice of you, Rocky," said Simon.

"Okay, *please* stop. I'm not a saint. I did what I had to do to save myself. I simply prayed to God to determine what I should do with *His* money. I learned in Vegas that I'm not here to get from God, but I'm here to give from God."

"Still, you gave up what most people dream of having. Was it hard?" Chip asked.

"As I climbed my way out of that gutter in Vegas, I came to realize that cocaine was a clear indication that I had way too much money. But seriously, I came to accept the fundamental truth that money and possessions will not make me happy. It's like Paul wrote in Philippians, 'I have learned what it is to have plenty. In any and all circumstances I have learned the secret of being well fed and of going hungry, of having plenty and of being in need. I can do all things through Him who strengthens me.'"

"What should I do with my fortune?" Simon asked.

"I don't know. Tech stocks maybe?"

"You know that's not what I mean, Rocky," Simon replied.

"Look, that's between you and God. Personally, I don't think I could handle the responsibility of the wealth. Money is not inherently evil, just the love of it. When Jesus said, 'Woe to them that are rich,' I have to believe that He was referring to people who tried to be faithful to God and money at the same time, or just money. Simon, I think you can do great things with your wealth during your life. God will use you and the gifts He's given you. In a sense, you're like the servant in the parable of the talents that wisely invested what was given to him, pleasing his master, and I was the brain dead one that handled my gifts foolishly. I don't think that someone is more spiritual just because he's poor. For every Mother Teresa who lives a life of poverty, there is a millionaire Christian who donates and tithes to feed the poor and help the sick."

"I see your point," Simon said.

"That's great, but if you don't mind, I really need to get some sleep," he said as he laid his head back against his pillow.

"Oh sure, Rock," Jim replied, "we'll pass on the good news that you're doing well."

Rocky was already asleep.

* * *

Three weeks passed, and Rocky's recovery surpassed his doctors' highest expectations. His friends supplied him with plenty of classic books to read as well as making time to visit him whenever they could. Bob had returned to Ohio, and the media, which had eventually played out the amazing tale of Rocky's life, finally stopped camping out at the hospital.

Rocky was able to attend the graduation ceremonies at Easton Theological Seminary. Although he had been looking forward to seeing many of his friends earn their diplomas, as well as seeing the fruits of his now legendary donation, he was hesitant to attend the ceremony for fear of upstaging the graduates who had earned their degrees, as well as stealing the spotlight away from God Who had made it all possible.

302

THE ROCKY RACCOON REVIVAL

Much to his dismay, he was given a seat of honor on the stage along with President Casper, Vice-President Williams, and other prestigious staff and faculty. During the introduction of those seated on stage, Rocky received a deafening standing ovation from everyone in attendance. Rocky was prompted by those sitting next to him to stand for the audience, and he did.

For the first time in the school's history, and in fact, the history of any American seminary, many major media outlets were covering the graduation ceremony. The Rocky Raccoon Revival was alive and well.

Dr. Casper gave an inspiring speech commenting on the impact of the revival upon New England and offered many testimonies from those touched by God during this great awakening. He did spare Rocky any mention of his donation and also made it a point to name several people involved in the revival in addition to Rocky.

"Today, I have the honor to announce this year's valedictorian, Thomas Ashcraft. Tom will receive a copy of the plaque displayed in the main lobby of the Lewis Center which commemorates the top student from each graduating class," Dr. Casper announced.

Tom stepped forward to shake Dr. Casper's hand and accept the plaque.

"Now, I'd like to announce the winner of this year's Aberdeen Scholarship award, who will receive an all expenses paid trip to study abroad at the historic Aberdeen College in Scotland," Dr. Casper said. "I'm happy to announce that this year's winner is James Eisen."

Jim was sincerely shocked to have won, since it seemed like a given all year that Tom would easily win. Everyone was happy for Jim, who had truly earned the honor. Even so, many in the seminary community understood why Tom did not win,

303

including Tom, who accepted it with grace.

Jim walked up and received a plaque honoring him for his achievement and had his picture taken with Dr. Casper.

Rocky was excited for his friend and happy that the Christ-centered event was broadcast by the national media. Now that the graduation ceremony was over, he knew that there was only one last thing for him to do.

Sojourner

Following the graduation ceremony, Rocky and a group of his friends went to Brubaker's Café in Salem to celebrate. Simon and Adam joined Rocky along with several of his Easton friends.

Becky came up to Rocky and gave him a kiss on the cheek.

"I owe this diploma to you," she said.

"I didn't take any of your tests for you. You *earned* it."

Tom, Martin, and Meredith shared a booth, and, like many of the Tuttle Hall gang, they realized it was time to say goodbye to one another.

Rick stood up and tapped his glass with a spoon to get everyone's attention.

"What a year this has been!" Rick exclaimed. "I'm really sorry to see so many of you go, yet in my heart I know that God is sending you all somewhere special. I am happy though, knowing that Rocky will watch over us after you smart graduates all leave."

"Amen!" was yelled out by several of the students staying at Easton.

Rocky stood up, nodded over at Rick, and then stepped up onto a chair.

"Thank you for making this the best year of my life. I am so proud of all of you, and I will continue to pray for you all. However, I am sad to say that I will not be here next year either. In fact, I'm packing my things up to leave tomorrow morning."

The air was sucked out of the café.

"Why, Rocky?" Steven asked.

"I could give you several reasons, Steven, like I don't want to be a janitor for the rest of my life or I want to go back to school or maybe I don't want to live somewhere where everyone knows my past. However, I will spare you all these reasons and simply say that God has called me to go elsewhere."

"Where, Rocky?" Adam asked.

"Elsewhere."

"That's just like you, Rocky," said Chip. "You came to us a mystery and now after we think we have you all figured out, you're leaving us a mystery."

"I'll be back again someday. For this year, I was exactly where God wanted me to be. Now, I must go where He leads me."

Simon got up and hugged Rocky. Several others followed Simon's lead and soon everyone was hugging Rocky goodbye. After that, Rocky excused himself so that he could say goodbye to the others who he had met and befriended during the year.

* * *

As upon his arrival to Easton, Rocky was able to pack his entire life easily into the backseat of a car. This time, however, he was packing his life into a new Honda Civic, which was a present from Simon following the totaling of Rocky's old car in the accident. He was pleased to find his trademark Ohio KEAGGY vanity plates on his new ride. As he drove down the winding road leading out of Easton Seminary, he thanked God for working through him to accomplish what many thought was impossible, a spiritual revival in New England.

He pulled into a Beverly gas station and filled his tank for the long trip before him. He did not know where he was going. He just knew that he'd know it when he got there. He paid the gas station attendant, hopeful that this would be the last person who would recognize him as *the* Rocky Raccoon.

He drove south down Interstate 95 and then merged onto 90 West. Twenty miles down the toll road, he noticed a car suddenly swerve from the left lane over to the right lane and then off to the side of the road. Rocky pulled over behind the car to see if the driver was okay.

"Hi there! Are you all right?" Rocky asked.

A young woman got out of the car and said, "Yes, I'm fine. I just blew my front right tire."

Rocky raised his left hand, which was still in a sling, "I'm afraid I can't be much help changing a tire."

"I don't have a spare, but thanks anyway."

"I can give you a lift to the next exit if you'd like."

"That would be great!"

"Hop on inside." He smiled.

"Thanks. Oh, by the way, my name is Lisa."

"My name is Michael."

"It's nice to meet you, Michael. You look familiar. Do I know you?"

"I don't think so. I just have one of *those* faces," he replied with a grin as he brushed back his long hair.

"Well, anyway, thanks for the ride."

Michael merged back onto the highway.

"So what does your license plate mean? What's KEAGGY?"

"I'm a fan of Phil Keaggy. He's a Christian musician and the greatest guitarist in the world."

"Are you a Christian then?"

"Yes, I am."

"This is *so* weird that I would meet you, Michael."

"Why is that?"

"I was just visiting my sister in Boston, and I went to her church which was the first time in like a decade I've set foot in a church. I'll tell you the truth. I left with so many questions but didn't want to ask my sister because she tends to be a real Bible thumper, if you know what I mean. However, I quietly prayed that I would meet someone I could talk to about God. I know it's not polite to talk about religion and politics, *but* would you mind if we talked a little about Jesus?"

"No, not at all," Michael looked over to Lisa with the smile that ignited the Rocky Raccoon Revival.

Michael C. Duell is a native of Northeast Ohio, and resides in north central Indiana with his wife and three children.

www.ingramcontent.com/pod-product-compliance
Lightning Source LLC
Chambersburg PA
CBHW070651180626
46817CB00006B/2327